He was lonely and vulnerable…

…and it would be very tempting to forget the past in a woman's arms. To block out the nightmares with a woman's kiss. A woman like Emily Townsend.

But Matthew had already hurt too many people as it was. He didn't need a new notch in his belt, and, instinctively, he knew Emily had had enough pain to last her a lifetime. He wondered if the faint shadow of hurt in her brown eyes had something to do with the subtle white circle around the third finger of her left hand.

None of his business, he thought with an inward curse as he stared at Jenny's grave. He had business to attend to. Old scores to settle. He didn't need a distraction right now. Couldn't afford one. Because this might be his last chance to put things right.

SAFE HAVEN

AMANDA STEVENS

Stranger in Paradise

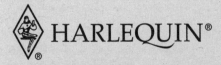

HARLEQUIN®

TORONTO • NEW YORK • LONDON
AMSTERDAM • PARIS • SYDNEY • HAMBURG
STOCKHOLM • ATHENS • TOKYO • MILAN • MADRID
PRAGUE • WARSAW • BUDAPEST • AUCKLAND

ISBN-13: 978-0-373-36158-8
ISBN-10:   0-373-36158-0

STRANGER IN PARADISE

AMANDA STEVENS

is a bestselling author of more than thirty romantic suspense novels. In addition to being a Romance Writers of America RITA® Award finalist, she is also a recipient of awards in Career Achievement in Romantic/Mystery and Career Achievement in Romantic/Suspense from *Romantic Times BOOKreviews*. Amanda currently resides in Texas. To find out more about past, present and future projects, please visit her Web site at www.amandastevens.com.

For Lucas and Leanne—the closest things to perfection I've ever created.

Chapter One

"Emily! Did you hear what happened? It's terrible! Just awful!"

At the sight of her sister-in-law marching up the sidewalk—a stroller preceding her and a four-year-old trailing her—Emily Townsend groaned inwardly. *Good grief,* she thought. *What did I do now?*

She'd been sweeping the leaves from her front porch, but now she stopped and leaned the broom against the wall, taking an extra moment to gather her patience. Then, squaring her shoulders, she turned to face Caroline Townsend, who had come to an abrupt halt at the bottom of the porch steps.

"What's wrong?" Emily asked.

"What's *wrong?*" Caroline repeated, adjusting the top of the stroller to shade baby Moira's face. Sunlight glistened like a halo off Caroline's long golden hair as she straightened and glared up at Emily. "Then you *haven't* heard!"

Emily was almost afraid to ask what Caroline was talking about, certain that her sister-in-law's dramatics had something to do with either Emily or the house Emily had just bought, or both. Her purchase of the old Talbot place had caused quite a stir in Paradise. She sighed in resignation. "I haven't heard anything, so just tell me."

"The sign out on the highway has been vandalized," Caroline said, obviously still shaken by the news.

Charles, Emily's nephew, climbed the porch steps and grabbed her hand. "They wrote a bad word," he said, beaming up at her.

"A bad word?"

"Someone painted over *Paradise* and wrote *H-e-l-l* in big red letters," Caroline explained.

"That spells *hell*," Charles offered.

Caroline glared at her son, aghast. "Charles! Where on earth did you ever hear such a word?"

"From Daddy," the four-year-old told his mother proudly. "I heard him on the telephone."

Emily grinned, imagining what her staid older brother would think if he could hear his son now. Her grin broadened as she visualized the sign out on the highway proclaiming *Welcome to Hell* in big red letters. She'd have to make a special trip out there, just to see it. Maybe even take a picture or two.

But she was smart enough not to say as much to her sister-in-law. Caroline and Stuart Townsend were very prominent and very proud citizens of Paradise. They took Stuart's position on the town council very seriously. So seriously, in fact, that he'd decided to run for the state legislature this year.

As if he weren't stuffy enough, Emily thought.

She couldn't resist pointing to the shingle hanging from her porch and asking innocently, "Does this mean I'll have to change the name of my bed-and-breakfast to the Other Side of Hell Inn?"

Caroline's mouth thinned into one long line of disapproval. "This is not a laughing matter, Emily Townsend.

You know good and well Paradise depends on its tourism. How's that sign going to look to folks who're just driving into town? What kind of impression will it make? They'll think we're a bunch of hooligans around here.''

At twenty-eight, Caroline was only two years older than Emily, but Emily had always thought her sister-in-law dressed and acted much older. Emily supposed Caroline's manner and appearance were a result of Stuart's careful tutoring. He was twelve years older, having married Caroline when she was just out of college, then he'd set about molding her into his idea of the perfect wife.

''I would assume Mayor Henley will have someone out there working on the sign today,'' Emily said, although it had taken her nearly two months to get the proper permit from his office to open her bed-and-breakfast. It seemed no one in town approved of her buying the Talbot house.

Caroline was not mollified. ''You know why this happened, don't you? Stuart says it's because of that article Mike Durbin wrote about this house.'' She waved a scornful hand at Emily's front porch. ''Why you insisted on using the last of your trust fund to buy this…this *monstrosity,* I'll never know. Your poor parents would turn over in their graves if they knew about this. You've made us all a laughingstock, using such an…unfortunate incident in the town's past to promote a bed-and-breakfast.''

Emily raised an incredulous brow. ''Unfortunate incident? It was a murder, Caroline. A murder that has gone unsolved for fifteen years.''

''That's nonsense. Everyone in town knows that stranger did it. That Wade Somebody-or-Other. He killed that poor girl in cold blood. *In your house!*''

''He was never found guilty.''

''Because he skipped town before he could be arrested. Just up and disappeared. If that didn't prove his guilt, I don't know what would. How you could drag up all that old business now, after all these years—''

Emily folded her arms and rolled her eyes, waiting for Caroline's tirade to come to a conclusion. Not that Caroline had anything new to offer. Both she and Stuart had made their opinions of Emily's decision to buy the house perfectly clear from the start.

Are you crazy? Stuart had shouted. *You'll be throwing good money after bad, trying to fix up that old place. Who'd want to stay there anyway?*

The Talbot house had been vacant off and on, mostly off, ever since Jenny Wilcox had been murdered in one of the upstairs bedrooms, fifteen years ago, and rumors of a haunting still occasionally surfaced, usually around the anniversary of the murder.

Details of the old tragedy had recently been rehashed in Mike Durbin's article for the *Paradise Herald.* The article had been picked up by several other papers, and interest in the Other Side of Paradise Inn had skyrocketed, which, of course, was exactly what Emily had intended. She'd gotten calls from as far away as Nashville, and she wasn't even officially open for business yet.

And they said she'd never be a businesswoman, she thought with a satisfied smile.

Caroline saw the look on Emily's face and shook a thin finger at her. ''Don't look so smug,'' she said, assuming the tone Stuart always used with his sister. ''This whole venture could still blow up in your face, just like everything else—'' Caroline stopped short, as if realizing she might have gone too far, even for her.

Neither Stuart nor Caroline ever missed an opportunity to remind Emily of what a failure she'd been at most of the career choices she'd made—and she'd made quite a few over the years, she had to admit—or of the mess she'd made of her life.

After all, it was Stuart who had adamantly opposed Emily's engagement to Eugene Sprague all those years ago. She'd eloped with Eugene when she was only nineteen years old. Now, seven years and a lot of heartache later, here she was, back in Paradise.

It was so easy to read Caroline's mind, Emily thought, giving her sister-in-law a surreptitious glance. *You should have stayed in Paradise and married Trey when you had the chance, Emily. Then you'd be living in the Huntington mansion, instead of trying to fix up a broken-down old house with a sordid past.*

But that was one of the reasons Emily liked the Talbot place so much. She felt a certain kinship with the house. They both seemed unable to live down their reputations.

"Auntie Em?" Charles said, calling her by her nickname.

Emily looked down into her nephew's sweet little face and felt a rush of affection. "What's up, Charley Horse?"

"Can I see the bloodstains now? You promised."

Caroline gasped in outrage. "Charles Townsend, where on earth—"

"Auntie Em said—"

Emily quickly clapped a hand over the child's mouth and smiled. "Kids say the darnedest things, don't they?"

"Emily, please don't be putting ideas into the boy's head. Children are impressionable enough. It's certainly a good thing you don't have little ones of your own," Caroline said, smoothing a hand down her cotton print skirt. She gazed critically at Emily's porch, as if seeing the fresh paint job for the first time. "Oh, Emily. Red shutters?"

"I like red," Emily said, lifting her chin a notch and trying to smother the flash of pain Caroline's careless comment about children had caused. "I think it gives the house pizzazz."

"Makes it look like a bordello, if you ask me," Caroline said, wrinkling her nose. "So when exactly is the grand opening?" She bent to pop a pacifier into Moira's mouth the moment the baby awakened and whimpered. Emily would have liked to pick up the fretting child, but she knew Caroline wouldn't approve. She said it spoiled a baby to always pick it up the minute it cried.

Unable to resist, Emily walked down the steps and peered into the stroller. Five-month-old Moira immediately spit out the pacifier and gave her aunt a wide, hopeful grin.

"I'll officially open for business two weeks from today, on October twenty-third," Emily said, tickling Moira's adorable chin. "The fall leaves should be at their peak by then, and, of course, the Fall Folk Festival starts the week after."

"October twenty-third," Caroline mused. "Why does that date sound familiar to me?" A light dawned, and Caroline's light blue eyes widened in horror. "Isn't that the anniversary of the murder? Why, that's positively ghoulish, Emily!"

And positively brilliant, Emily thought. With Mike Durbin's help, the publicity for her opening could be phenomenal.

As soon as Moira realized her aunt wasn't going to pick her up, she started to howl. Emily glanced expectantly at Caroline, but she was gazing down the street. "What is that infernal noise?"

At first, Emily thought Caroline was referring to Moira's sobs, but then, over the sound of the baby's cries, came a low thrum that steadily grew louder.

"I think it's a motorcycle," Emily said.

"A *motorcycle?* In *Paradise?*"

The words were barely out of Caroline's mouth when a big black Harley came into view. Both Caroline and Emily stood with open mouths as the powerful machine glided to a stop at the curb, the engine was killed and the rider got off.

And what a rider!

Dressed in jeans, boots and a black leather jacket, the stranger striding up her walkway had longish dark hair, a tall, athletic build, and—when he took off his mirrored sunglasses—eyes that were the most striking shade of light gray Emily had ever looked into.

"Oh, my…" she heard someone whisper. Caroline poked her in the ribs, and Emily realized the words had come from her own mouth.

"I'm looking for a place to stay," the man said, gazing at her with those beautiful gray eyes. His voice was low and dark, infinitely sexy. Emily felt a delicious shiver along her backbone.

Caroline, who had been silent for at least one full minute—a record for her—said primly, "Emily isn't open for business yet."

"Oh, yes, I am," Emily put in, almost before Caroline had stopped speaking. Emily wasn't about to lose a potential customer, especially when Cora Mae Hicks, who operated the This Side of Paradise Inn across the street, was probably watching out her window at that very moment, ready to pounce on anyone Emily might turn away.

The bed-and-breakfast business in Paradise was fiercely competitive, and Cora Mae had ruled at the top of the heap for nearly twenty-five years. But Emily planned to change all that.

"Would you like to see the rooms?" she asked eagerly.

"I have some business to attend to first," the stranger said. "But I'll be back at six." He turned to leave.

At the sight of his retreating back, Emily had the almost overpowering urge to somehow make him stay. If he left now, he might never return. She might never see him again, and for some reason she couldn't have begun to explain, Emily desperately wanted to see this man again.

"Wait!"

He turned.

"What's your name? I...need it for the register."

He paused for a split second, and their gazes collided. Emily felt the impact all the way to her toes. "Just call me John," he said mysteriously, slipping on his mirrored glasses.

"John what?"

"Doe." Then he mounted his bike, started the engine and roared off.

They watched him in silence until he was out of sight, until only a faint hum could be heard from a distance, then Caroline turned to Emily and exclaimed in disbelief, "Did he just say his name was John Doe? Isn't that what they call a corpse?"

Emily shivered at Caroline's words. Still, dead or alive, the stranger who'd just ridden away on his motorcycle was the best-looking man she'd seen in years.

Finally, something interesting had happened in Paradise.

"TELL ME AGAIN who we're going to see," Mike Durbin, a reporter—the only reporter, in fact—for the *Paradise Herald,* instructed as Emily climbed into his ancient Plymouth. He glanced down at her legs, and Emily blushed, tugging at the hem of her short denim skirt.

"Her name's Miss Rosabel Talbot. She owned my

house at the time of the murder.'' Emily settled back against the shabby upholstery and gazed out the side window at the Talbot house. The *Townsend* house now, she reminded herself.

Oh, it did look good, she thought proudly, gazing at the sparkling white paint, the new latticework and, yes, even the red trim.

Emily loved everything about her new home, including the wide wraparound porch on the first floor and the tree-shaded balcony on the second, the diamond-paned bay window in the dining room and the stained-glass front door, which had cost her a small fortune to have restored. She loved the gardens in back and the maples in front, which were now turning the yard into a cornucopia of fall color.

The house was Emily's first real home in years. She and Eugene had moved around so much when they were married that no place had ever seemed like home to her. And before that, staying first with her grandmother, then with Stuart after her parents died, Emily had felt more like an unwelcome guest than anything else.

Now, for the first time since she was eleven years old, Emily finally had a place to call her own.

''I hope this isn't going to be a complete waste of time,'' Mike said, drawing her attention reluctantly back to him. ''Supposing the old girl doesn't remember anything about the murder? She's in a nursing home, isn't she? Mind's likely not what it used to be.''

''She sounded sharp enough on the phone when she agreed to see us,'' Emily said. ''Let's go. I have to be back by six.''

Mike lifted his eyebrows. ''Hot date tonight?''

Emily thought about the stranger, quickly conjuring up an image of his dark hair and light gray eyes. Excitement tingled through her. "Something like that," she murmured.

"I didn't know you dated."

Emily didn't like the speculative gleam in his eyes. Mike Durbin was not at all the kind of man she wanted to get mixed up with. For one thing, he had a kind of lean and hungry look about him that Emily didn't trust. For another, he reminded her too much of her ex-husband, and God knew that was reason enough to stay away from him.

"I don't date," she said impatiently. "My appointment this evening is strictly business. Now, shall we go?"

"You're the boss," Mike said, shifting the car into drive. The Plymouth hesitated, shimmied for a moment, then took off in a cloud of exhaust down the street. Emily would have offered to take her car, but her old VW didn't run much better, and besides, the heater was on the blink again, and after a sunny morning, the day had suddenly turned cold and drizzly.

Emily thought about the stranger on his motorcycle. Did he get cold, racing along the streets? Or did he feel exhilarated, with the wind blowing through his hair and the feel of the powerful bike between his thighs? Emily felt a little surge of adrenaline, just thinking about it. She'd never in her life ridden on a motorcycle, but she'd always wanted to. Especially now.

"I have to get back early myself," Mike was saying as he maneuvered the car through Paradise's narrow streets. "Gotta make a run out to the highway, check out that defaced sign. No doubt that'll be our lead story tomorrow," he said with open contempt.

In the short time Emily had known Mike, he'd never bothered to disguise his disdain for the small town in which he found himself living, or for the small-town paper for which he found himself working.

He'd once been an award-winning investigative reporter for the *Arkansas Democrat,* having lived in both
Little Rock and Washington, D.C. But after his fall from
grace seven years ago, no one in the print media would
touch him. The only job he'd been able to get was working for his uncle at the *Herald.*

Emily supposed the ensuing years of struggle and frustration explained the flashes of desperation she occasionally glimpsed in Mike's eyes.

She said now, "I really appreciate the time you're
spending on this story."

He shrugged. "I have to admit, I wasn't too keen on
the idea when you first brought it up, but I'm starting to
think you may be on to something. We've already had
quite a few complaints at the paper about that article.
Even a couple of anonymous threats."

"What kind of threats?" Emily asked in alarm.

"The usual crackpot stuff. People letting off steam. But
it does appear that some folks in Paradise get mighty
touchy at the very mention of the Wilcox murder."

"I hope your uncle hasn't changed his mind about the
series," Emily worried. She knew how important adver-
tisers were to a newspaper. If too many people com-
plained, Roy Travers, the owner of the *Herald,* might
want to kill the rest of the articles she and Mike had
planned.

"You let me worry about Uncle Roy. I know how to
handle him. Besides, do you know how long it's been
since I've written about anything other than who bought
what at the latest craft show, or which house received first
place for the best yard display at Christmas?" He glanced
at her, giving her an enigmatic wink. "I should be thank-
ing you for putting me on the right track, Emily. A good
murder is exactly what I need right now."

His tone was light, but something in his eyes—that look of hunger, that flash of desperation—made Emily uneasy, and she couldn't help remembering why Mike had been fired from the *Democrat* seven years ago. According to town gossip, he'd fabricated a story that won him all kinds of industry accolades and awards. When the truth eventually came out, his career had been in ruins.

Emily stared at Mike's profile, wondering what a man like him might be willing to do to recapture all that he'd lost.

The thought left Emily unsettled, and both she and Mike fell silent. Neither of them spoke again until they pulled into the parking lot at the Shady Oaks Nursing Home in Batesville, over an hour later.

"Let me do the talking," Emily said as they walked through the front door. "I've known Miss Rosabel for years, but she might be a little nervous around you."

Mike looked around, wary. "Fine by me," he said, fiddling with the collar of his shirt.

Funny how some people got nervous around old people, Emily thought. She'd once worked in a nursing home while she was still married to Eugene. She'd gotten along fine with the residents. It had been the management and their medieval policies she couldn't handle.

At least Shady Oaks had a nice homey quality to it, Emily noticed with relief, taking in the beautiful needle-point wall hangings and lush potted plants decorating the lobby.

Miss Rosabel was sitting in a rocking chair by the window when they walked into her room. She wore an intricately crocheted shawl of sky blue that highlighted her gray hair and her brilliant blue eyes. She had once been Emily's piano teacher, and even though Emily hadn't seen her in years, she would have recognized Miss Rosabel anywhere.

"Miss Rosabel," she said, hurrying across the room to kneel beside the old lady's chair. "You haven't changed a bit."

"You have," Miss Rosabel said bluntly. "What have you done to your hair?"

Emily fingered the short curls at her nape. "I got it cut a few months ago. I figured it was time for a change," she said, offering an explanation where none was needed. Stuart had almost had apoplexy when he first saw her.

A woman's crowning glory is her hair, he'd said disdainfully. *And you've just cut all yours off.*

"You had the most beautiful long hair when you were a little girl. Dark and glossy as a raven's wing," Miss Rosabel reminisced. She ran a critical eye over Emily, until Emily began to fidget, just as she had years ago. Finally, Miss Rosabel nodded and said, "This style suits you, though. You always were an original. And I imagine all that long hair was a tangled mess in the mornings."

"It was," Emily agreed, surprised by the old woman's perceptiveness. "But I wish you'd explain that to Stuart."

"And how is your dear brother?" Miss Rosabel asked the question mildly, but her voice was tinged with sarcasm. Emily remembered that while she was staying with Stuart, he and Miss Rosabel had had one or two run-ins over Emily's lack of discipline in her music. Emily had wanted to play her own compositions, with Miss Rosabel's enthusiastic approval, while Stuart had wanted her to learn the classics. She'd never become an accomplished pianist by pecking out that racket, he'd said.

Emily smiled a little at the memory now, even though Stuart's words had hurt at the time. "He's running for the state legislature this year," she told Miss Rosabel.

"I suppose he and Trey Huntington are still thick as thieves." Miss Rosabel's gaze sharpened on Emily, making her wonder uneasily just how much the old woman remembered about Emily's relationship with the illustrious Trey Huntington. She wondered if Miss Rosabel held the same opinion everyone else in town seemed to have—that Emily had been out of her mind to turn down a man like Trey.

"They're still friends," Emily said carefully. "In fact, Trey's handling Stuart's political campaign."

Miss Rosabel raised her eyebrows at that, but said nothing. Emily kept quiet, too, letting the brief silence make the transition from idle chitchat to business matters. Then she said, "Look, Miss Rosabel, the reason we're here—"

"You want to know about the murder." The blue eyes moved from Emily to Mike, who had been standing surprisingly patient through their small talk. "You must be that reporter fellow Emily told me about. The one who faked a story and got himself fired off the *Gazette* a few years ago."

Two bright spots of color ignited Mike's cheeks. "It was the *Democrat*," he said, stepping forward.

"Well, they're one and the same nowadays," Miss Rosabel pointed out.

"So they are. I hope you won't hold my past transgressions against me," Mike said with false levity. "I've learned from my mistakes."

"Have you?" Miss Rosabel made it seem doubtful as she gave him a thorough once-over, then returned her gaze to Emily. "What is it you want to know about that poor girl's death?"

"Everything," Emily said. "Mike wants to do a series of articles about the house to coincide with the anniversary of the murder. It'll be terrific publicity for the grand opening of my bed-and-breakfast. You know how people love a mystery.''

"Except for the good citizens of Paradise," Miss Rosabel said dryly. "They won't like having their dirty laundry aired in public, and they won't be happy about me talking to you two."

"Why not?" Emily asked, even though, judging by Caroline and Stuart's reaction to Mike's first article and by what Mike had said about the complaints and threats the paper had received, she knew that what Miss Rosabel said was true.

"I imagine they have their reasons," Miss Rosabel evaded. She gazed out the window for a moment, as if gathering her thoughts, then said, "It happened such a long time ago. I don't know if I can remember everything."

"Tell us what you do remember," Emily offered encouragingly, settling herself on the throw rug at Miss Rosabel's feet.

Mike sat on a footstool and brought out his recorder.

"What's that thing?" Miss Rosabel asked suspiciously.

"A tape recorder, to make sure I quote you accurately."

"I've never seen one that small," Miss Rosabel said, her disdain obvious in her tone. Then her sharp eyes lifted to Mike's. "Are you sure it works?"

"Oh, it works, all right. Trust me," Mike said, with an odd little smile that sent a sudden, unexplainable chill down Emily's spine.

Chapter Two

"She was a beautiful girl." Miss Rosabel's eyes looked dreamy and far away, and Emily knew that the old woman had transported herself back in time, to fifteen years ago, when she'd first met Jenny Wilcox, the young woman who had been murdered in Miss Rosabel's bed-and-breakfast. Emily's bed-and-breakfast now.

"She came to Paradise as a substitute for one of the high school teachers, who'd broken her leg. Since she didn't know how long she'd be needed, she rented a room from me rather than trying to find a house. It was off-season, so I gave her a good price. My niece, Nella, was also staying with me, and the two of them hit it off right away, even though Nella was a few years younger, just seventeen that summer.

"I remember feeling relieved, because Nella never had any friends, and we were all so very worried about her. She was always shy and withdrawn, especially after her mother died so suddenly...." Miss Rosabel drifted off, but then, with an effort, seemed to regroup her thoughts.

"Anyway, that's why her father had sent her to me, hoping a new town, a new school, would bring her around. But nothing I did helped until Jenny came along. Jenny had this way about her, you see. People were drawn to her. All the men in town were half in love with her before that first week was out. Trey Huntington and your brother, Stuart, both came around the inn to see her, but Tony Vincent fell the hardest for her. And because the other two men were his friends, they backed off.''

Emily remembered Tony Vincent. He was about Stuart's age, and she vaguely recalled that the two of them had been friends of a sort. Unlikely friends, because Tony had been a real jock back then, and Stuart had always considered himself an intellectual, a part of Trey Huntington's elite group.

But even though he came from a poor background, Tony's feats on the football field had earned him a place of honor in Paradise. He'd been captain of his high school football team and had later attended the University of Arkansas on a full football scholarship. After that, he'd been drafted by the St. Louis Cardinals, but his professional career had been somewhat of a disappointment. He'd suffered a lot of injuries to his knees, and there'd been rumors of a serious drinking problem, Emily recalled.

''Well,'' Miss Rosabel continued, drawing Emily's attention back to the story. ''The September that Jenny Wilcox came to Paradise, Tony had just been released from his contract with that professional football team. Knowing that he was down on his luck, Jenny went out of her way to be nice to him. That's the way she was. Well, Tony was so smitten that he proposed to her just a week after they'd met, right there in the inn, in front of Nella and myself and a number of other guests. Oh, it was very romantic,'' Miss Rosabel said, her eyes sparkling.

''What did Jenny do?'' Emily asked, getting caught up in the woman's excitement.

''She turned him down, of course, but in such a charming manner that Tony fell for her even harder. He was determined to win her over, and he and Jenny began spending a great deal of time together. I remember how I used to hear her slipping out of the inn in the middle of the night sometimes, and I was sure she was going to meet Tony. Nella and I both thought a wedding would be imminent by the end of October. Then, a few weeks after Jenny arrived, a stranger came to Paradise, and everything changed.'' Miss Rosabel's eyes darkened. The hand clutching her shawl trembled.

''What was this stranger's name?'' Mike asked.

''Wade Drury. He was handsome as the very devil, but you only had to look into his eyes, those beautiful gray eyes, to know he meant trouble. Nella was quite taken with him. He rode this big black motorcycle, you see, and—''

Emily's head jerked to attention. ''Did you say motorcycle?''

Miss Rosabel nodded. ''Yes, and the minute he saw Jenny, he was just as enamored as everyone else in town was, though he tried not to show it. But you could tell how he felt by the way he looked at her when he thought no one was around. She was the only reason he hung around Paradise for as long as he did,'' Miss Rosabel said. ''He didn't have family in town, no job that I ever knew about. What other reason could there be?''

He rode a motorcycle, Emily thought. Wade Drury, the man who killed Jenny Wilcox, had ridden a big black motorcycle. And he'd had gray eyes. Beautiful gray eyes.

Emily shuddered. ''What happened after Wade came to town?''

''Tony became insanely jealous. He hated the idea of Jenny staying in the same house with Wade Drury, even though Nella's room was between Wade's and Jenny's. One night Tony saw Jenny and Wade talking, and Tony's temper got the better of him. He'd been drinking, and he and Wade fought bitterly. Nella and I tried to help Jenny break them apart, but it didn't do any good. All we could do was watch helplessly while the two men tried to kill each other over Jenny. I finally had to call the sheriff to come stop the fight.''

Miss Rosabel paused and took a deep, shuddering breath. ''The next day, Jenny's body was found in her room, covered in blood. She'd been stabbed to death with a butcher knife.''

Even though Emily had heard bits and pieces of the story for years, she still felt the sickening shock of Miss Rosabel's words.

''Who found the body?'' Mike asked.

Miss Rosabel's eyes closed. ''I did.''

''It must have been awful for you,'' Emily said softly.

''I've never seen anything like it. I still dream about all that blood.…''

Emily took the old woman's hand and held it between hers.

Mike said, ''What happened after you found the body?''

''The sheriff came. We were all questioned, but Wade Drury was nowhere to be found. Tony swore that Jenny had told him Wade was making unwanted advances toward her, that Wade had even tried to break into her room one night. Jenny was terrified of the man, according to Tony.

''It was easy to believe Wade was guilty. No one knew anything about him, you see. He'd just shown up in town one day and stayed on. He was a drifter, a stranger in Paradise, and Tony was one of our own. Everyone assumed he was telling the truth.''

''Even you?'' Emily couldn't resist asking. Her gaze

met Miss Rosabel's, and Emily thought she saw a faint glimmer of doubt reflected in the depths of the old woman's eyes.

"I didn't know what to think," Miss Rosabel finally admitted. "The whole town was outraged that a brutal murder could occur in our peaceful little community. The citizens were incited to almost a mob frenzy by Trey Huntington, who demanded justice. Wade Drury was guilty, Trey insisted, and had to be punished. But the night after the murder, someone claimed they saw Wade leaving town on his motorcycle, and he was never heard from again."

"Didn't the investigation continue?" Mike asked.

"The sheriff asked a few more questions, some outsiders came to town and made a few inquiries, but nothing ever came of it. When no family came forward to claim Jenny's body, the town buried her, and both she and Wade Drury were soon forgotten. Until you two came along and started stirring things up," Miss Rosabel finished.

Emily glanced at Mike. She'd never seen him look so animated, so excited. His pale blue eyes were almost glowing with anticipation, but there was still something about him that disturbed Emily. That hunger...

She had a sudden sick feeling in the pit of her stomach that perhaps she'd started something she wouldn't want to see finished.

"What happened to your bed-and-breakfast after that?" Mike asked, seemingly oblivious of Emily's misgiving.

"It was doomed." Miss Rosabel shrugged her frail shoulders. "Nothing I could do to stop all that talk. I remember the day I left the house for the last time. Cora Mae Hicks was standing on her front porch, gloating, as I walked down the street. I actually heard her laugh. Can you imagine?"

A vision of Cora Mae's cold black eyes and her thin, unsmiling mouth formed in Emily's head, and it wasn't too terribly difficult to picture the woman's glee over her rival's misfortune.

Miss Rosabel sat up suddenly, her eyes snapping with anger. "I've thought about this a lot over the years, made a lot of notes about the murder and such, and there is only one person I can come up with who actually benefited from that murder. My bed-and-breakfast was giving the This Side of Paradise Inn a run for its money. I wouldn't be a bit surprised to learn Cora Mae Hicks killed that poor girl herself, just to drive me out of business."

Emily looked at Miss Rosabel, in shock. "Surely you don't think—"

Miss Rosabel glared at Emily. "In my opinion, Cora Mae has always been one brick shy of a load, and she's ferociously protective where that bed-and-breakfast of hers is concerned. You be careful, Emily. You're the competition now, and in Cora Mae's eyes, that makes you the enemy."

ALL DURING THE DRIVE back to Paradise, Emily couldn't get Miss Rosabel's story out of her mind. Emily had known about the murder, of course, but she'd been only eleven at the time, and she hadn't given it much thought over the years. But somehow, hearing the tragedy in such detail from Miss Rosabel made it seem more immediate.

Poor Jenny. No one had come forward to claim her body. The town had buried her, then forgotten her. It was the saddest thing Emily had ever heard. Had Jenny's family even been notified? Or, fifteen years later, were they still wondering about her, waiting for her to come home?

After Mike dropped her off at the inn, Emily went out back to cut some chrysanthemums from the garden and gather fall leaves from the maples to make an arrangement for the table in the foyer. But, on impulse, she carefully laid the flowers and leaves in the front seat of her car and headed out to the cemetery. She had the strangest urge to see Jenny Wilcox's grave, to pay her respects and maybe even to grieve for a moment for the young woman who'd had no one come forward when she died.

Emily parked the car near the wrought-iron gate and got out. She hadn't been to the cemetery in years, not since the day her parents were buried. That day had been overcast, too, with a misty rain blowing down from the mountains, making the whole scene seem surreal. Emily had stood between Stuart and her grandmother and watched as her parents' coffins were simultaneously lowered into the frozen ground.

Emily tried to shake the memory as she walked through the gate. Still, a cemetery was a natural place for gloomy thoughts, she decided.

The wind kicked up, blowing dead leaves across the graves as she made her way to the section in which she vaguely remembered Jenny Wilcox had been buried. The grave was marked by a flat, nondescript headstone that Emily might easily have missed, except for one thing. A man was standing over Jenny's grave.

Emily hesitated, not quite sure what to do. The man's head was bowed, as if he were deep in contemplation, and even though she couldn't see his face, Emily recognized the dark hair and the leather jacket. The man standing next to Jenny Wilcox's grave was the stranger who called himself John Doe.

A shiver of apprehension coursed down Emily's spine. Suddenly, though she couldn't have said why, exactly, she didn't want him to see her there. Didn't want him to know that she'd seen him.

She started to turn away, but before she could, the stranger looked up and Emily found herself trapped by his stare, found herself left breathless once again by the intensity of his beautiful gray eyes.

"So we meet again," he said.

Emily managed to shrug, even though her heart was pounding inside her chest. *Keep it light,* she told herself, and forced a smile. "I brought flowers," she said, looking down at Jenny's grave. "For her."

"Did you know her?"

His question was casually spoken, but Emily sensed something in his voice. A hint of the same intensity that simmered in his eyes. "No, I didn't know her," Emily admitted. "But I...feel sorry for her."

"Because she was murdered?"

"Yes. And because she died all alone."

Her answer seemed to surprise him. Something moved in his eyes, a flash of pain that was gone in an instant. He let his gaze fall back to Jenny's grave.

Emily stood silently by, unable to keep her own gaze from straying to the stranger's face. He had such striking features—high cheekbones, dark brows and lashes that were in dramatic contrast to the lightness of his eyes, and lips that were neither thin nor thick, but somehow sensuous nonetheless.

Emily took a deep, shaky breath. "Did you know her?"

Droplets of mist glistened on his leather coat and in his hair as he moved a step or two away from the grave, as if distancing himself from a memory. "I like old mysteries," he said with a shrug. "You might say I have a fascination with unsolved crimes. I read Mike Durbin's article in a Memphis newspaper—it must have been picked up on the wire—and decided to come here, out of curiosity."

''You're from Memphis?'' Emily asked, out of her own curiosity.

He looked up, and his gaze held hers just long enough to start her heart pounding again. Then he glanced away. ''I'm originally from Memphis, but I've lived here and there.''

''Where do you call home now?''

''Wherever I happen to be at the moment.''

''You just roam around the countryside on your motorcycle, looking for old crimes to solve?'' Emily asked skeptically.

A faint smiled touched those sensuous lips. ''Sometimes.''

Emily looked around. ''Speaking of your motorcycle, I didn't see it when I drove up.''

''I parked it over there,'' he said, indicating the side of the cemetery next to the road.

Emily saw the big bike parked at the curb, near the iron fence. ''What did you do, climb the fence?''

Again, the hint of a smile. ''Something like that.''

His evasiveness was beginning to disturb her. Emily huddled inside her denim jacket as the wind rattled leaves across Jenny's grave and a deep silence fell between them.

She suddenly became aware of how alone the two of them were, how isolated the cemetery was. It was growing colder, too, colder and foggier, and she was starting to have that feeling again that the entire scene was somehow unreal.

A chill seeped through her jacket, and she shivered as she bent to lay the flowers on Jenny's grave. Her fingers shook slightly as she straightened the arrangement to her satisfaction, then stood.

''I should be getting back,'' she said, shoving her hands into her pockets.

For one brief moment, Emily could have sworn the stranger's gaze lingered on her lips, making her feel warm and trembly all over. Then his eyes darkened, and her stomach clenched.

"See you at six," he finally said.

"See you," Emily echoed, then turned to leave. She could feel the stranger's gaze on her as she made her way back to the car, and by the time she climbed inside, her hands were shaking so badly she could hardly turn the ignition.

HE WATCHED HER climb into her battered Volkswagen, admiring the long legs beneath the short skirt, the slender waist and hips beneath the denim jacket. Emily Townsend was a very attractive woman. Not drop-dead gorgeous, as Jenny had been, but undeniably appealing in an offbeat sort of way, with that funny little haircut and those big brown eyes that looked as if they could peer right into a man's soul.

He shifted uncomfortably, making himself look down at Jenny's grave again.

A woman like Emily Townsend could be a dangerous thing for a man like him.

For one thing, he'd gone a long time without female companionship. A very long time. He was lonely and vulnerable, and it would be very tempting to forget the past in a woman's arms. To block out the nightmares with a woman's kisses.

A woman like Emily Townsend.

But he'd already hurt too many people as it was. He didn't need a new notch in his belt, and instinctively he knew Emily Townsend had had enough pain to last her a lifetime. He wondered if the faint shadow of hurt in her brown eyes had something to do with the subtle white circle around the third finger of her left hand.

His guess would be that she was recently divorced, and judging by the wounded looked in her eyes, it hadn't been her idea. Funny how that notion filled him with regret and maybe just a little bit of jealousy. What kind of jerk had let her go?

None of your business, he thought with an inward curse as he stared at Jenny's grave. He had business to attend to. Old scores to settle. He didn't need a distraction right now. Couldn't afford one. Because this might be his last chance to put things right.

And maybe then, after fifteen years, they could all finally rest in peace.

Chapter Three

As Emily pulled into her driveway and parked, her thoughts were still on the stranger she'd seen at the cemetery. She couldn't get over the shock she'd felt, finding him standing over Jenny Wilcox's grave.

And she still wasn't quite convinced that his presence there had been due solely to curiosity, his interest in old mysteries, as he'd claimed.

His eyes were what gave him away, Emily thought. They were too intense. Too deep and dark and full of secrets.

She shivered now, just thinking about him, thinking about the way he'd looked at her. The way those eyes had lingered on her lips…

Stop it, Emily told herself firmly as she got out of the car and walked across the yard to her porch. She couldn't afford to let her imagination get the better of her, or to think things that just weren't so. The man was a stranger. He had no interest in her except as the owner of the bed-and-breakfast where he was about to spend his first night in Paradise.

Assuming, of course, that he came back.

Emily started up her porch steps, but as she did so, something—a feeling of being watched—made her glance quickly over her shoulder. Her gaze was caught by a movement across the street, at the This Side of Paradise Inn. A curtain at an upstairs window in Cora Mae's house fluttered, and Emily knew without a doubt that the old woman was up there, watching her.

Cora Mae had been watching every move Emily made ever since she'd moved into the Talbot House. Cora Mae had even threatened to sue when Emily named her bed-and-breakfast the Other Side of Paradise Inn.

Before today, Emily hadn't paid much mind to the old woman's threats or to her open hostility, but now Emily couldn't help shuddering as she remembered Miss Rosabel's parting words. *I wouldn't be a bit surprised to learn Cora Mae Hicks killed that poor girl herself, just to drive me out of business.*

PROMPTLY AT SIX, Emily heard the motorcycle pull up out front. Even though she'd been listening for it for the better part of an hour, the sound still startled her, and in her nervousness, she dropped the bowl of rose-scented potpourri she'd been carrying. Luckily, the crystal bowl didn't break, but the potpourri flew in every direction.

Emily was down on her hands and knees, scooping up dried rose petals and throwing them back into the bowl when the front door opened and the stranger walked in. From her vantage, she saw his boots first, then his jeans, then the leather jacket, and finally his face as her gaze traveled slowly upward. He stared down at her for a moment, then squatted, putting their eyes on a more even keel.

"Have an accident?" he asked in that deep, liquid voice of his.

"As usual," Emily admitted, feeling the butterflies in her stomach start to flutter. She'd never been this close to him—close enough to smell the leather of his coat and the wind in his hair and the faint, irresistible scent of after-shave. His eyes, striking from a distance, were positively magnetic up close. Emily found herself unable to look away.

Or was it simply because she didn't want to? The view, after all, was pretty spectacular.

"Let me help you," he said, reaching down to scoop a handful of potpourri from the floor.

"Oh, don't bother," Emily said, putting her own hand down to stop him. Their fingers touched, then jerked apart. "I'll…get the vacuum," she finished. "I'm sure you're anxious to get settled in." She got awkwardly to her feet, and he followed her, rising in one smooth movement that left Emily marveling at his grace.

"Did you get to see much of the town this afternoon?" she asked, walking over to the antique mahogany desk she'd placed near the foyer. What she really wanted to know, of course, was how long he'd stayed at the cemetery after she left, and how long he'd been there before she arrived. And what he'd been doing out there in the first place.

"I saw enough," he said, gazing around with obvious interest.

The large, airy front room, with its hardwood floors and French doors, made a wonderful first impression, Emily thought. She'd placed a small grouping of furniture near a cozy window alcove, another in front of the fireplace, and yet another overlooking the gardens. Here, guests could come and read the paper in relative solitude, or chat with fellow travelers, or simply sit quietly and stare at the magnificent scenery of the Ozarks.

"This is nice," he said. "Very impressive. Somehow I hadn't pictured it as quite so—"

"Normal? Homey?" Emily smiled. "That's exactly why I wanted Mike Durbin to do the article. I wanted people to know that the Other Side of Paradise Inn is a far cry from the dark, sinister murder scene written about in the past. Well," she said briskly, trying to ignore the commotion of her heart as she looked at him. "If you'll just sign the register, I'll show you up to your room." She pushed the book across the desk and waited for him to sign.

He hesitated for a moment, then picked up the gold pen and scrawled his name across the blue line. Emily almost expected to see John Doe written across the page, but when she turned the book around, she saw that he'd signed the register as Matthew Steele.

She looked up at him. "I thought you said your name was Doe."

"I said you could call me that."

"Why would you want me to call you that, if it's not your name?" she asked in confusion.

Matthew shrugged. "It's a private joke. You wouldn't understand."

What was it Caroline had said? *Isn't that what they call a corpse?*

"You're not a ghost, are you, Mr. Steele?"

He leaned against the desk. "Do I look like a ghost, Emily?" His gray eyes stared deeply into hers. Too deeply for such an ordinary conversation. But nothing seemed ordinary about this stranger, Emily realized. Quite the contrary.

"How did you know my name?" she asked breathlessly.

"I read it in Durbin's article."

"Oh, yes. I'd forgotten. Well, shall I show you to your room?"

Emily led the way up the stairs and opened the first door off the landing. In her opinion, it was the best room in the house, with a south window that allowed plenty of light, and a spectacular view of the gardens in back and the mountains in the distance.

Matthew stepped inside and looked around, taking in the handmade quilt on the bed, the lace curtains at the window and the framed watercolors hanging on the walls. Emily hadn't noticed what an undeniably feminine room it was before she saw how undeniably masculine Matthew Steele looked standing inside.

He said, "It's very nice, but do you have anything facing the street?"

"Facing the street?" Emily echoed with a frown. "Well, there's the blue room, but the view isn't nearly as good—"

"That sounds fine."

Dutifully Emily led the way down the hallway, but before they reached the blue room, Matthew stopped at the room across the corridor. The door was open, Emily noticed. She could have sworn she'd closed it when she finished hanging the curtains that morning.

"What about this room?" Matthew asked, shoving the door open wider.

"I'm...not really finished in there."

Matthew stepped inside. "It looks fine to me."

"But I—"

"Is this where it happened?" He turned to face her, his gray eyes capturing hers in a gaze so intense, Emily felt her breath leave her in a rush.

She managed to nod as she followed him into the room. Though Emily didn't believe in ghosts, she always had a strange feeling when she entered this room, a rush of conflicting emotions she couldn't have begun to explain.

"The furniture has all been changed, of course," she said quietly. "The wallpaper's new, and the floors have been sanded and refinished. There's nothing left of that terrible tragedy in this room."

"Do you really believe that?" He was looking at her again, staring at her in that most disturbing way he had. Emily found herself growing even more nervous.

"They say houses have personalities," he said. "They take on the emotions and feelings of those who have lived in them. The more violent the emotion, the longer it lingers, until the house itself becomes almost a living, breathing entity."

"A house is wood and brick and mortar," Emily said, not quite as convincingly as she would have wished. "Nothing more, nothing less."

Matthew walked over to the bed and stood staring down at it, as if he could see something Emily couldn't. She shivered at the dark, absorbed look on his face. "This house has secrets," he said softly, so softly Emily wasn't sure she'd heard him correctly. Then, as he lifted his gaze to hers, he said, "I intend to find out what they are. If it's the last thing I do."

EMILY TRIED to put the conversation out of her mind as she drove to the town council meeting that night, but something about Matthew Steele, about the way he'd looked in that tragic room, wouldn't let her forget him. Or was it what he'd said that disturbed her so much?

This house has secrets. I intend to find out what they are. If it's the last thing I do.

Emily shivered, just thinking about Matthew Steele. Who was he, she wondered, and why had he come to Paradise?

"Why do you care, Emily?" she muttered as she pulled

into a parking space in front of the town hall. Matthew was a customer, her first one, and her only one at the moment, and he should have no more significance to her than that.

But why had he been standing over Jenny Wilcox's grave? Why had he looked so sad, so intense?

Maybe for the same reason Emily herself had felt compelled to take flowers to Jenny's grave. Maybe the story had touched them both.

But whatever Matthew Steele's reason for being here, Emily couldn't afford to waste time worrying about it now. She had other, more pressing concerns at the moment, and she knew she'd better clear her mind of everything else before facing her brother and the rest of the town council. Not to mention Trey Huntington.

At the mere thought of Trey's name, Emily squirmed. During the time she'd been back in Paradise, she'd made a point of avoiding him. Their parting had not been an amicable one, and she dreaded seeing him again.

Emily sighed as she stared out the window of her car. The Huntingtons were practically worshiped in these parts, and no one, least of all Trey, could understand how Emily Townsend, who had never accomplished anything in her life, could have turned down his marriage proposal.

So what if she'd only been nineteen at the time and he'd been thirty-three? She'd obviously needed someone to take care of her.

So what if she and Trey had hardly seen eye-to-eye on anything? Trey would bring her around in no time. With the Huntington and Townsend history, theirs would be a match made in heaven.

So said everyone in town, and then Emily had up and eloped with Eugene Sprague, a wannabe country-and-western singer who'd known about as much success in his life as Emily had in hers.

She'd realized the marriage was a mistake from the first, but she'd hung in there, through Eugene's refusal to hold down a steady job and his string of infidelities, until she was forced to admit defeat. The last straw had come when he finally made it abundantly clear to Emily that he had no intention of ever giving her the children she so desperately wanted.

So here she was back in Paradise, Emily thought as she got out of the car and headed up the sidewalk toward city hall. Maybe she was foolish to come back to a town where she had never really felt she belonged, but at this point in her life, Emily had badly wanted to put down roots somewhere. The only family she had lived here, and though she and Stuart might disagree on just about everything, she still loved him and knew deep down that he loved her.

The door to the meeting room opened directly from the outside of the building. Emily slipped into the room and took a seat at the back near an open window.

A breeze blew in, but rather than close the window, Emily pulled her jacket more tightly around her. She liked the feel of the wind on her face and hoped that the chill would keep her alert through Stuart's long-winded opening speech.

A shadow passed by the window, but before Emily had time to wonder who might be out there in the darkness, her brother called the meeting to order and a hush fell over the room.

As Emily had expected, the meeting was less than ten minutes old when someone brought up the subject of Mike Durbin's article. Just as predictable was the identity of the person voicing the complaint—Cora Mae Hicks.

"As we're heading into the fall tourist season, we certainly don't want a reminder of an…unfortunate incident in the town's past to keep people away."

It seemed that *unfortunate incident* had become a euphemism in Paradise for *murder*. Emily raised her hand to speak. When Stuart ignored her, she jumped to her feet. "I'd like to be allowed to speak on this subject," she called. Every head in the room turned in her direction. Stuart had no choice but to recognize her, though he did so with obvious reluctance and a look on his face that clearly said, *Don't you dare embarrass me.*

Emily took a deep breath and said, "I'm sure most of you will agree that Mike's article was tastefully done. He didn't dwell on the more gruesome aspects of the murder, nor did he sensationalize the few details that are known about the case. What he did was write a human-interest piece about a crime that has gone unsolved for fifteen years, and he did so in a way that has piqued people's curiosity for miles around. That article has generated a whole new interest in Paradise."

"We don't want that kind of interest, Emily," a deep voice said from the front of the room. Trey Huntington slowly stood, and for the first time in seven years, Emily stood face-to-face with the man she'd once rejected.

Her first thought was that he'd aged well. At forty, he was still extremely handsome, in a *GQ* sort of way, but on closer inspection, Emily saw the gray wings at his temple, the deep lines around his mouth and eyes. His dark eyes were still just as piercing, still just as relentless, but there was a coldness in them now, an icy scorn for anyone who didn't happen to share his opinion.

He had once intimidated Emily with that stare. She realized now that he still did, but thankfully, she'd had a lot of experience in hiding her true emotions in the past few years.

She lifted her chin just a fraction and glared right back at him. "Interest is interest," she said. "What do you care what brings people to town, as long as they come and spend money? I'm not even open for business yet, and because of that article, I already have bookings. Doesn't that prove my point?"

"We've always prided ourselves on being a peaceful little community here. We don't even have to lock our doors at night. Using a murder to publicize a business could destroy that image, and will more than likely bring the sort of people into town that we don't want," Trey argued. He stopped short of saying "undesirables," even though Emily had heard him use that term before.

"I disagree," she replied. "The pictures Mike ran with the article showed what a beautiful, charming home the Talbot house is. It went a long way to dispel the rumors that have run rampant about that place for years, just as talking in public about what happened fifteen years ago will help quiet the whispers of a cover-up in Paradise."

There was more than one gasp from the audience, and then everyone started talking—some shouting—at once. Emily ignored the outraged exclamations. She concentrated instead on putting Trey Huntington in his place for once. Actually, this would be twice, she thought in amusement as Stuart brought the meeting back to order.

Trey, however, did not share her humor. If it was possible, his eyes grew even frostier. "That's a dangerous word to be tossing about so carelessly, Emily. There was no cover-up. Everyone knew Wade Drury committed the crime. He fled town before he could be arrested."

"If it was all so cut-and-dried," Emily said, "then no one should care if I do a little investigating on my own."

Trey raised an incredulous brow. "To what end, Emily? Don't tell me you're actually planning to try and solve the murder yourself?"

Emily felt her face grow hot as snickers erupted around her. She knew exactly what Trey was implying, and so did everyone else. She'd never been able to accomplish anything in her life, let alone solve a murder.

Emily's face burned with humiliation. She turned her gaze to Stuart, hoping that just once he would take up for her. But he wouldn't even look at her. There was no doubt in Emily's or anyone else's mind who was now in charge of the meeting.

That was the way it had always been, she thought bitterly. Trey Huntington ran Paradise, just as his father had run the town before him. That was why her own parents had died on an icy road coming home on Huntington business. Because William Huntington had insisted that her father—Huntington's attorney—return that night, despite the dreadful weather conditions.

As the old memories crowded around her, Emily became even more determined not to back down. If her father had stood his ground, he and Emily's mother might still be alive.

Emily trained her gaze on Trey. "I'll tell you exactly why I want to investigate that murder," she said. "To find out what really happened back then. To lay old ghosts to rest. No matter how much you and everyone else in here might wish to believe otherwise, that murder has always hung like a dark cloud over this town. For everyone's sake, it's time to find out the complete truth about that night fifteen years ago, and for the life of me, I can't understand why anyone in this room would have an objection."

Emily paused, letting her gaze scan the crowd, before

adding in an ominous tone, "Unless, of course, someone here has something to hide."

A stunned silence fell over the room. Emily took a moment to enjoy the deep scowl creasing Trey Huntington's brow, the thunderstruck expression on her brother's face. Then she turned and walked out of the room.

Outside, the night was cold and clear, with a waxing moon glowing palely against the sky and the stars so low they seemed to hang just above the purple silhouette of the distant mountains. The clock in the town square struck ten, the chimes thin and plaintive in the deep stillness of night.

Matthew Steele drifted out of the shadows. He didn't make a sound, just slipped from the darkness like a spirit in the night. Emily felt her heart start to pound when she saw him. "What are you doing here?"

He was standing perhaps six feet away. Moonlight fell between them, throwing angled shadows across his face that made his expression difficult to read. He looked ghostly in the moonglow, a haunting figure from the netherworld.

When he spoke, his tone was light, but his voice still had the power to send chills up and down Emily's spine. "I saw the lights, heard the shouting, and my curiosity got the better of me."

Emily thought about the shadow she'd seen pass by the window earlier and wondered if it had been him. Had he followed her here?

She cast a glance toward the open window, speculating about whether or not anyone could see them out here. She doubted they could be overheard. The meeting was still in an uproar. No one would hear anything. Not even a scream, Emily thought, as Miss Rosabel's words came back to haunt her. *You only had to look into his eyes, those beautiful gray eyes, to know he meant trouble.*

As if reading her thoughts, Matthew stepped forward, more fully into the light, and Emily thought she saw his gray eyes flash with amusement. "Congratulations," he said. "If your intention was to cause a sensation, you certainly succeeded. Makes you wonder what they're all so afraid of, doesn't it?"

For a moment, it was all Emily could do not to retreat. Her heart hammered painfully inside her chest as he stared down at her, the amusement in his eyes turning to something darker and deeper. Something that frightened her.

"You'd best be careful, Emily," he said in a low, menacing tone that chilled her to the bone. "Solving an old murder can be a deadly business."

"Wh-what do you mean?"

"Some people don't take kindly to having old secrets dug up." He took another step toward her.

Emily's heart thundered inside her. Her breath was coming in jerks, and she knew, suddenly, from the way he was looking at her, that he was going to kiss her. Right out here, with her brother and Trey Huntington and the whole blessed town only a few feet away, Matthew Steele was going to kiss her.

Excitement spiraled through her. Her blood heated and her senses spun. She'd always liked living on the edge, and somehow Emily knew that kissing Matthew Steele would definitely be embracing danger. Courting disaster.

She swayed toward him.

Everything about her tensed and waited.

"Quite a little ruckus you caused in there."

The voice definitely did not belong to Matthew Steele. Emily opened her eyes and spun around, searching the darkness. Matthew was nowhere in sight. It was as if he'd vanished into thin air.

Without kissing her.

And Mike Durbin stood there, staring at her as if she'd taken leave of her senses. "Emily? You okay?"

She shrugged, feeling like a fool. "I guess so."

A gust of wind blew through the trees, sounding like rain as it stirred the dying leaves. Feeling chilled, she folded her arms across her chest, hugging herself tightly against the cold. A dog barked in the distance, the sound eerily mournful in the silence that fell around her.

"What's wrong?" Mike asked. "You look as if you've seen a ghost."

"I'm fine," Emily insisted, but in truth, she wasn't sure how far off the mark Mike Durbin might be. If not a ghost, Matthew Steele was certainly a mystery. "I'm glad you came out here," she said, taking a few steps away from the spot where Matthew had been standing. "I want to talk to you. I guess you heard what I said in there."

"About solving the murder?" Mike shook his head and chuckled. "Wish I'd had a video camera. The expression on Trey Huntington's face was priceless. Obviously, you hit a nerve."

"Obviously, I opened my big mouth when I should have kept it shut," Emily said. "Mike, you know I never had any intention of trying to solve the Wilcox murder. All I wanted was some free publicity from your articles. I don't know what came over me. I don't know the first thing about solving a crime."

"Well, luckily, I do, because I think we're on to something big here, Emily. I have a feeling—" He broke off when someone called his name.

Trey Huntington stepped out of the building's shadow, making Emily wonder whether he'd been there all along, eavesdropping. Somehow, she doubted it, but not because she thought Trey wouldn't stoop to something that low. She knew he would, but he'd more than likely hire someone to do it for him.

"Durbin," he said as he came to stand between them. Mike and Emily stepped back, allowing Trey to take center stage, as always. "I'd like to have a word with you," he said to the reporter.

"Seems I'm a popular guy tonight," Mike quipped, but he shot Emily a look that told her he wasn't nearly as confident as his words sounded. "What can I do for you, Mr. Huntington?"

"I trust you'll use discretion in your reporting of this meeting."

"I'll be fair and accurate," Mike said. "Beyond that, I make no promises. Maybe you'd be willing to give me an interview. You could tell me everything you remember about Jenny Wilcox's murder. From your own perspective, of course. As I understand it, you were one of the first ones to demand Wade Drury's arrest."

Even in the darkness, Emily could see Trey's face harden in anger, and she caught her breath. Mike Durbin, whether he realized it or not, was playing with fire. Trey Huntington was a powerful man in Paradise. If he wanted a story killed, all he had to do was make one phone call to Roy Travers. Mike had to know that. He had as much to lose here as she did, but he wasn't backing down, and Emily couldn't help but admire him for that.

Trey said, "You're making a serious mistake, Durbin."

"It won't be the first one," Mike said, and suddenly Emily understood the game he was playing. He was willing to risk everything, because he didn't have anything to lose.

Emily remembered the desperation she'd glimpsed in

Mike's eyes on occasion, and wondered again just how far he'd be willing to go to get his story. He'd already made a very powerful enemy.

Trey turned to her, and Emily had a sinking feeling that she might not be able to hold up under his scrutiny as well as Mike had. She'd done fine in the meeting, but that had been in front of a crowd. Alone, one-on-one, she wasn't nearly as sure of herself with Trey. She knew first-hand what he was capable of, and the memory of their final parting still had the strength to frighten her. Trey Huntington could be a very dangerous man when crossed.

He took Emily's arm and propelled her away from Durbin.

In spite of her fear, Emily jerked her arm free and glared up at him. "What do you think you're doing?"

"What do you think *you're* doing, Emily?"

"Trying to run a business the best way I know how," she retorted.

She could almost see Trey's smirk in the darkness. The faint scent of his cologne—*Égoiste,* she thought—drifted to her. "You're hurting your brother again, that's what you're doing. How could you do this to him, Emily? After everything you've put him through in the past."

It was a low blow, bringing her past indiscretions into the argument, but when had Trey Huntington ever played fair?

"I'm not doing anything to Stuart," Emily said defensively. "All I want to do is make a success of my bed-and-breakfast. How can that possibly hurt Stuart?"

"It can't have escaped your notice that your brother is in the midst of a hotly contested campaign for the state legislature. Publicity about the Wilcox murder could kill his chances."

Now wasn't the time to point out the irony of Trey's

words, Emily decided. She said instead, "How? What does a fifteen-year-old murder have to do with Stuart's election to the legislature? They're two separate issues, aren't they?" She stared up at Trey, waiting for an answer. When he didn't respond, she said slowly, "You know, Trey, if I didn't know better, I'd think you were afraid of what I might find out in this investigation."

He moved very close, watching her face in the dim light spilling from the windows of the building behind them. His eyes were like bits of black stone, and his voice was like ice. "You don't frighten me in the least, Emily."

The look in his eyes, the coldness—so incongruous with the casual way he spoke—brought a spasm of fear to Emily. She forced herself to smile up at him. "Well, maybe I should frighten you," she told him challengingly. "Maybe everyone else in this town *is* afraid of me, because of what I might find out. Maybe that's why they're all so against me. What do you think?"

For a moment, he didn't say anything. Even the wind seemed to still, as if the night were holding its breath. Then Trey said, in a deceptively soft voice, "I think you should forget all this nonsense about the murder, Emily, before you make yourself—and your brother—look even more foolish than you already have."

Emily managed a small laugh, and was quite proud of herself for the way it came out, with just the right mix of humor and incredulity and even a hint of disgust. "You can't tell me what to do like you do everyone else in this town. I'm my own person, Trey. You, of all people, should know that by now."

She didn't want to use her rejection of Trey to hurt him, but turnabout was fair play. With Trey Huntington, she had to use any measures available to defend herself. She knew he would do the same.

His voice was carefully controlled, as if he were having to struggle very hard to keep his temper at bay. "You may not be as independent as you think." His frigid gaze claimed hers in the darkness. Emily felt an unpleasant chill wash over her. "You're back in Paradise now. This is my town."

"You may own the buildings and the land and everything else, but you can't own people."

He lifted his hand and took her chin, caressing her at first. Then his fingers tightened, trapping her. "You are so naive, Emily. I'm glad to see you haven't changed."

"Oh, but I have," she said, moving away from his cold touch. "You have no idea."

She saw his smile in the darkness, the sardonic twisting of his lips, but before he could deny her words, the sound of a motorcycle blasted through the night. The powerful bike, hardly more than a blur, raced down Main Street, and neither Emily nor Trey nor anyone who had come out of the building behind them said a word until the sound had long since faded in the distance. Then an excited murmur drifted through the crowd.

Emily's heart pounded against her ribs. She'd had hardly more than a glimpse of the stranger, but that was all it had taken. All that she'd needed to reassure herself that Matthew Steele was indeed real, and that he was still here in Paradise.

And tonight he would be sleeping in her house.

They would be completely alone.

Anything could happen with a stranger.

Emily glanced up, absorbing Trey's features. He was handsome, powerful and wealthy. An irresistible combination, some might think, but to Emily he'd never seemed less attractive, less appealing. She could muster up no feelings for him whatsoever, not even regret, and yet just one glimpse of a stranger on a motorcycle had set her pulse to pounding like the pistons of a runaway locomotive. The sound was so loud in her ears, Emily thought Trey must surely hear it.

But she needn't have worried. Trey had forgotten all about her. His gaze remained focused on the street, where the powerful bike had passed only seconds before. The look in his eyes, the expression on his face, startled Emily. She'd seen it once before, when she'd told him in no uncertain terms that she wouldn't marry him if he was the last man on earth.

It was a mixture of disbelief, fear, and cold black rage.

Chapter Four

Emily stared at the newspaper the next morning, unable to believe what she was reading. A shaft of sunlight streamed in through the bay window in the kitchen, highlighting the headline that read Bed-and-breakfast owner vows to solve fifteen-year-old murder.

She groaned, cradling her head in her hands. Mike Durbin had certainly wasted no time in moving the story to the front page, and Emily had no doubt that he would do whatever was necessary to keep it there, in spite of Trey's warning last evening.

And now, if she didn't at least make some token attempt to solve the murder, she'd look like a complete fool, which was exactly why Trey had goaded her into that ridiculous position in the first place. All the publicity and interest Mike's initial article had generated in the Other Side of Paradise Inn would die down if people thought Emily was just another crackpot.

Of course, everyone in Paradise would naturally assume that this was just another of her harebrained schemes, anyway, and that sooner or later she would fall flat on her face, just like all the other times when she'd tried to dazzle them with her cleverness.

Emily could hear Stuart and Caroline's endless tirades

now, and her head ached, just from thinking about it. She wished with all her heart that for once in her life she could be the one to look her brother straight in the eye and shout, *I told you so! I told you so!*

But there was only one way she could do that now. She had to prove Stuart was wrong about her. She had to prove to him and to the whole closed-minded town that Emily Townsend *could* succeed at something when she set her mind to it.

Sighing, she got up to start a fresh pot of coffee. It was early, and she had no idea what time Matthew would appear for his breakfast, but she was determined to be ready. Publicity was all well and good, but the final proof of her success would be in her ability to keep guests coming back once she had attracted them. Matthew was her first customer and she wanted to make a good impression.

For more reasons than one. The thought fleeted across her mind as she pulled a pan of freshly baked cinnamon buns from the oven. Emily slid the pan onto a cooling rack and flung off the oven mitt, annoyed with herself for the direction of her thoughts.

Didn't she have enough to worry about without making a fool of herself over a stranger? Wasn't it enough that she'd made a fool of herself over this murder business? The "unfortunate incident" in Paradise's past?

"Good morning."

Emily whirled at the sound of Matthew's deep voice. He'd managed to startle her, even though he'd been on her mind all morning.

"Good morning."

Emily ran a quick assessment of herself through her mind. Had she forgotten anything important when she'd dressed this morning? Decent jeans, soft leather boots, flannel shirt with a pink camisole peeking through the neckline. So far, so good.

"Beautiful day, isn't it?" she asked as Matthew walked into the room. She couldn't help noticing the way he was dressed, also. The faded jeans that molded his long legs, the black T-shirt that hugged his muscular arms and chest, the way his own dark hair glistened with moisture, as though he'd just stepped from the shower.

A tantalizing image, that.

He was undeniably attractive, undeniably masculine, and undeniably powerful, in a way Trey Huntington would never be, and he affected Emily as Trey—with all his money and prestige—never had and never would.

Matthew Steele's appeal was far more subtle, more indefinable, and Emily had the feeling that, to her at least, it could be far more dangerous.

His gaze dropped to the paper lying open on the table. "I see you've made the front page."

Emily grimaced. "Don't remind me."

"Having second thoughts about solving the murder?"

"Try third and fourth thoughts." Emily poured Matthew a cup of coffee and offered him cream and sugar, which he declined. "If you'd like to go into the dining room, I'll bring in your breakfast."

"What's wrong with in here?" Matthew asked, indicating the breakfast alcove in the kitchen. "The paper's already here, the sun's shining in, and something smells delicious."

"Cinnamon rolls. You can eat in here, if you want." Though his nearness would probably make her so nervous she'd break half the dishes in the kitchen.

Matthew sat down in the sunshine, and Emily bustled about, setting the table, replenishing his cup, and when they'd cooled sufficiently, she brought him a plate of rolls.

Matthew sampled one. "My grandmother used to make cinnamon rolls like this," he said. "I haven't tasted anything so good in years."

His warm gaze rested on Emily, and she blushed just like a kid with her first crush. Good grief, it wasn't as if she hadn't been around the block a time or two. Or three.

While Matthew read the paper and savored his coffee and rolls, Emily savored the moment. There was something so exquisitely intimate about serving a man breakfast in the kitchen.

She thought about all the mornings she'd eaten alone during her marriage. Eugene had never gotten out of bed before two in the afternoon, and when he did get up, it had only been to stumble into the kitchen for a cup of coffee that he immediately carried back to the shower with him. He'd never sat and read the paper with her, never even kissed her good-morning. Sometimes a careless wave of his hand had been the only indication Emily had that he even knew she was there.

Eugene had hated her cinnamon rolls.

Matthew's plate was already empty. Emily gave him seconds, and he smiled his appreciation.

"Don't know why I'm so hungry," he muttered.

"It's the mountain air," Emily said. "It always affects appetites that way."

"I think you may be right." His dark gaze held hers, then moved downward and over her, in a manner so smooth and covert, Emily might have thought she'd imagined it, except for the delicious tingle running up and down her spine.

The attraction between them was almost a tangible thing. Emily thought that if she could capture and market this feeling, she'd be an overnight millionaire. As it was, all she could do was fumble with the top button of her flannel shirt and shift from one foot to the other.

"Why don't you sit down," Matthew said, indicating the chair opposite his, "and tell me how you plan to solve this murder?"

His words were like a splash of ice water. For a few moments, Emily had managed to put that predicament out of her mind while she contemplated this new and more exciting predicament. Now she had to turn her thoughts to murder again.

She sighed heavily and dropped into the wicker-backed chair. "I haven't a clue," she said morosely. "I don't even know where to start."

Matthew pushed back his empty plate. "Why don't you start at the library? Look up all the old newspaper accounts of the murder. Maybe something will click and give you a lead."

Emily snapped her fingers. His suggestion made so much sense. "Now, why didn't I think of that?"

"I'm experienced," Matthew said. Then he added, "Like I told you yesterday, mysteries are somewhat of a hobby of mine. I like solving them. That's why I came to Paradise."

"Then you want to solve the Wilcox murder, too?"

"I'm interested in the story," Matthew said, his tone noncommittal. Then he shrugged. "I might be able to help you. Why don't you tell me what you know?"

Emily hesitated. Could she trust him? *Should* she trust him? But what harm could there possibly be in telling him the story that Rosabel Talbot had told her? Besides, he'd soon be reading all about it in Mike's articles, anyway. And if he could help, so much the better. Emily needed all the assistance she could get.

told him about her and Mike's conversation with Miss

Rosabel, all about Jenny Wilcox and Wade Drury and Tony Vincent, and when she'd finished, she sat back and folded her arms across her chest.

"So you see, everyone in town believed the stranger was guilty. There were no other suspects, and the fact that he just up and disappeared like that made him look even more guilty. The way I see it, all we really have to do is find out what happened to Wade Drury. Then the case will be solved."

Matthew's expression remained the same, one of polite, casual interest, but something flashed behind his eyes, a look that made Emily's heart jolt as he said softly, almost indifferently, "But what if Drury didn't do it?"

Emily faltered for a moment, taken aback by the look in Matthew's gray eyes. Then she said, "But…he had to have done it. If he didn't, that would mean that the murderer might still be alive and well and…living… here…in…Paradise." Her voice trailed off as the very air between them became electric with awareness. Not sexual tension this time, but something far more dark and deadly.

Their eyes measured each other for a long, silent moment. Suddenly, for the first time since she and Mike Durbin had started digging into the past, the impact of what she was doing hit Emily. She was looking for a murderer, someone who had viciously stabbed a young woman to death. Someone who had covered up the brutal crime for fifteen years.

Someone, possibly, that Emily had known all of her life.

Or someone, possibly, that she had just met.

So now she knew it wasn't a game.

Murder was never amusing, Matthew thought as he

watched Emily from the front window of her house. She got into her dusty blue Volkswagen, shifted into reverse and backed the little car out of the driveway. Then, shifting again, she headed down the street toward town and the Piggly Wiggly store where she'd said she did all her grocery shopping.

Don't bother locking up if you go out, she'd added. *Nothing ever happens in Paradise.*

Nothing except murder.

Matthew started to turn away from the window. Now that Emily was safely out of the house, he had some investigating of his own to do. But a movement caught his eye, and he stilled. A curtain fluttered at an upstairs window in the house across the street, then fell back into place, as if someone had turned away from the window the moment Emily was out of sight.

Matthew frowned. There was something ominous about the house across the street. The turrets and towers and lacy scrollwork were all pleasant enough, but the massive oaks surrounding the yard cast huge shadows over the house, giving the place an air of perpetual gloom, even in midday. Perhaps in the heat of summer the shady yard would offer welcome respite, but in October, with the promise of the first snowfall not so very far away, the house looked cold and bleak and empty. Soulless.

As he continued to watch, the front door opened and a woman stepped out on the wide wraparound veranda. Her gaze settled on the Other Side of Paradise Inn. She walked down the porch steps, never taking her eyes off the front of Emily's house. As if lured by some strange, irresistible force, the woman crossed the street and came to a standstill on the sidewalk in front of the inn.

Matthew drew back from the window, but he continued

to watch the woman. She was sixty at least, thin and wiry, with scraped-back hair, a narrow face and piercing black eyes. The term battle-ax came to mind, but Matthew knew looks were often deceiving. However, in this case, he very much doubted that his immediate impression of the woman was far off the mark.

There was something about the absorbed expression on her deeply creviced face as she stared at Emily's house that brought an uneasiness to Matthew. He didn't ignore the feeling. In his line of work, he'd been trained, and had learned from his own experiences, to discount nothing, especially his own instincts. There was something about this woman he didn't trust.

As he continued to watch her, her gaze lifted, and Matthew thought she must be looking at the window of his bedroom. The window of the room in which Jenny Wilcox had been murdered. She raised her hand—it was her only movement—to absently caress the wrinkled skin at her neck, and Mike Durbin's account of the murder suddenly came rushing back to Matthew. *Jenny Wilcox had been brutally stabbed fifteen times. The fatal wound was the one to her throat....*

Matthew crossed the room, opened the door and stepped onto the porch before the woman had time to leave. She glanced at him and visibly started. The color drained from her face, leaving the unattractive features, the bulging eyes, the hawklike nose and the lipless mouth, to stand out starkly. The hand at her throat moved to her heart. For a moment, Matthew thought she might actually pass out.

He walked down the steps into the sunlight, her gaze following his every move. "It's Cora Mae, isn't it?" he asked softly. "Cora Mae Hicks?"

Her eyes narrowed on him. "Do I know you?"

Matthew smiled. "I thought you looked as if you recognized me."

"I was mistaken," she said quickly. "You couldn't be— Never you mind. How do you know *my* name?" Her dark eyes flashed with an emotion Matthew was hard put to define.

He said truthfully, "When I was looking for a place to stay in Paradise, your name was mentioned. You own a bed-and-breakfast, don't you? The one across the street. The This Side of Paradise Inn, isn't it?"

As if connected by a common string that had suddenly been yanked, their gazes moved to the shingle hanging from Emily's front porch. The Other Side of Paradise Inn. Clever girl, Matthew thought approvingly.

Cora Mae obviously didn't share his opinion. "I could sue her for that," she snapped. "She has no right using that name, capitalizing on all my hard work. I've operated the This Side of Paradise Inn for over a quarter of a century. It's the best one in town. In the whole county. Everyone knows that. Now here she comes along with all her highfalutin ideas, trying to steal away my customers by stealing the name of my inn. Well, I won't stand for, I tell you. I won't let her get away with this."

Matthew couldn't believe the venom in the old woman's voice. He wondered if Emily had any idea of the extent of Cora Mae's resentment. He tried to make his tone sound only mildly interested when he said, "So you've operated your bed-and-breakfast for over twenty-five years. That means you were right there across the street when Jenny Wilcox was murdered."

Cora Mae's lips thinned to nothing more than a jagged line. "Who are you?"

"My name is Matthew Steele."

She considered the name for a moment. "Used to be

some Steeles lived down in Newport, but I heard tell they moved away years ago. Worthless lot, best I recollect. You any kin to Delbert and Fannie Steele?''

"I don't think so."

"I don't think so, neither," she said. Her words seemed to have a double meaning. "What brings you to Paradise?"

"I read Mike Durbin's article in a newspaper, and it grabbed my attention. I decided to come see for myself where the murder occurred."

"Why?" Cora Mae demanded, her eyes glinting with cold suspicion.

Matthew shrugged. "Call it curiosity." *Or revenge.*

Cora Mae's gaze went back to the upstairs window. Her eyes took on a sort of feverish glee. "That girl was stabbed, you know. Fourteen times in the heart and in the face." Her gaze darted back to Matthew's. "And once in the throat. A crime of passion, they called it."

"So I read." Matthew felt a chill creep over him as the old woman continued her unblinking regard.

"Rosabel Talbot owned this place then. Tried to make a go of her bed-and-breakfast, but she weren't no competition for me, and after the killing, her business was finished anyhow. The bloodstains wouldn't come up. They never do. Don't matter what you use on them. No one wanted to stay in the house after that."

"I guess that was a lucky break for you, wasn't it?" Matthew murmured.

But Cora Mae was staring up at the window again. "This place should have been burned to the ground a long time ago. Emily Townsend is doing the devil's work, opening it up again. She's inviting evil back into Paradise." Cora Mae paused for a moment, her gaze flashing back to Matthew. "Unless someone does something to stop her."

Demented, Matthew thought. Undoubtedly certifiable. But that did nothing to alleviate his unease about Cora Mae Hicks. If anything, she was even more dangerous than he'd first thought. Matthew would have given a lot to know her exact whereabouts on the night Jenny was killed.

He watched Cora Mae turn and make her way across the street. When she reached the safety of her own porch, she looked back and made the sign of the cross in the air, as if to ward off evil spirits.

Matthew wasn't sure whether the gesture had been directed toward Emily's house, or at him.

As EMILY DROVE through the tree-shrouded streets of Paradise that afternoon, she couldn't help but admire the beauty of the town. The fall foliage was nearing its peak, and the maples lining Main Street were on fire in the sunlight.

Quaint little houses—painted pink or country blue or white—had been turned into art galleries, craft stores and restaurants with window boxes spilling over with purple pansies, red geraniums, and showy bronze chrysanthemums.

But beneath the sunlight and beyond the charming pastel houses and the windswept hillsides, a darkness simmered. Paradise wasn't at all what it seemed, Emily thought bitterly, remembering her unhappy childhood. The people here were sheltered, secluded from the rest of the world, which sometimes bred narrow-mindedness and intolerance. Oh, they put on a good show for the tourists, but if one of their own stepped out of line, they could be mean-spirited and sometimes merciless.

And one of them, Emily thought grimly, might even have committed murder.

In spite of the sunshine streaming in through her windshield, she shuddered. It was a day to go berry-picking and cloud-watching. Not a day to have murder on one's mind, but, unfortunately, Emily couldn't seem to think of much else. Especially since her conversation with Matthew that morning.

She pulled her car into the parking lot of the Paradise Town Library, which was situated two blocks over from Main Street and near the park. The library was housed in a charming little redbrick building that had once served as a one-room schoolhouse. An old-fashioned bell still hung near the entrance to the building, and the trees sprawling across the spacious lawn still bore the scars from dozens of initials painstakingly carved into their bark.

Inside, however, the library was surprisingly modern, even computerized, and Nella Talbot, the librarian, was more than eager to help. She stood over Emily's shoulder as Emily scrolled through screen after screen of fifteen-year-old newspaper articles.

"What exactly are you looking for?" Nella asked.

"I wish I knew." Emily looked up and smiled. She hadn't seen Nella in years, but the woman hadn't changed much. She was still extremely thin, with the quiet, athletic grace of a ballet dancer, and her fair hair was pulled back from her face and secured with a plain silver barrette. She wore glasses, which Emily didn't remember, but instead of detracting from her appearance, the lenses seemed to magnify the violet-blue of her eyes, giving them a dreamy quality.

Everything about the woman was soft and quiet and

understated—exactly the attributes one would desire in a librarian.

Nella said shyly, "I wondered when you'd come by." She shifted the heavy reference book she carried from one arm to the other and gave a sheepish little shrug. "I happened to be at the meeting last night. I heard what you said about solving the Wilcox murder."

"I suppose you've read the paper this morning, as well," Emily said dryly.

A smile hovered at the corner of Nella's lips. "It was hard to miss," she admitted. She set the book on the table beside her, then, hesitating for only a moment, sat down beside Emily at the computer. "I think it's great what you're doing. Solving an old murder. It's so exciting."

Nella Talbot was full of surprises. She was the first person in town to show Emily the least bit of support, and that made her instantly warm to the librarian.

"Not many people in Paradise share your opinion," Emily replied. "I think a few would even like to string me up for causing so much trouble."

"But that's the way you've always been," Nella said. Emily glanced at her, but from the placid expression on Nella's face, Emily could tell the comment wasn't meant to be mean.

"I guess I have always been a bit of a rabble-rouser," Emily agreed.

Nella's eyes gleamed. "I remember hearing about some of the things you used to do in high school, organizing sit-ins and walkouts and what have you. I could never do anything like that."

"All it takes is a lack of good judgment."

Nella laughed quietly as she adjusted the skirt of her blue shirtwaist, then crossed her legs primly, as if she were settling in for a nice long chat. It came to Emily suddenly that the woman must be lonely. There probably wasn't much traffic at the Paradise Town Library, and as best Emily could remember, Nella had always been something of a loner anyway. An outsider who never quite fit in. Emily felt a certain kinship with her for that.

Nella said, "What made you come back to Paradise, anyway? I mean, there aren't exactly a lot of opportunities around here."

"No," Emily agreed, "but it is home."

Nella nodded vaguely. Her eyes were trained on the computer monitor, and Emily turned. The screen had stopped on an article about the Wilcox murder. The picture above the text was of Miss Rosabel Talbot, and the young woman beside her was Nella.

"You were there, weren't you?" Emily asked.

Nella's blue eyes took on a faraway look, much as Miss Rosabel's had the day before, when she related the details of the murder to Emily and Mike Durbin.

"It was terrible," Nella said, in a soft, anxious voice. "Horrible. It's something I'll never forget. All that blood…"

"Your aunt said the same thing," Emily told her. "I drove down to Batesville to visit with her yesterday."

Nella looked surprised. "You did? But…why?"

"She seemed the obvious person to talk to first." Emily paused for a moment, then said, "Were you with Miss Rosabel when she discovered the body?"

Nella shook her head. "I'd already left for school. I didn't hear about the murder until later that day, but I…I helped Aunt Rosabel clean the room once the… investigation was over."

Emily grimaced, imagining what it must have been like for a seventeen-year-old to have to deal with something so grisly. Jenny Wilcox had been stabbed fifteen times.

The walls and floors must have been splattered with blood. "Your aunt said you two witnessed a fight between Tony Vincent and Wade Drury the night before Jenny Wilcox's body was found. Do you remember much about it?"

Nella pushed her glasses up her nose with one slim finger. "I remember that Tony had been drinking. He was drunk, in fact, and when Tony drank he became... unreasonable."

"Violent?"

Nella shrugged. "I'd heard so, but that night was the first time I'd ever seen his temper firsthand. I really thought he was going to kill Wade Drury. He probably would have, if it had been anyone else, but Wade knew how to handle himself. He wasn't as strong as Tony, but he was smarter. Tony had worked himself into a drunken rage, and he let his emotions get in the way. But Wade was so cool. Like ice water. He could have killed Tony if he'd wanted to."

"But he didn't."

"No. When he knew Tony had had enough, Wade just got up and walked away."

"Doesn't sound like the actions of a cold-blooded killer," Emily mused.

"But then, no one knows exactly how a killer acts, do they? Until he murders someone, I mean." Nella stood and brushed the wrinkles from her cotton skirt. "Well, I'd better get back to work. If you need anything else, just holler." She picked up the reference book from the table, and started to turn away. Then she said hesitantly, "I wonder...that is...would you mind if I dropped by your inn sometime? I haven't been in that old house in years, and I'd love to see how you've fixed it up. With your flair, I'm sure it must look wonderful."

Emily couldn't help being flattered. It was the first time anyone in town had shown the least bit of interest in her renovations to the Talbot house. She smiled warmly. ''I'd love to have you drop by. Come anytime. Maybe we can have coffee or something.''

Nella's own smile seemed shy and almost pathetically grateful. ''I'd like that,'' she said. ''Well, back to work.'' She patted the encyclopedia in her arms, then turned and disappeared into the rows and rows of books.

Emily went back to her own work. Absorbed in the articles, she hardly noticed the shadow that fell across the computer screen a few minutes later. The deep voice that spoke behind her, however, could not be ignored. He said, ''Any luck?''

Emily turned and found Matthew lounging against the desk behind her. A little thrill raced through her as she took in his appearance—the leather jacket, the jeans and the boots. The half smile playing at the corners of his tempting, tantalizing mouth.

Be still, my heart, she thought as she tried to remain outwardly calm. ''Not much,'' she told him. ''The local newspaper accounts were pretty sparse.''

He straightened and moved toward her. Emily could smell the wind on his clothes as he bent over her shoulder and scanned the article she had pulled up on the screen. ''What about the Little Rock papers?''

His breath was warm on her neck. Emily thought the hairs at her nape must be curling. Not to mention her toes.

''The major papers only go back ten years.''

''Too bad. We'll have to look elsewhere for a lead, then.''

Emily turned her head just a fraction. It was thrilling how close they suddenly were. So close, Emily could see the tiny lines that fanned out around his eyes and mouth, and the faint masculine shadow of his beard. So close, she could look deep into his eyes and see the hint of secrets that lurked somewhere in those intriguing gray depths. So close, everything stilled within her.

"We?" she breathed.

As if the proximity were getting to him, too, Matthew straightened and backed away. He sat down in the chair Nella had vacated, sprawling his long legs in front of him. "I told you this morning I might be able to help you."

"Yes, you did," Emily said. "But I've been wondering since then why. Are you a reporter?"

"No."

"A cop?"

"I just like mysteries."

"And you came all the way from Memphis to Paradise, Arkansas, just because you read about an old murder in the paper?"

"Well," he said, "there was a picture of you with the article."

Emily said, "Oh," and quite literally felt as if the breath had been knocked clean out of her. Matthew's smile deepened, and she thought, *Please, no more. I can't take a killer smile on top of so much charm.*

The combination was positively lethal, and Emily had no doubt that at any moment she'd say or do something to make a complete idiot of herself.

So she said nothing at all. Did nothing at all. And meanwhile, her heart raced inside her chest.

Matthew cocked his head slightly. "Did I say something wrong?"

"No, it's just—"

"You still don't trust me."

"Well—"

"I understand. I'm a stranger, and from what I've seen,

strangers aren't exactly welcomed with open arms in Paradise. At least not all strangers.''

''You have to look like a tourist,'' Emily explained. ''And you don't.''

''Should I be hitting all the art galleries? Browsing the craft shows? Taking long walks in the woods and gathering wildflowers?''

It was an incongruous picture. Emily said bluntly, ''It wouldn't help. You'd never pass for a tourist.''

''Why not?''

''Because you look too—''

One dark brow arched. ''Too what?''

She searched for the right word. ''Intense. Brooding. You don't look like you're on vacation. You look like a man with a mission.''

The amusement in his eyes vanished. His features seemed to harden before Emily's eyes, and she shivered, glimpsing a darkness inside him that she had no wish to see. Matthew Steele had seen things, done things. It frightened Emily to think of what sins his immortal soul might harbor.

''You look like a man with a definite purpose in life,'' she said softly, mesmerized in spite of herself by the very qualities inside him that frightened her.

He shook his head. ''I might have once,'' he said, with what sounded like regret to Emily. ''But not anymore. I'm free to do whatever I want, and right now, all I want is to help you solve a fifteen-year-old murder.''

''Which brings us back to my original question,'' Emily answered. ''Why?''

''Why not?''

Because she didn't know anything about him, Emily told herself. She didn't even know whether Matthew Steele was his real name, or what his real purpose for coming to Paradise was. Stuart would have a conniption if he knew she was contemplating spending time alone with this tall, dark, handsome stranger who might or might not be a murderer.

And, after all, Stuart had been right about Eugene Sprague all those years ago. He'd warned Emily that Eugene was no good, and his assessment couldn't have been more on target. If Emily had listened to her brother back then, she might have saved herself a lot of grief.

Emily knew what Stuart would say to her if he was here right now. He'd tell her to run as far and as fast as she could from a man like Matthew Steele. He'd tell her to use her brain instead of her heart for once in her life. He'd tell her she'd be a fool to be taken in a second time by a good-looking man who practically oozed sensuality.

Emily's gaze met Matthew's. Her mind was made up. She knew what she had to do. She took a deep breath and said, ''I think we should go talk to Miss Rosabel Talbot again. She may have remembered something else since Mike and I were there yesterday.''

''Let's go, then,'' Matthew said, standing.

''Just let me clean up a little here first.'' Emily turned back to the computer. A loud bang at the front of the library startled her, and her fingers slid off the keyboard. Both she and Matthew whirled toward the noise.

Nella Talbot stood in the doorway of her office, wearing an expression Emily could remember having seen only once before in her life, when a deer had been caught and paralyzed by the headlights of her car.

Like that deer, Nella remained motionless, mesmerized, staring straight at Matthew Steele.

Lying at her feet was the stack of books that had tumbled from her arms.

Chapter Five

"What in the world was that all about?" Emily asked as she and Matthew left the library. "Did you see the way she was staring at you?" Granted, Emily liked looking at Matthew herself—who wouldn't?—but Nella's stunned expression had hardly been one of admiration.

Matthew stopped beside his motorcycle and turned to her. "Maybe she didn't hear me come in. She was probably just startled to see someone else in the library."

Emily wasn't convinced. She shook her head. "I don't think so. I mean, she was surprised, all right, but she was staring at you as if she recognized you."

Matthew shrugged. "I have the kind of face that always reminds people of someone they know."

Emily started to contradict him. Matthew Steele reminded her of no one but himself. She'd never met anyone even remotely like him. But he was handing her a helmet. Emily gazed down at it. "What's this for?"

"We're going to see Miss Rosabel, aren't we?"

"On your *motorcycle?*"

"Why not?"

Emily stared at the Harley. She'd always wanted to ride on the back of a bike, but now that she was actually confronted with the opportunity, the thing looked huge and powerful, and Emily realized she had no idea what kept it from toppling over.

Matthew straddled the bike. "Ready?" He sat there waiting for her, his black leather jacket gleaming dully in the late-afternoon sunlight and his mirrored sunglasses revealing only a distorted image of herself. Emily had no idea what he might be thinking.

She took the helmet—she noticed he didn't have one—and tugged it on her head. "As ready as I'll ever be, I guess." She climbed on the back of the Harley, fumbled for the correct place to put her feet, then slipped her arms around Matthew's waist.

"Hang on."

He didn't have to tell her twice. Emily clung to him for dear life as he gunned the engine and put the bike into gear. Then, with a jerk and a roar, they were off.

Nella stood watching them from the front window of the library, and Emily wanted to wave, but she didn't dare release her death grip on Matthew. Nella didn't wave, either, merely stared after them as they left, and Emily wondered again about the librarian's strange reaction to Matthew.

Actually, Emily was having a pretty strange reaction to him herself. She found she liked being this close to him and having her arms around him. She liked the way his body felt against hers. It was a nice place to be, she decided. A very nice place to be.

As they rode down Main Street, Emily glanced up at the window of her brother's office, wondering what he would think if he could see her now. He wouldn't be surprised. Nothing she did would surprise him anymore, just as nothing she did would ever please him.

She felt a pang of sadness at the thought. Stuart was the only family she had left, and the distance between them hurt her. She wished things could be different, but, unfortunately, the fourteen years separating their ages made Stuart seem more like her father than her brother. It was his nature to try to tell her what to do, just as it was Emily's nature to rebel against his advice.

The houses thinned as they neared the highway, the pastel colors and flower boxes giving way to graying wood, peeling paint and ragged yards strewn with bicycles, tire swings and dirty toddlers grubbing about in sandboxes. In a way, Emily had always liked this section of Paradise better than the picture perfect image of downtown. It was more honest. More real.

Within moments, they were out on the highway, passing the sign that still bore the graffiti message Welcome to Hell. Matthew turned his head and shouted something to her, but over the roar of engine and wind, Emily couldn't hear him. She shrugged, and Matthew turned his attention back to the road.

Chiseled through the rocky hillside, twisting and turning, the road was buttressed on the right by soaring, jagged limestone bluffs, while on the left it fell away to a steep embankment jutted with boulders and tree trunks. The highway had recently been paved, so the surface was smooth and unblemished.

Matthew drove fast, handling the Harley with what seemed to Emily terrifying competence, leaning into the curves, opening the throttle on the tiny stretches of straight road, barely slowing for the breathtaking rollercoaster plunges downhill.

The stunning fall scenery passed by in a red, gold and apricot blur. Emily's heart stayed in her throat, but she still loved the sensation. It felt as if they were soaring through time and space, riding the waves of some vast and invisible sea. The feel of the wind in her hair and the vibrating speed of the powerful bike were both terrifying and exhilarating.

Emily laid her head against Matthew's leather-clad back, shielding herself from the sharp sting of wind against her face as they roared downhill. In spite of the speed and the cold and the death-defying road, she felt warm and oddly protected so near him. A part of her wished she knew more about him, and a part of her was glad she knew nothing at all. She didn't want anything to diminish the thrill of the moment.

But by the time they arrived in Batesville, the thrill had diminished a little on its own. Emily was frozen, and when she got off the bike her legs were stiff and her butt was numb. It wasn't quite the sensation she'd been expecting.

Matthew got off the motorcycle and reached down to remove her helmet. He laid it on the seat behind him. When Emily took a few hobbling steps away from him, he said sympathetically, "It takes a little getting used to. You have to be somewhat of an aficionado to appreciate riding a bike—even a Harley—in this kind of weather. Or maybe you just have to be plain crazy," he added with an ironic smile. "Next time, we'll take your car, if you want."

"That takes a little getting used to, too," Emily said, trying without much success to fluff her flattened hair with her fingers. "Especially when you have to push it uphill."

They walked up the steps of the nursing home, and Matthew held the door for her. Emily stepped through, relishing the warmth. The thermostat was set high, and by the time they'd been ushered down the long hallway to Miss Rosabel's room, Emily had removed her coat and slung it over her arm. Matthew did the same.

The attendant who accompanied them pushed open

Miss Rosabel's door and stuck her head inside. She called gaily, "Miss Rosabel, you have visitors. That nice young woman from Paradise is back. And she's brought another young man to see you."

The attendant, who had to be fifty if she was a day, slanted an admiring look up at Matthew as she turned away from the doorway and disappeared down the hallway.

Maybe Nella *had* been reacting to Matthew's looks, Emily thought, but when they went inside Miss Rosabel's room and the old woman's gaze fell on Matthew, the same expression of astonishment crossed her features.

What in the world is going on? Emily wondered.

Miss Rosabel was sitting by the window again, and as if suddenly chilled, she pulled her blue shawl around her shoulders.

Emily, made uneasy by Miss Rosabel's reaction, said hesitantly, "May we come in and talk to you for a few minutes?"

Miss Rosabel motioned for them both to enter, but her eyes never left Matthew. She watched him cross the floor, and when he and Emily were standing in front of her, the old woman's hand fluttered to her heart. Her voice shook when she said, "I don't believe my eyes."

Emily knelt beside her. The look on the old woman's face alarmed her. "What's wrong, Miss Rosabel?"

"He's the spitting image," she muttered. The hand clasping her shawl trembled.

"Spitting image of whom?" Emily asked. When Miss Rosabel still didn't answer, Emily touched her arm, and the woman visibly started. Emily said, "Are you all right, Miss Rosabel? Can I get you something?"

Miss Rosabel batted Emily's hand away. "I'm fine,"

she snapped. "I'm not the one you should be concerned about."

Matthew knelt beside them. "My name is Matthew Steele," he said in a soft, reassuring voice.

"Matthew Steele," Miss Rosabel repeated. She looked at once relieved and doubtful. "For a minute there, I thought you were someone else," she murmured.

"He has the kind of face that always reminds people of someone they know," Emily repeated dryly, giving Matthew a look that clearly said, *Just what is going on around here?*

"Yes, that must be it," Miss Rosabel agreed, but her gaze never left Matthew's face.

Emily was beginning to feel as though she'd stepped into the "Twilight Zone." Why was everyone acting so strangely? Was it because Matthew was so devastatingly attractive and so obviously appealing? Or was it something else? Something more sinister?

Was it because he rode a motorcycle and had gray eyes? Did he remind everyone of Wade Drury, the man accused of a brutal murder?

Did everyone in town know something Emily didn't?

Your paranoia is showing, Emily scolded herself. She said briskly, "Matthew read Mike Durbin's article in a Memphis paper and became interested in the murder. We'd like to talk to you about it, if you don't mind."

"I don't mind. I'm glad to have the company." Miss Rosabel finally tore her gaze away from Matthew and looked at Emily. "I don't know what more I can tell you, though."

"Sometimes, the more you talk about an incident, the more you remember." Emily paused for a moment, then continued, "I went to the library this morning to do some research, and I spoke with your niece."

Miss Rosabel's eyes seemed to sharpen on Emily. "You saw Nella?"

Emily nodded. "We talked about the night Wade Drury and Tony Vincent had their fight."

Miss Rosabel's lips thinned almost imperceptibly.

"Nella said Wade Drury could easily have killed Tony that night, if he'd been of a mind to. She said Tony started the fight, but Wade was the one who walked away. You told Mike Durbin and me yesterday that the sheriff had to come in and break up the fight, remember?"

"Did I?" Miss Rosabel frowned, evidently trying to recall. Her eyes clouded a bit. "The sheriff did come. I remember that plainly, but I think Nella's right. Wade had ended the fight before Willis ever got there. At any rate, Nella would remember more about that night than I," she murmured.

"Why?"

There was a long silence, then Miss Rosabel said, "Well, she's younger, of course. Her memory's bound to be clearer." Her logic made perfect sense, but for some reason, Emily didn't think that easy explanation was what Miss Rosabel had been thinking at all.

Emily, wondering why Matthew was being so quiet, decided to try another tactic. "I got the impression from something you said yesterday that Nella had a crush on Wade Drury. Did she?"

Miss Rosabel turned to stare out the window. Her frail shoulders lifted and dropped as she gave a long, weary sigh. "I guess you were bound to find out sooner or later," she said softly. Her gaze met Emily's again, and there was something in the older woman's eyes that Emily couldn't quite discern.

"You have to understand how it was for Nella," Miss Rosabel explained. "She was new in town and didn't have many friends. Wade was kind to her. He was handsome and mysterious, and more than a little wild, I suspect.'' Her gaze drifted back to Matthew.

''Those qualities are devastating to any teenager, but to someone like Nella, well… She felt things more deeply than most girls her age. She'd had…infatuations before, you see, one rather serious. That's why her father had sent her to me that year. She'd fallen madly in love with one of her teachers, and there was some trouble, because the man was married. There was a lot of talk, and, well, we decided—my brother and I—that it would be best for everyone if Nella came to stay with me until all the fuss blew over.''

Emily couldn't have been more shocked. She would never have guessed that quiet, unassuming Nella Talbot was a woman with a sordid past. But still waters ran deep, and far be it for Emily, with her own less-than-sterling past, to cast stones at anyone else.

Matthew said grimly, ''Did Wade know how she felt?''

''He'd have had to be blind not to. But he was never anything but kind to Nella. She was just a child, and he never led her on. Truth be told, I don't think Nella ever expected, or even wanted, anything else from him. It was so obvious which direction the wind was a-blowing as far as his own affections were concerned, and Nella adored Jenny. In spite of the differences in their ages, Jenny was the first real friend Nella ever had.''

The plot thickens, Emily thought, glancing at Matthew. A romantic triangle had certainly been motive for murder before, and if you added the volatile angle that was Tony Vincent, who knew what might have happened that night?

Matthew stood and moved to the window, staring out with a brooding frown. Emily studied his profile—the strong, chiseled jawline, the bold slash of dark brows over beguiling gray eyes, and she thought, as she'd thought a dozen times since she'd first laid eyes on him, *Who are you, Matthew Steele? Who are you really?*

Miss Rosabel was obviously still affected by him, too. Her faded blue eyes, bright with an emotion Emily couldn't quite decipher, watched Matthew with an absorbed, unblinking regard, and Emily tried to tell herself, *Well, why not?* The woman was old, not dead. She could appreciate a good-looking man the same as anyone else. But Emily had the impression that Miss Rosabel's interest in Matthew was more than just admiration for an attractive man. She seemed fascinated, intrigued, and maybe just a little bit frightened by him.

And so had Nella.

Matthew turned from the window, and Emily thought she saw Miss Rosabel catch her breath as he trained his gray eyes upon her.

"Did you ever hear of a group that called themselves the Avengers?"

There was no mistaking the fear that flashed in Miss Rosabel's eyes. "Oh, no," she said. "Don't tell me they're at it again."

"Not that I know of," Matthew said. "I just wondered what you could tell me about them."

Again Emily had the distinct and unpleasant feeling that she was on the outside looking in. She said, frowning, "'The Avengers' was an old TV show, wasn't it?"

"Would that that were true, child," Miss Rosabel said cryptically. Then, to Matthew: "How in the world do you know about them, unless—?"

Matthew cut her off. "I've done some research."

He glanced down at Emily, and she glared up at him. Obviously, he'd been holding out on her. Emily didn't say anything, but she knew the look on her face told Matthew plainly enough that when they left here, he had a lot of explaining to do.

Miss Rosabel, unaware of the silent tension between her two visitors, said, "I haven't heard anything about the Avengers in years. Hadn't even thought about them. No one talks about them, you know. We never did."

"Who were they?" Emily asked.

"No one really knew. It was a secret society. All the members dressed in black clothing and wore ski masks to cover their faces. They called themselves vigilantes, but they were little better than thugs," she said in disgust.

"What did they do?"

"What didn't they do? They roamed the streets of Paradise one whole summer, upholding law and order, they claimed, but it got so innocent folks were afraid to go out at night. Afraid the Avengers might accuse them of some crime for which they'd have no defense. Those few months when they prowled the streets at night were a terrible time. People afraid in their own homes. Young boys beaten up because they'd had the misfortune to be caught out on the streets after midnight. Property vandalized. One poor family run clean out of town." Miss Rosabel shuddered. "There was nothing they wouldn't do."

"Were they operating in Paradise at the time of Jenny Wilcox's murder?" Matthew asked.

"The summer before Jenny came to town they were. Their activities had let up some by fall, but I've often wondered…" Miss Rosabel faltered. She tugged her shawl around her again, then, lifting her chin, said, "I've often wondered if they didn't have something to do with Wade Drury's disappearance."

Emily gasped. "You mean…you think they *did* something to him?"

"I'm not saying they hurt him," Miss Rosabel rushed

to explain. "Not physically. But I wouldn't put it past them to have threatened him in some way. I think Wade was afraid to hang around town to try and clear his name. He knew the Avengers—not to mention the sheriff— would have railroaded him into a conviction."

"Then you don't think he killed Jenny?" Matthew asked.

Something flickered in the old woman's eyes. "There was a darkness inside him. Make no mistake about that. I saw it when he went after Tony that night. But Wade knew how to control it. He knew when to walk away. I never could bring myself to believe he was a killer."

"But...if he didn't kill Jenny Wilcox," Emily said slowly, "haven't you wondered all these years who did?"

"Every night of my life."

"Then why didn't you ever say anything to anybody?" Emily asked in amazement.

Miss Rosabel shrugged. "Nobody ever asked until now. And besides, who was I supposed to tell? The sheriff? I always suspected he was in up to his eyebrows with the Avengers. Everyone in town wanted to believe Wade Drury was guilty. It was easier that way."

Emily let out a long breath. "My God," she said. "I can't believe this. I can't believe that Jenny's murder has gone unsolved all these years. And I can't believe a bunch of thugs dressed up in Halloween costumes used to roam the streets of Paradise, frightening people half out of their wits. And no one knew who they were? Forgive me, Miss Rosabel, but in a town the size of Paradise, I find that very hard to believe."

"Oh, we had our suspicions," Miss Rosabel allowed. "But we kept them to ourselves. We didn't dare do otherwise."

"This is unreal," Emily said, rising from the stool. She

dragged her fingers through her hair. "How come I never knew anything about this group? I lived in Paradise until I was out of high school. There was never any talk about a vigilante group, or any other kind of group, that I remember."

"They were only active for a short time, that one year, and like I said, the whole thing was kept hush-hush. If word had gotten out, it could have hurt the tourist trade, and I don't have to tell you, Emily, that other than Huntington Industries, tourism is about the only thing Paradise has going for it."

"So this group of turkeys got away with murder, more or less, because the good citizens of Paradise were afraid of bad publicity." The more things changed, the more they stayed the same, Emily thought bitterly.

"Groups like this were hardly unique to Paradise," Matthew said. "Fifteen, twenty years ago, just like now, there were a rash of paramilitary groups cropping up all over the country, usually in small communities and rural areas. Among them were survivalist groups and militias, but the vigilante groups like the Avengers were the most dangerous, because they didn't have a cause. They didn't believe in anything. Their actions weren't motivated by fear of big government or anything else. They were power-hungry, pure and simple. They wanted absolute control over the people who lived in their communities, and they used violence and fear to get it."

"How could I not have known about this?" Emily demanded. "How could I have been so blind?"

"You were only a child," Miss Rosabel reminded her. "And you'd lost your parents that same year. Your brother would have naturally wanted to protect you from anything else that might have been distressing to you."

"*Distressing?* I would have been outraged. I *am* outraged. No wonder I never fit in in that town,'' Emily said, whipping her hand through her hair again. ''I should never have come back.''

''But the Avengers aren't around anymore,'' Miss Rosabel pointed out kindly.

''Maybe not as a group,'' Emily said. ''But the people who hid behind those black ski masks and terrorized innocent people are still living in that town, just as…'' She paused, taking a deep breath as her gaze met Matthew's. She didn't bother saying the rest. She didn't have to, because she knew they were both thinking the same thing.

Just as Jenny Wilcox's murderer might still be living in Paradise.

''How COULD I not have known?''

It was late afternoon, and the sun was setting, as Matthew and Emily strolled around the manicured yard at Shady Oaks, talking over what they had just learned. Matthew took Emily's arm, steering her toward a wooden bench that had been placed beneath the gnarled branches of one of the old trees from which the nursing home had taken its name.

They both sat down, and Matthew rested one arm along the back of the bench, barely touching Emily's hair. She felt his touch, though. Felt it all the way to her toes.

She concentrated very hard on a verdigris sundial situated in the center of the garden. A gray squirrel, foraging for acorns, scattered the red and gold leaves blanketing the flower beds.

Matthew said softly, ''Don't beat yourself up over this, Emily. You were just a kid. There was nothing you could have done about it.''

''Except close my eyes and pretend nothing was wrong, like everyone else in town did.'' Emily shook her head.

"I can understand why some people would have been too afraid to step in or speak up, but my God, the sheriff, of all people, should have done something."

"Miss Rosabel seems to think he might have been involved."

"Comforting thought, that, isn't it?"

Matthew shifted his arm, and his hand brushed her hair again. Emily wanted to lean back and rest her head against his arm. She wanted to close her eyes and forget all about the murder and the Avengers and everything else that had gone on in Paradise fifteen years ago.

She wanted to concentrate on the here and now, this very moment, to savor the new and exciting emotions Matthew Steele had awakened inside her. She wanted to turn her head and look at him for as long as she desired, to drink in every nuance of his masculine countenance and explore every line and angle of his handsome face.

She wanted badly to kiss him, and the yearning became an almost physical ache inside her. They were sitting so close, and Emily knew that if she gave the slightest signal, showed him even a hint of what was in her heart, he would probably grant her wish.

But if Emily had learned anything in the past few years, it was that her impulses could be, and often were, dangerous. She'd gotten herself into trouble more times than she cared to remember by following her heart instead of her head, and after her disastrous marriage to Eugene, she no longer trusted her own instincts. She didn't dare give away her heart again, because she was tired of having it broken.

So she kept her eyes straight ahead and said, "What I can't understand is how people like my brother could have let something like that go on. In many ways, Stuart is the typical Southern redneck. He's always had an almost fierce devotion to truth, justice and the American way, and a group like the Avengers, who took the law into their own hands, would have been abhorrent to him. The only thing I can think is that he must not have known about them, either.''

''I suppose that's possible,'' Matthew said slowly. He gazed at Emily for a very long time, wondering if he could trust her. Could she really not have known what was going on back then? Was she really as guileless as she seemed? After all that Matthew had lived through, all that he'd seen, it was hard to believe that anyone could be so artless.

But sitting there in that dying garden, with the wind ruffling her dark hair and her huge brown eyes full of warmth and sincerity and just a hint of wariness, Matthew found himself drowning in the possibilities. In her jeans, cotton flannel shirt and denim jacket, she looked soft and petite, but there was nothing girlish about her. Emily Townsend was all woman, and Matthew found himself responding to her in a very masculine way.

He wanted, suddenly, to kiss those full, lush lips of hers, to pull her close and hold her against him for a very long time. He wanted to unbutton her jacket, slip his hands inside her shirt and feel the smoothness of her pale skin. He wanted to hear her moan beneath him, then have her reach for him again....

But there was something else. Something far more disturbing than the desire.

In the fading light, she looked young and innocent and strangely vulnerable, and Matthew realized, almost too late, that what he wanted to do more than anything was to protect her. Shield her from his suspicions. Spirit her away before she could learn any more distressing revelations.

That there would be more disclosures, perhaps even more disturbing than what they had uncovered today, Matthew had no doubt. Paradise was full of secrets, and he wouldn't rest until he'd exposed every single one of them.

And Emily, he very much feared, would be caught in the cross fire.

There was no help for that. He had sworn to do everything he could to find out what had really happened in Paradise fifteen years ago, and if Emily Townsend got hurt, if she lost her innocence in the process, well, that was just too damned bad.

TWILIGHT FELL as they snaked their way back up the road to Paradise. Without the sunshine, the wind was merciless, and a fine mist had descended from the mountains. Emily huddled against Matthew's back, wondering miserably how he stood the sharp lashing his face must be taking. He was still bareheaded, and now, with dusk settling all around them, he didn't even have sunglasses to protect his face from the cold.

But if he suffered, he suffered in silence. Emily had no indication that he was even aware of the nasty weather. Or of the road conditions. He still drove fast, even though the misty dampness made the pavement slick and treacherous.

Emily wanted to call out to him to please slow down, but for some reason, she didn't dare. After they left the nursing home, he'd grown silent and moody, and Emily had the distinct impression that there were times when some internal demon drove him. Tonight was one of those times.

And so she kept her silence and clung to him, and every once in a while she would glance toward the edge of the road, where the steep embankment plunged headlong into the deeper darkness of the valley below. The other side, the cliff side, was even darker, a sheer black wall where rank upon rank of cedars charged up the looming side of the mountain.

A car came around one of the hairpin curves, taking it fast, crowding the motorcycle to the far outside. The rear tire touched gravel, spun, then gripped the pavement. Matthew slowed, regaining control of the Harley.

Emily couldn't hear anything over the roar of the engine, but she could imagine the stones that had been loosened tumbling down the embankment, rolling over and over into the blackness. She shivered, wishing they were home, wishing for a fire and dry clothes and a steaming cup of hot chocolate.

Matthew turned his head and shouted over his shoulder, something that sounded like "You okay?" but the wind tore his words away.

Emily nodded and clutched him tighter. He seemed satisfied with that as an answer, for he opened the throttle and they were once again plunging through darkness, sailing without a care up that steep and winding hillside.

What made her look up, Emily never knew. It wasn't a sound that drew her attention, for the roar of the motorcycle obliterated all else. It wasn't a movement, for in the darkness, with only a hint of moonlight glimmering sporadically off rock, visibility was limited. But something caught Emily's attention. Something made her glance up, and as she stared up the sheer face of the cliff, her heart leaped into her throat.

There were signs all along the road warning of rockslides, but in all the time Emily had lived in Paradise, she'd never actually seen one. Until now.

It looked as if a huge piece of the mountain had broken

away and was now hurtling toward the bottom, gaining momentum with every rotation and loosening a treacherous shower of smaller stones and gravel.

Emily clutched Matthew's arm. She pointed toward the mountain. The boulder was rolling faster now, and it was almost upon them. There was no way they could out run it, nothing else Matthew could do. He released the throttle and hit the brakes. The tires screamed in protest and slid sickeningly on the wet pavement. The motorcycle lurched sideways, still sliding. Emily screamed and clung to Matthew for all she was worth as he fought valiantly for control of the bike.

The boulder, like a giant bowling ball, rolled over everything in its path, soared off a jagged precipice and struck the pavement mere inches in front of them, bouncing like a rubber ball over the side of the embankment.

The motorcycle careened out of control toward the edge, as if following in the wake of the boulder. Matthew threw his weight against the momentum and put a leg down to balance the bike. Finally, after heart-stopping seconds of madness, everything came to a swift and silent standstill.

By some miracle, they were still upright. The rear of the bike was precariously close to the steep slope, and as Emily looked down, she grew dizzy, just thinking about what could have happened. They had come within inches of either being smashed to bits by the boulder or being sent crashing down the side of the embankment.

Even now, Emily imagined that she could hear the sound of the boulder rolling over and over as it raced toward the bottom. But when Matthew killed the engine, there was nothing but eerie silence.

They both got off the bike, and Matthew pushed it back up on the pavement. The center of the highway, where the boulder had struck, looked like the shell of a cracked Easter egg. Emily shuddered, looking at it.

Feeling light-headed and slightly nauseous, she reached up and jerked the helmet off her head. She gulped in the cold mountain air, trying to steady her nerves. "We could have been killed," she gasped.

Matthew was staring up the side of the cliff. In the distance, Emily heard the sound of a car engine and thought fleetingly that they should probably move off the road. After narrowly avoiding one disaster, she certainly didn't want to get hit head-on by another one. However, the sound faded, and she guessed the car was traveling in the opposite direction.

Matthew turned to her suddenly, as if he'd just remembered she was with him. "Are you okay?"

"Fine," she said. "Peachy."

"That was too damned close."

"I've heard of rockslides before," Emily said. "I even had a friend in third grade whose uncle was killed by one, but that's the first time I've ever seen it firsthand. What do you suppose could have loosened a boulder that large?"

"Good question." Matthew's gaze moved back up the side of the mountain.

Shock was beginning to set in for Emily, and she started to tremble. Her teeth were chattering, too, and in a moment, she knew, she'd probably burst into tears. She wasn't good with disasters, she'd discovered. Narrowly missed or otherwise.

Matthew saw her shaking and put his arm around her shoulder. "Sure you're okay?"

"I've never been so frightened in my life," she admitted. He tightened his arm around her, and Emily clung to his warmth. He felt solid and strong, and she buried her face in his shoulder. His other arm came around her, pulling her even closer.

"Hey, it's okay," he murmured. "We made it. We're safe."

"I know, but…we could have been killed," Emily said. Her breath caught on a sob, and she thought, *What a time to lose my nerve.*

She would have liked to impress Matthew with her bravery and her careless disregard for life and limb, but she'd just had the daylights scared out of her, and there was no way she could pretend she was having fun.

"I want to go home," she whispered against Matthew's shoulder.

"I'll get you there," he promised. He wove his hands through her hair and lifted her face, saying softly, "Emily, I'm really sorry."

"For what? You didn't send that boulder crashing down the mountainside. It was just a…a freak accident. These things happen."

"Maybe." But he didn't sound convinced. He pulled her to him, and Emily's breath caught again—not from fear this time, but from his closeness. From the way he held her. From the way his voice sounded when he whispered her name.

They stood gazing at each other in the darkness, awareness a tangible thing between them. The silence seemed to stretch forever. Finally, without taking the time to consider the consequences, Emily lifted her hand to Matthew's cheek.

He closed his eyes, as if relishing her touch, and drew a ragged breath. "Emily."

"Yes?"

"This thing between us." He drew another breath and looked away. Emily let her hand drop from his cheek, feeling a little knot of dread settle in the pit of her stomach. He forced his eyes to meet hers. ''It can't happen.''

Emily felt as if he had just slapped her. Her pride stung from the blow, and she took a step or two backward, reeling from shock and humiliation. ''You're married,'' she blurted.

''No. It's not that.''

''Involved, then.''

''There's no one else. It's just—'' Matthew broke off, shoving his fingers through his hair.

''Please,'' Emily said. ''Say no more. I understand, and it doesn't matter. I'm not exactly in the market for a relationship, either. I haven't even been divorced a year, and God knows I don't need another complication in my life right now—'' She broke off, realizing she was babbling to cover her embarrassment. She turned away.

''Emily, it's not you.''

Of course it was her. Why else would an unattached man reject a woman who was practically throwing herself at him? It had to be her. But Emily managed to shrug nonchalantly. ''I know.''

''No, you don't know, but it's the truth.'' She had her back to him. His hands closed over her arms, but he didn't try to turn her. Instead, he pulled her back gently against his chest and rested his chin on the top of her head.

''It's not you,'' he repeated, his voice a deep, rumbling vibration in his chest as Emily tried to relax against him. ''It's me. I can't get involved with anyone right now. There are too many things in my past that have to be resolved first. I've done some terrible things, Emily.''

Emily's heart began a slow, painful dance inside her chest. Now that the desire between them had been diluted by his rejection, the immediate situation in which she found herself became crystal-clear. She was standing on a dark and lonely road, miles from anywhere, with a handsome stranger she knew nothing about. A stranger that others seemed to fear.

She shuddered. ''What kind of things?''

''Things someone like you wouldn't understand.''

''Does it have anything to do with why Nella and Miss Rosabel had such strange reactions to you?''

His hands tightened on her arms for a moment. ''I've never been to Paradise before,'' he told her. ''I've never met any of these people. If they react to me, it's probably because I'm a stranger.''

A gray-eyed stranger who rode a motorcycle. Perhaps that was all it was, Emily thought. But deep in her heart she knew there was more to Matthew Steele than he had told her. So much more.

She thought she felt his lips against her hair, and the movement—imagined or not—made her want to turn in his arms and stare up at him. But she was afraid to. Afraid of what she might see in those beautiful gray eyes.

As if he sensed her doubts, his hands dropped from her arms. He said abruptly, ''We'd better head back.''

Emily felt bereft. A part of her wanted to stay there on that lonely mountainside with Matthew forever, and another part of her—the wiser part, perhaps—wanted to run. She turned slowly to face him. ''Matthew?''

He was walking toward the Harley, and he didn't turn.

Emily got the message. Enough had been said for one night. She followed him, and he wordlessly handed her the helmet. She put it on, then climbed on the bike behind him. Her arms went around him, and for the briefest moment, he laid his hands over hers. It was a tender, reassuring gesture that for some insane reason made Emily want to cry.

Chapter Six

Emily tried to avoid Matthew's eyes when they walked into the brightly lit kitchen at the inn, but it was difficult in the close confines. They kept bumping into each other, setting off little explosions of awareness inside Emily.

Finally, in exasperation, she took the coffeepot from his hands and said, "Here, let me do that. You're a paying guest."

"We're also partners," Matthew said, but he relinquished the coffeepot and the sack of coffee beans as if he, too, were bothered by the constant contact.

Emily's heart took a bounce at his words, but she managed to say calmly, "Partners, are we? Then how come I feel as if you're the one with all the answers?"

"That's only an illusion," Matthew assured her. He opened a cupboard, searching for cups.

"Next one," Emily directed him as she placed the beans in the grinder. For a moment, the noise silenced their conversation, but once she was finished, Emily picked right up where they'd left off. "You knew exactly what you wanted to ask Miss Rosabel before we went to see her, didn't you?"

"I told you I was interested in the case," Matthew said. "I did some research before I came here."

Why did she not believe him? Emily wondered. Or, at the very least, why did she think there was more to his story than he was telling her?

"Tonight proves we're on the right track," he said grimly.

Emily glanced up. "What do you mean?"

"I'm talking about the boulder. That was no accident, Emily."

Emily gasped. "What are you saying?"

"I'm saying someone was on that mountain, waiting for us. I'm saying they deliberately sent that boulder crashing down on us."

Emily stared at him in astonishment. "You mean you think…someone tried to kill us? Why, for God's sake?"

"To stop us from asking questions."

Emily felt stunned. When she'd first approached Mike Durbin about doing a series of articles on the murder, she'd had no idea how quickly things could get out of hand.

"My God," she breathed. "Do you actually think someone tried to kill us?"

"I don't know." Matthew gestured impatiently with his hand. "Maybe they just intended to frighten us and the boulder came closer than they meant. Didn't you hear a car start up?"

"Yes, but I just thought—"

Matthew broke in. "I don't think it was a coincidence. I think they were up there waiting for us, and when the trap was sprung, they drove off in a big hurry."

"But how could they have known when we would be coming back along that particular stretch of road? It doesn't make sense."

"It does if they followed us down. They knew we'd be coming back sometime today. They could have rigged up some kind of trigger or lever under the boulder while we were talking to Miss Rosabel. Then all they had to do was sit tight and wait for us. How many motorcycles did you see out on the road today?''

Good point. Emily said, ''Who do you think it was?''

''I have no idea. But I do know one thing. Someone is getting nervous about our little investigation.''

''Which means someone in town has something to hide.''

''Exactly.''

Emily poured the coffee and brought the two steaming mugs over to the table. She pulled out a chair and sat down. ''Do you think we should go to the sheriff?''

Matthew shrugged. ''I don't think it would do much good. We don't have any proof, and besides, you heard what Miss Rosabel said. She thinks the sheriff was involved with the Avengers. And if the Avengers were somehow involved in Jenny's murder or Wade's disappearance, I don't think we can look to the sheriff for help.''

Emily shivered as his words sunk in. ''Do you really think someone tried to kill us tonight, Matthew?''

He gave her a long, measured look. ''I honestly don't know. But if you want to pull out of this thing, Emily, no one's going to blame you.''

No one but herself. Emily thought about the warnings she'd gotten, first from Trey Huntington, then from her brother. It made her angry to think of the way they were still treating her, like a not-too-bright child who needed to be told what to do.

Well, Emily wasn't a child. She was a grown woman, and if she'd had any doubts about that before, she sure didn't now. Not after her reaction to Matthew earlier, out there on the highway.

But he'd made it perfectly clear there could never be a romantic partnership between them, and now that the initial sting of his rejection had faded, Emily had to admit his decision was probably a wise one. She'd made too many mistakes in the past, too, and she certainly didn't want Matthew Steele to be another.

She was attracted to him. No doubt about that. But Emily had always been drawn to a walk on the wild side, and as she gazed at Matthew now, she had the feeling that was exactly where a relationship with him would take her.

With her track record, she was definitely better off keeping her distance. At least as much as their new partnership would allow.

Partners. Emily couldn't help admiring the way the word sounded, and all that it entailed. Respect. Sharing. Equal in every way.

She liked that. Liked it very much.

She said to Matthew, "I don't want to back out now. We've only just started."

"It could get dangerous, Emily."

"Do you trust me to be your partner, Matthew?"

"Implicitly." He smiled, but there was a hint of darkness in his eyes. A faint suggestion of regret.

Emily chose to ignore it. She took a deep breath and reached for her cup. "Let's get on with it, then."

"SO WHERE EXACTLY did you read about the Avengers? According to Miss Rosabel, everyone around here was afraid to utter a word about them."

It was half an hour later, and they were still sitting at the kitchen table, the remains of their evening meal littering the surface as they rehashed everything they knew about the fifteen-year-old murder. The microwave dinged, and Emily got up to remove the leftover cinnamon rolls they were having for dessert after hastily prepared ham sandwiches.

Matthew hesitated. "I don't remember exactly where."

Emily sat down at the table. She stared at him reproachfully, sensing his evasiveness.

"Emily," he said softly. "Does it matter how I know? I ran across a reference to them somewhere, and I took the chance that Miss Rosabel might know more about them."

"And she did."

"And she did."

"How lucky for you," Emily said sardonically.

"How lucky for you that you have such a clever partner." He grinned and helped himself to a cinnamon roll.

"Yeah, right." Emily had the feeling that luck had very little to do with it. She also had the feeling that they weren't exactly equal partners. Not yet, anyway. Matthew was still a man with secrets. Emily wondered if he would ever feel he could share them with her. Or, for that matter, if she even wanted him to.

I've done some terrible things, Emily.

Her appetite suddenly gone, Emily pushed her plate away. "Tell you what," she said. "Why don't we make a list of our suspects and jot down everything we know about them?"

"I've never been big on lists," Matthew said. "But why not? You write and I'll eat."

"What a deal." Emily rose and searched for paper and pencil in her catchall drawer. She sat down at the table again and stared at the blank sheet. "Who's first?"

"Wade Drury, of course."

Emily looked up in surprise. "But Miss Rosabel said she didn't think Wade was guilty."

"That's only her opinion," Matthew reminded her.

"True. All right, Wade Drury, then. What do we know about him?"

"He was a stranger," Matthew supplied. "No one in town knew anything about him."

Except that he had gray eyes and rode a motorcycle, Emily thought, but she said instead, "And he was in love with Jenny Wilcox."

"Again, according to Miss Rosabel."

"It seems we're hinging a lot of our leads on her, doesn't it?" Emily said with a frown. "I think I should go talk to Nella again."

"All right, but meanwhile, why don't you put Nella down as suspect number two?" Matthew finished his roll and pushed away his plate.

"Nella?" Emily stared at him in astonishment. "You don't honestly think she had anything to do with Jenny's death?"

"If she was in love with Wade, and Wade was in love with Jenny…"

"I know, but she's—"

"A woman?" Matthew arched an amused brow. "You don't think a woman is capable of murder?"

"Well, yes, I guess so, but Nella is so…fragile. I can't imagine her hurting a fly."

"Can you imagine her involved with a married man when she was only a teenager?"

"Touché," Emily said. She wrote Nella's name down, then scribbled a few pertinent facts beside it. "Suspect number three has to be Tony Vincent. Although, for my money, I think he should be suspect number one."

"What do you know about Vincent?" Matthew asked, getting up to pour himself another cup of coffee. He leaned against the counter and crossed his feet as he regarded Emily from across the room.

"Well," Emily said, "he was a friend of my brother's back in high school and college. He was a major football jock, and from what I remember, half the girls in town were in love with him."

"So he wasn't used to getting rejected by women."

"None of them were. That whole group—Tony, Stuart, Trey—all of them had their pick of girls. Of course, I was only a kid then. But I do remember how Tony always drove around town in this really cool Mustang convertible, and how he always had at least one girl with him. Come to think of it, though, I don't know how he was able to afford a car like that. His family was dirt-poor. He went to college on a full football scholarship."

"Schools have been known to pay for play. What did he do after college?" Matthew asked, sipping his coffee.

"He was drafted by a pro team, but that didn't last long. He never quite measured up to the big boys, and rumor had it his drinking eventually got the better of him. Last I heard, he owns a garage here in town. Works on cars for a living. That's what his dad used to do, too."

"Maybe we need to pay Mr. Vincent a little visit," Matthew said, setting down his cup and strolling back over to the table. He stood behind Emily, reading over her shoulder. "Better put Cora Mae Hicks on that list."

Emily gaped up at him. "But she's a—"

"Woman?"

"Not only that, she's got to be sixty if she's a day."

"Which would have made her around forty-five at the time of the murder. And from what I saw today, she's still got plenty of spunk left in her. Not to mention anger."

"You met Cora Mae today?"

Matthew gave a sober little laugh. He rested his hands on the back of Emily's chair, making her acutely conscious of his presence. "Oh, yeah. Thank God it was daylight. I don't think I'd want to meet up with her after dark.''

"She is pretty scary,'' Emily conceded. "All of us kids used to avoid her house like the plague on Halloween. Chucky Freed swore she put a razor blade in an apple she gave him once. Of course, that was after he heard of a similar incident on '60 Minutes.' ''

"Were you aware she regards you as an enemy?'' Matthew asked.

Emily nodded. "Because of the name thing. The Other Side of Paradise Inn. I probably shouldn't have done that, but it seemed so perfect.''

"You could have named the place Heartbreak Hotel and it wouldn't have mattered. The fact that you opened a bed-and-breakfast in Paradise at all is reason enough for her to hate you. I got the definite impression that Cora Mae takes a very dim view of competition.''

"That's what Miss Rosabel said the first time Mike Durbin and I went to talk to her,'' Emily admitted. "In fact, she went so far as to say she wouldn't put it past Cora Mae to have murdered Jenny herself, just to run Miss Rosabel out of business.''

"Well, there you are—suspect number four.'' Matthew straightened and moved away.

Emily tried not to notice. Tried not to think about how very much she liked having him so near, or about the way he'd held her earlier, out on the mountain, when she was so scared. She tried not to think about how much she'd wanted him to kiss her. How much she still wanted him to.

She gave a nervous little laugh. "I'm running out of room.''

"So start a new page.'' Matthew was standing by the sink, staring out the window. Emily had the feeling that another dark mood was descending over him. Amazing how already she was beginning to interpret his temperament.

She tried to lighten his mood again by saying, "At this rate, we could have a book in the making. And we haven't even started on the Avengers yet."

"No," he said grimly, "we haven't even started on the Avengers." He turned away from the sink, and the look in his eyes made Emily's breath rush out of her.

For one split second, she had a glimpse—just a hint—of the terrible things he had done. Then the shutters came down, and his expression once again became inscrutable. "I think we've done enough for one day," he said. "I'm beat. What do you say we call it a night?"

Emily felt too keyed up to sleep, but she shrugged, gathered up her paper and pencil and said, "Sure, why not? Tomorrow's a new day, right?"

MATTHEW DREAMED about Jenny that night. He saw her so clearly, the way she'd looked the last time he saw her, with her crystal-blue eyes, her shimmering blond hair and her radiant smile. A smile like sunshine after a rainstorm.

When Matthew awakened, he tried to hold on to the image, even considered for a moment trying to force himself back to sleep. But if he closed his eyes now, he knew the nightmares would come. Jenny's fragile image would be replaced by the screams. The blood. The horrible guilt.

No, he wouldn't go back to sleep. Not now.

Matthew got up and slipped on his jeans. He crossed the room to the window and stood staring out at the darkened streets of Paradise. He thought about Emily Townsend.

Was she asleep? he wondered. He pictured the way she would look, her dark hair against a white pillow, her sweet face even more peaceful and serene in repose. Something stirred inside Matthew, and he tried to block the image of Emily, but he couldn't. Not after tonight.

Out there on the mountain, he'd known the exact moment when her fear turned to desire. Her soft brown eyes had deepened soulfully and her lips—those luscious, perfect lips—had parted ever so slightly. And in that instant, a powerful longing had swept through Matthew. A need so great it had taken every ounce of his strength, every shred of whatever decency remained within him, not to haul her up against him and kiss that sexy, innocent mouth of hers until neither of them could think straight.

But that would have been a mistake, Matthew thought. A terrible, tragic mistake that he'd made once before. There had been another woman who had looked at him the way Emily Townsend had looked at him tonight. Desire mingling with caution. Trust warring with fear. Matthew had wanted that woman, too, so much so that he'd let his emotions ruin his judgment, and the consequences had been disastrous.

Matthew wouldn't make that same mistake with Emily. He wouldn't let her fall in love with him.

Because every woman who had ever loved him had ended up dead.

EMILY AWOKE with a start. She'd been dreaming about a loud noise, like shattering glass, but as she lay there in the darkness, she heard another sound, muffled and distant, like footsteps running down the street. She sprang upright, realizing that the shattering noise had been just as real as the footsteps.

Her first thought was that Matthew was up and had perhaps dropped a glass. But he wouldn't have been running outside, would he?

There was something distinctly sinister about footsteps running away in the night, and as Emily sat there in bed, huddled beneath her covers, she began to tremble with dread.

Don't panic, she scolded herself. *And don't let your imagination run away with you.*

After all, she was the owner of the inn, and the welfare of her guests rested upon her shoulders. If anything was amiss at the Other Side of Paradise Inn, she was the one who had to investigate.

Her heart hammering in her throat, Emily got up and padded across the room, drew back her door and crept through it. Her bedroom was downstairs, at the end of a longish hallway that led directly into the large front living area. As silent as mist, Emily slipped down the darkened corridor, letting the faint moonlight glimmering through the French doors guide her.

As she emerged from the hallway, the French doors were across the room, directly in front of her. To her right was the foyer, and to her left, the staircase. She took a few steps into the room, and then something—someone— touched her arm.

Emily screamed and tried to bolt, but the hand tightened around her arm, holding her fast. In the next instant, Emily's breath rushed out in relief as she recognized Matthew's towering silhouette in the darkness.

''Matthew,'' she said, her hand flying to her heart. ''You scared me half to death.''

He put a finger to his lips, commanding her silence as he moved around her. ''Stay here,'' he whispered. ''I'm going to have a look around.''

And it was then, as he moved away from her, that Emily saw the gun in his hand, glinting in the moonlight. She gasped again. ''Matthew!'' But it was too late. He'd disappeared through the archway into the dining room, and then Emily heard the telltale squeak of the swinging door that led into the kitchen.

She stood there in the darkness, hugging her arms around herself and shivering. She gazed around the room, her eyes traversing the familiar nooks and crannies that were somehow made foreboding in moonlight.

Taking a few more steps into the room, she saw at last what had caused the shattering noise. The stained-glass panel from the front door lay in glistening jewel-tone fragments on the herringbone-patterned wood floor. Emily gasped in outrage. That door had cost her a small fortune to have restored.

She hurried across the room, now oblivious of the lurking shadows. Barely suppressing her tears, Emily dropped to the floor and began picking up the pieces.

After a few moments, Matthew came back into the room. His shadow fell across the floor in front of her, and Emily looked up. "Did you see anything?"

He shook his head, walked over to turn on the light, then came back to kneel beside her. Emily noticed that he'd put the gun away. "Whoever did this is long gone by now. I didn't find so much as a footprint."

Emily stared at him for a moment, trying to decipher his expression. Finally she said, "This may seem a strange question, considering what just happened, but...do you have a permit for that gun?"

"Yes. It's nothing for you to be concerned about."

"But it is. This is my home, Matthew. I don't like guns being brought in here without my knowledge." Her challenging gaze met his.

"I don't like guns, either," he said softly. "But considering everything that's going on around here, I don't think we can be too careful."

"But…did you bring it with you when you came here, or did you go out and buy it?" Somehow the distinction was important to Emily, though she couldn't have said why.

"I brought it with me. It's just for protection, because I'm on the road a lot. But if it makes you feel better, I'll get rid of it. Okay?"

She nodded, not sure anything would make her feel better after tonight. Gazing down at the glistening fragments of colored glass scattered on the floor, she said miserably, "Why would someone do this? I don't even know if I have enough money to have the glass repaired again. That door is antique. It's irreplaceable."

Leaning over, Matthew retrieved a rock the size of a baseball from a corner of the foyer. In her distress over the door, Emily hadn't even noticed it. Something white was fastened to the stone, a piece of paper, and Matthew carefully removed it.

"What does it say?" Emily demanded.

Wordlessly, Matthew handed her the note. The words—cut from magazines and newspapers—jumped out at her. *Let the past rest in peace. Or else you won't.*

As Emily gripped the paper, a smear of blood appeared on the side, and she lifted her hand, palm up, and peered at her finger. She'd nicked herself on one of the stained-glass fragments, and the streak of blood on the note made it seem more threatening somehow. More portentous.

Matthew removed the note from her fingers and laid the paper aside. He held her hand in his. "Here. What have you done to yourself?"

The blood trickled down Emily's finger. She felt weak, but whether from the cut or the note, or even Matthew's nearness, she wasn't quite sure. She said in a tremulous voice, "It's just a nick."

"Let's get it cleaned up and make sure." Matthew stood and, still holding her hand in his, pulled her up. He led her down the hallway to the bathroom and flipped on the light. Emily, distressed and more than a little confused from all that had happened, sat down on the edge of the bathtub and numbly directed Matthew to the first-aid kit.

"I guess we've had our second warning," she said. "Do you suppose whoever loosened the boulder earlier threw that rock through my door?"

"I'd say that's a pretty good bet."

"So what do we do now?"

"Keep shaking things up until something breaks loose," Matthew said. "And in the meantime, we keep up our own guard."

Emily thought about his gun. "You certainly seem to take all this in stride," she said, her tone suspicious.

Matthew shrugged as he closed the medicine cabinet and turned toward her. "I've traveled around a lot. I've learned it pays to be careful."

He knelt in front of her and took her hand. Emily winced as he swabbed away the blood, then applied antiseptic.

"Ouch!" She tried to jerk her hand away, but he held it fast.

"Luckily, it's not deep. You'll live," he predicted, glancing up. He smiled, and Emily's heart fluttered inside her.

Whether it was from fear or adrenaline or just plain old-fashioned hormones, she didn't know exactly, but suddenly a deep shiver ran through her as she became acutely aware of the fact that she was sitting before Matthew Steele, clad only in a pair of white satin pajamas, and he was wearing nothing but a pair of jeans.

Her gaze unwillingly dropped, taking in the broadness

of his shoulders, the deepness of his chest, the hardness of his muscles. And something stilled inside her. A kind of breathless waiting came over her. In spite of herself, Emily felt her hand tremble in his, giving away her emotions.

His gaze slowly lifted to meet hers, and she could tell by the dark, knowing look in his eyes that he was feeling the attraction, too. Feeling it as strongly as she. As Emily watched helplessly, he brought her hand up to brush his lips across her wounded finger. His tongue flicked across her palm, and Emily drew a sharp breath.

"This can't happen," she whispered.

"I know," he said, his eyes on her.

"What are we going to do?"

"I don't know about you," Matthew said, "but I think I'm going to kiss you."

"I think I'll die if you don't—"

Emily's words were lost as his arms came around her and he drew her to him. His mouth sought and found hers as his hands moved over her, every inch of her. She felt their hardness against the soft folds of her satin pajamas, and the sensation was extraordinary, exquisite.

Trembling from head to toe, Emily wrapped her arms around Matthew's neck and pressed herself against him, and they tumbled backward, letting the thick bathroom carpet cushion their fall.

Emily landed on top, and she pulled back to stare down at Matthew. His eyes were deep and dark and full of mystery, full of promise. She shuddered to think what it all meant, but in the next instant, she wasn't thinking at all. With his hand on the back of her neck, he drew her back down for another soul-shattering kiss.

Emily's heart pounded against Matthew's. She had never felt so overwhelmed, so overcome. When at last he broke the kiss, she buried her face in his neck, marveling at the way her body had blossomed at his touch.

He tangled his hands in her hair. "Emily."

"I know." She sighed deeply. "This can't happen."

"It can't. Not again."

Emily raised up so that she could look down at him. "Matthew, why not? And please don't tell me I wouldn't understand."

"All right, I won't." He lifted her so that he could slip out from beneath her and sit. Then he leaned back against the tub and drew his knees up, resting his arms across them. Emily knelt beside him.

His eyes had grown dark and bleak, and he wiped the back of his hand across them, as if he could erase the painful images he saw. "There was a woman." His voice was wooden, emotionless.

Emily's heart pounded in desperation. She wasn't sure she wanted to hear any more, but she couldn't seem to stop herself from asking, "Were you in love with her?"

He rubbed his hand across his eyes again. "I thought I was. I'm not sure anymore. It was…a relationship that never should have happened. It ended in disaster."

"What happened?"

His eyes met hers. Emily thought she had never seen such darkness. Such guilt and agony. But his voice still betrayed nothing when he said, "She died." And Emily felt the world as she knew it come crashing down around her.

She put a tentative hand on his arm, and he flinched, as if he could no longer bear her touch. Emily drew her hand back, hurt.

"I can't afford to get involved with anyone, Emily. I don't trust myself. Especially not with someone like you."

Emily knew she should ask no more questions. Knew that she should get out of that room while the getting was good. But she couldn't move. She was mesmerized, rooted to the spot by a kind of sick fascination that made her ask, "Because you still love her?"

"No." His gaze bored into hers. If it was possible, his eyes grew even darker. "Because I killed her," he said.

Chapter Seven

"*My dear!* This place is positively *vibrating* with psychic emanations!"

Emily could only gape at the woman who was walking—no, sailing—through the inn's front door. Large, rawboned, with unlikely wisps of red hair peeking from beneath the wide brim of a lavish hat, the woman reminded Emily of nothing so much as a large purple battleship plowing full speed ahead as she steamed into the Other Side of Paradise Inn.

With a flourish, she presented Emily her card, then turned and gazed around the room. Beneath the purple knit suit the woman wore, her generous bosom jutted to attention as she flung her arms wide and closed her eyes in ecstasy.

Emily, unable to do anything but stare wide-eyed at such an awe-inspiring sight, finally tore her gaze away and glanced down at the pale lavender card that proclaimed in dark purple ink:

Mrs. Grace DeVere
Pine Bluff Psychics League

"*Why* have I not heard of this place before?" the woman demanded, opening her eyes to glare an accusation at Emily.

"Well, I…"

"If my dear cousin Fayetta hadn't had the good fortune to run across the article in the *Bald Knob Banner,* and if she hadn't had the presence of mind to clip the story and send it to me, I would have remained in the dark about this house for the rest of my natural born days."

"How fortunate that didn't happen," Emily said doubtfully. "What can I do for you, Mrs., uh, DeVere?"

Grace DeVere had stepped away from the desk to once again gaze in rapture around the room, but now she spun back. "What can you do for *me?* Young woman, a better question to ask is what can *I* do for *you?*"

Oookay, Emily thought. "Exactly why are you here, Mrs. DeVere?"

"To help you contact the spirits who inhabit your home," Mrs. DeVere said matter-of-factly. "Tell me, have you experienced any unusual psychic phenomena since you moved in?"

Emily wasn't sure she would know a psychic phenomenon if she met one, unusual or otherwise, but she said gamely, "Not that I know of."

"No cold spots? No levitation? No unexplained noises in the middle of the night?"

Emily thought about the noise the rock had made last night, when it crashed through her front door. The cause of that had hardly been supernatural, but she almost wished it had been. It would certainly be no less of a mystery.

"I haven't experienced any of those things," Emily said.

Mrs. DeVere looked crestfallen, but then she perked up. "Well," she said, "we're obviously dealing with a shy spirit, one reluctant to make contact. It may take a few days to break through the barrier.''

''Barrier?''

''That separates the known world from the unknown one. Now, if you would be so good as to show me to my room, the quicker I settle in, the quicker the spirits will become accustomed to my presence.''

Emily said, ''Mrs. DeVere, I'm afraid there's been some mistake. I'm not yet open for business.''

Mrs. DeVere, obviously not one to be daunted by such a minor detail, said, ''The article mentioned something about a grand opening on October twenty-third. That's only a few days away. Surely an allowance can be made.''

Actually, allowances had already been made. Emily hadn't exactly turned Matthew away, now had she? And after last night, after what he had told her, she wasn't so sure her decision had been a wise one.

Emily made a few mental calculations. If she let Mrs. DeVere stay, she could put the extra money toward the repair of her front door, which had been taken down this morning and was en route to Bradford, where a stained-glass maker Emily knew had agreed to start work on it immediately. A plain wooden door had been temporarily installed in its place.

''You do understand there may be some inconveniences,'' Emily explained. ''I'm still working on some of the rooms.''

''I understand, and don't worry, my dear. You won't even know I'm here.''

Emily very much doubted that. Mrs. Grace DeVere wasn't exactly the type—or of the stature—to fade into the woodwork. However, Emily forced herself to say cheerfully, ''If you'll just sign the register, I'll take you up now, and someone will bring up your bags in a few minutes.'' Someone like her, but Emily didn't mention that fact to Mrs. DeVere.

Using her own pen, Mrs. DeVere scrawled her name across the register in purple ink, then followed Emily up the stairs to the room at the top of the landing. Mrs. DeVere entered, gazed around for a moment, then stated, ''This will do nicely. Now show me to the murder room.''

''I'm sorry, but that room is occupied at the moment.''

''Of course it is. Restless spirits always return to the scene of the crime. That's why I'm here, my dear.''

Emily strained for patience. ''I don't mean that. I have a real flesh-and-blood guest in that room right now.''

Mrs. DeVere smiled mysteriously. ''Why don't you let me be the judge of that? If the vibrations are as strong as I suspect they will be, I know at least two or three other psychics who will come at once to join me.''

Emily hesitated. The last thing an innkeeper should do was violate a guest's privacy, but to have the bed-and-breakfast at full occupancy so early in the season would be a real coup. The fall foliage wasn't even at its peak yet, and the Fall Folk Festival wouldn't start until the weekend of the twenty-fifth, two days after Emily's grand opening. Cora Mae Hicks would be pea green with envy.

And, besides, Matthew was gone. He'd been gone ever since last night, when he'd walked out on her after their disturbing conversation in the bathroom. Emily wasn't sure he was ever coming back, and she thought, with more than a flicker of regret, that perhaps it would be for the best if he didn't. How could she trust him now, after what he'd told her? After what he *hadn't* told her?

''Well?'' Mrs. DeVere demanded, drawing Emily's attention back to the present. ''Are you going to show me the murder room or not?''

Emily shrugged. "Why not?" she said, and led Grace DeVere down the hallway.

Emily opened the door and glanced inside. The room was just as she'd left it earlier that morning, when she'd been in to change the linens on the bed and leave fresh towels.

Mrs. DeVere looked positively ecstatic as she stepped inside. She sought the center of the room, closed her eyes, and went very still. A tiny humming sound emanated from the back of her throat. After a moment or two, Emily began to get the creeps.

Mrs. DeVere reached out with one hand, groping like a blind woman. "She's here. The young woman who was violently murdered. I feel her all around me. Her spirit roams restlessly, searching for peace." The clutching hand stilled and her breathing became shallow. She splayed her other hand across her ample bosom. "I feel another presence here, as well. An evilness…"

The dramatics were straight out of *Poltergeist,* Emily thought, but a sudden movement in the hallway caught her attention, and she jumped in spite of herself.

Matthew stood in the doorway. The sunlight spilling in through the window at the end of the hallway surrounded him with a golden aura. For a moment, his form seemed to waver in the light. He looked misty, ethereal, not quite of this earth.

Then he stepped into the room, and the illusion shattered. The look in his eyes told Emily that he was a flesh-and-blood man, all right, and a damned angry one at the moment.

"I'M REALLY, really, *really* sorry," Emily said again, for perhaps the tenth time. "I know it was inexcusable of me to invade your privacy that way, and I don't blame you for being angry, but it was just that…she wanted to see the room, to—''

''Experience the psychic vibrations. I know,'' Matthew said dryly. They were in Emily's little Volkswagen, headed toward Tony Vincent's garage. ''And I told you, I'm not mad.''

''But you were. I could tell.''

He sighed. ''All right, I was. But I'm not now. Let's just get on with our business, okay?''

And pretend last night never happened.

Though he hadn't said it, Emily sensed that was what he meant. But she wasn't at all sure she could do that. Like it or not, Matthew Steele had gotten to her. Big-time. The kiss last night had proven to her just how much she had come to care for him in such a short period of time.

Was there such a thing as love at first sight? Destiny? Emily had never really believed in any of those things before, but from the moment she laid eyes on Matthew, she had felt something. Something…significant. Something more than just physical attraction.

Something that frightened her a little.

Especially after what he'd told her last night.

She glanced at him. His head was turned, and he was staring out the side window. Emily wondered whether he was thinking about last night, too, and what he had told her.

Because I killed her.

The unspoken words seemed to hang in the air. Emily took a deep breath. ''Matthew.''

He turned his head and looked at her.

She bit her lip. ''We have to talk about last night.''

One brow rose slightly. ''About the kiss, or the confession?''

''Both, I guess.'' Emily was feeling miserable and was

suddenly wishing she hadn't even brought up the conversation. But when a man told you he'd killed someone, and when that man was staying in your home, when he'd *kissed* you— Well, Emily didn't see that she had a choice. For her own peace of mind, she had to know the truth.

"About the kiss," Matthew said slowly. "You and I both know it should never have happened, but I can't honestly say I'm sorry it did."

"And the confession?" Emily managed to ask, her heart fluttering inside her chest like the wings of a caged bird. "Do you regret that?"

There was a long pause, and then Matthew said, "You're still here, aren't you?"

"Yes. I'm still here." *For better or for worse.* Emily swallowed. "The woman you told me about last night…"

"What about her?" Matthew's tone was flat, expressionless, giving away nothing of what he might be feeling. They might have been talking about a social event or a football game instead of…

Emily couldn't even bring herself to think the *M* word. She took another deep breath. "Did you really…I mean…you know…"

"Kill her?" Matthew seemed to have no such compunctions. He said the words bluntly, without hesitation. "I won't lie to you, Emily. I was very much responsible for her death."

"But being responsible…that's not the same thing as… I mean, the implication was that…you…you…" Emily lifted one hand from the steering wheel and gestured helplessly.

Matthew said nothing.

"What I mean is…her death was an accident, wasn't it?" she asked softly, braking for a stop sign. She turned and looked at him.

Something flickered in Matthew's expression, a denial. Then he said with a weary sigh, "Okay. It was an accident. But that didn't make me any less to blame," he said harshly. "I was careless, irresponsible, and someone died." He glanced away for a second. "There are a lot of things about my past I can't explain. That I don't want to explain. But I will tell you this." His eyes were dark and mysterious, oddly seductive for the conversation they were having. He said, almost reluctantly, "You have nothing to fear from me, Emily. I would never hurt you."

Their gazes clung for a moment. Emily's eyes dropped to his lips, searching their contours as she remembered the way his mouth had felt on hers, the way his body had molded against hers. If Matthew hadn't stopped the kiss. If he hadn't pushed her away—

Emily lifted her gaze to his. His eyes were deep and knowing. A shiver raced through her, because she knew he was thinking exactly what she was thinking.

Forcing herself to look away, Emily checked both ways, then drove through the intersection. "Well," she said, trying to keep her tone light. "I guess I just have one more question, then."

"What?"

"Are you wearing…do you have your gun with you today?"

"No. Does that make you feel better?"

"I'm not sure," she admitted. "I guess I'm worried about what's going to happen when we talk to Tony Vincent. I mean, we can hardly just waltz in and ask him if he killed Jenny Wilcox."

"Why can't we? You just asked me."

Emily blushed. "That was different. I mean…well, it just was. But I don't think Tony's likely to admit to anything, do you?"

''Maybe not overtly.''

''What does that mean?''

''It means we watch his expression, study his actions,'' Matthew explained. ''We let him do all the work and hope that he gives himself away.''

''Well, I, for one, haven't a clue as to how to do that,'' Emily assured him. ''So I hope you're up on your Ellery Queen routine.''

''I'll try to muddle through.''

She didn't doubt it for a minute. Matthew Steele seemed quite capable of anything. She tried to ignore the little voice inside her that demanded, *Even murder?* as she pulled into the gravel parking lot of Vincent's Auto Repair and killed the engine.

When she and Matthew got out of the car, she could hear a loud banging noise coming from the interior of the garage. ''Sounds like Tony's hard at work on something.''

''Yeah, but what?'' Matthew took her elbow and steered her to the open bay and the noise.

A man with greasy orange coveralls was bent over a table scattered with an assortment of parts and wires and springs that, connected, might once have been an engine. He looked up when Emily and Matthew entered the garage, and the hammer he'd been using to straighten a metal pipe dropped to the table with a clang.

He stared at Matthew.

By now, Emily was used to the reaction. She called out, ''Hello, Tony. I don't know if you remember me or not, but you and my brother used to be friends. I'm Stuart Townsend's sister, Emily.''

''I know who you are.'' Tony picked up the metal pipe as he came around the worktable and walked over to meet them at the doorway. He limped slightly, favoring his left leg.

He was a big man, tall and broad-shouldered, and even though there were telltale signs of his drinking etched into his face, his body, beneath the coveralls, looked hard and muscular, the still-powerful physique of a man who had once been an all-collegiate running back.

Feet planted apart, a scowl creasing an already deeply lined forehead, he swung the pipe up and slapped it against the palm of his other hand. "What do you want?" His voice was coarse and gravelly, the voice of a man driven to excess.

"We just want to talk to you," Emily said. "We're hoping you can answer some questions for us. This is Matthew Steele."

Tony glanced at Matthew. "That name supposed to mean something to me?"

"I don't know," Matthew said. "Does it?"

At just over six feet, with the lean, conditioned body of a runner, Matthew had neither the height nor the bulk that Tony did, but as Emily stared at the two men confronting each other, it was Tony who seemed diminished.

He might have felt it, too, for he smacked the pipe against his palm again, harder this time. The resounding thud created by metal hitting flesh made Emily wince. Tony moved his gaze from Matthew to Emily. "Your brother know you're here?"

"I don't report to my brother," Emily assured him. "Look, all we want to do is ask you a few questions about the night Jenny Wilcox was murdered. You were with her earlier in the evening, weren't you?"

"I don't have anything to say about Jenny," he said sullenly. "To you or to anyone else."

"What about Wade Drury?" Matthew asked. "Do you have anything to say about him?"

Tony's expression changed rapidly from surly impatience to outright hostility. The metamorphosis was astounding. "What do you want to know about that murdering bastard?"

Matthew said calmly, "I take it the two of you were hardly friends. Word has it, you were jealous of Drury. You even picked a fight with him that night. Was it because you thought Jenny preferred Wade to you?"

"You're crazier than you look if you think that," Tony said hotly, and Emily thought that Matthew had probably gotten the kind of reaction he'd been talking about. How to decipher it, though, she had no idea.

"Jenny had no more use for that no-good drifter than I did. She was afraid of him. He even tried to break into her room once, after she told him to get lost. She told me so herself."

"Did she? I wonder," Matthew mused.

"Yeah, well, you go do your wondering someplace else," Tony snarled. "I've got work to do. And unless you have some repairs you want done on that rattletrap you drove up in, I'll thank you to vacate my premises. *Now.*"

"But wouldn't you like the chance to tell us more about Jenny?" Emily asked. "Give us your thoughts on the murder?"

"My thoughts are on the record," he said. "I talked to the police plenty after that night. They knew, right along with the rest of us, that Drury killed her in cold blood. Killed her because he couldn't have her." Tony paused for a moment, shoving a lock of dark hair from his forehead.

Then, like a chameleon, his expression underwent another rapid change. His features seemed to crumple, and his eyes grew misty. He was either a consummate actor or a raging psychopath, Emily thought, not at all comforted by the notion.

His voice softened as he said, "I won't talk about Jenny. I won't tarnish her memory like that. She ought to be allowed to rest in peace."

Let the past rest in peace. Or else you won't.

The message taped to the rock thrown through her window came back vividly to Emily as Tony Vincent stared down at her, his eyes brimming with tears.

"SO WHAT DID YOU THINK?" Emily asked as they got into her car and drove away.

Matthew shrugged. "The man's definitely got problems."

"Yes, and he definitely still has a thing for Jenny. Did you see the way he looked when he talked about her? I thought he was actually going to cry. He's still in love with her, Matthew."

"*Obsessed* might be a better word," Matthew said, his expression dour. "People with obsessions have been known to commit murder, usually in the name of love."

Emily shuddered, thinking about a love like that. A love that would make someone want to kill. For some reason, Trey Huntington's image materialized in her mind. She shook her head, wanting the vision to disappear. She didn't like thinking about Trey. Didn't like remembering what he had almost done to her once. In the name of love.

She said, "Did you happen to notice all those empty beer bottles lined up on the counter near the refrigerator? Several of them were recently emptied, like in the last hour or two."

Matthew turned to her, amusement glinting in his gray eyes. "And just how did you deduce that, Miss Marple?"

Emily smiled, grateful that he had decided to lighten

the moment. Her thoughts had grown way too dark for such a beautiful day. "Elementary, my dear Watson. The bottles were still sweating."

"Very good, Emily. I'm impressed."

"Thank you," she said, glowing a little at his words of praise. She turned down her street. "So what do we do now? We didn't get anything out of Tony. Not really."

"We got a reaction—actually, several—and at this point, that's about all we can expect."

"So we just keep talking to people? Making general nuisances of ourselves?" Emily asked skeptically.

"You got it." Matthew fell silent for a moment, then said, "I may be away some for the next few days, Emily. Something's come up."

Pulling into the driveway of the Other Side of Paradise Inn, Emily turned off the engine and faced him, trying to keep her tone one of mild interest. "Where are you going?"

Matthew shrugged. "It's just some business I have to attend to. But while I'm gone, I want you to promise me something."

"What?"

The way he was looking at her made Emily's heart start to pound. His eyes always had such a profound effect on her. Emily tried to remind herself that the man was virtually a stranger and, by all indications, was emotionally unavailable to her. He'd pushed her away more times than Emily cared to remember.

But even with all that, she couldn't seem to keep her pulse from racing, her heart from skipping a beat, when he reached over and took her hand in his.

Emily's fingers trembled inside his. Their gazes met, and for just a split second she saw her own emotions, her own desire, mirrored in the gray depths of his eyes.

''I want you to be careful while I'm gone, Emily. I have a feeling things are really going to heat up around here from now on, and I don't want you to put yourself in danger.'' He paused for a moment, then said softly, ''I don't want anything to happen to you.'' There was an edge of regret in his voice that Emily didn't understand.

She wanted to ask him why he cared what happened to her, but she didn't dare. She'd learned a long time ago, when she asked her ex-husband point-blank if he was having an affair, that unless you really wanted to know the answer, unless you were willing to deal with the consequences, you'd better not ask the question.

So all Emily said was ''I'll be careful, Matthew.''

Chapter Eight

"The Other Side of Paradise Inn," Emily said brightly into the telephone. It was the next day, and she was alone in the inn.

"I'd like to speak to Emily Townsend, please."

"This is she."

"Miss Townsend, this is Thelma Dickerson. I'm the director of the Shady Oaks Nursing Home, down here in Batesville."

"Yes, Miss Dickerson. What can I do for you?"

"Well, I hate to be the one to break this to you, especially over the phone and all, but Miss Rosabel Talbot passed away last night."

"Oh, no! How did it happen?" Emily asked, sudden tears stinging her eyes.

"Heart attack, most likely. One of the aides found her this morning. The reason I'm calling you is, well, we didn't exactly know who else to notify, and we found your name and phone number in her room."

"I don't understand," Emily said, frowning.

"I know this is going to sound strange, but Miss Rosabel had one of our orderlies fetch a box of her personal belongings out of storage last evening and bring it over to the nursing home. Fred said she told him it was urgent.

He said she seemed quite anxious to have the box in her possession.''

"That does seem odd," Emily agreed. "Do you know what was in the box?"

"I'm getting to that," Ms. Dickerson assured her. "Fred was worried about Miss Rosabel's agitated state, so he agreed to go get the box for her when he went off duty. He said she was still up and waiting for him when he got back, around ten or so, and she immediately wrote your name on the lid, without even looking at the contents. Then she told him to make sure the box got to you if anything happened to her."

Alarm bells sounded inside Emily's head. "If anything happened to her? Was she sick?"

"I suspect that at her age and in her frail health, Miss Rosabel knew she could go at any time. I've seen this sort of thing happen before. They sense the end is near and begin to make their preparations, poor things."

Emily still wasn't satisfied. "I'm afraid I don't understand. If the box contains Miss Rosabel's personal belongings, shouldn't her next of kin have it?"

"She didn't have any relatives," Ms. Dickerson said. "Miss Rosabel was all alone in the world."

"No, but, she does…did have relatives," Emily told her. "She has a niece who lives right here in Paradise. Surely you have her name and number somewhere in Miss Rosabel's file. Nella Talbot?"

There was a long pause, then the woman said, "I don't know anything about a niece, or anyone else in Miss Rosabel's life. Until you came to see her a few days ago, she hadn't had a visitor in years."

WHEN MATTHEW CAME IN shortly afterward, Emily anxiously filled him in on all the details of the phone call. "I suppose I should go see Nella,'' she said.

Emily was seated behind her desk, and Matthew was perched on the corner. As she gazed up at him, she tried not to think about how sexy he looked in his black leather jacket and black jeans. His dark hair was tousled, as if someone had recently spent a lot of time running her fingers through it.

Emily's palms itched to do exactly that, but after last night, when she heard his motorcycle start up and drive off just before dawn, she'd resolved to keep her emotional distance from Matthew. He obviously didn't trust her enough to tell her where he was going, and Emily had to protect herself. She was already feeling more for him than was wise.

Matthew glanced at his watch. ''It's after six. I doubt the library is still open. Do you know where she lives?''

''No, but I can find out,'' Emily said. She opened a desk drawer and took out Paradise's sparse phone book. Leafing through the pages, she located Nella's number and dialed. Before anyone picked up, Emily palmed the mouthpiece and said, ''I don't want to tell her over the phone. I'll just ask her if I can drop by—'' Nella's answering machine clicked on.

Under the circumstances, Emily didn't feel she should leave a message. She hung up, frowning. ''I guess I'll try again later.''

''Meanwhile, why don't we drive down to Batesville and pick up that box?'' Matthew suggested. ''If Miss Rosabel went to so much trouble to have it brought over to the nursing home, and then made sure someone got it to you if anything happened to her, there might be something important inside.''

''It's that 'if anything happened to her' part that's bothering me so much,'' Emily confessed. ''You don't think someone…you know…did something to Miss Rosabel, do you? Because she talked to us?''

Matthew's grave expression was hardly reassuring. ''I can't say the same thought hasn't crossed my mind. I'd like to talk to the nursing home director, if she's still around tonight. Then, tomorrow, I'll try to see the coroner, though I doubt there'll be an autopsy. If it appears Miss Rosabel died of natural causes, there wouldn't be a reason for one.''

''Not even if we tell them our suspicions?''

''Who'd believe us? We don't have any proof. And maybe she *did* die of a heart attack. It wouldn't be that unusual. Not for someone her age.''

''I guess you're right,'' Emily said, worrying her bottom lip with her teeth. She looked up at Matthew. His eyes were studying her intently, as if he had something more on his mind than what they were discussing.

Almost imperceptibly, his gaze moved to her lips. Emily's heart jolted inside her. She had a hard time gathering her thoughts and keeping them focused on murder.

''Don't…you find it strange that the nursing home didn't know anything about Nella?'' she forced herself to ask. ''Since she was the next of kin, you'd think they'd have her name and number in Miss Rosabel's file.''

''Not if Miss Rosabel didn't supply them. Maybe she and Nella had some kind of falling-out.''

''I guess that's possible,'' Emily mused. ''But why didn't either one of them say anything about it to us?''

''Sometimes it's difficult to talk about family problems,'' Matthew said, and Emily could see his point. She certainly didn't relish discussing her and Stuart's disagreements with anyone else.

"Come on," Matthew said. "Let's go find out what Miss Rosabel wanted you to know."

"WHAT IS IT?" Emily asked. She stared at the box on her kitchen table as Matthew cut the twine and pulled the flaps loose. "What's in there?"

Matthew withdrew a handful of old letters, receipts, and bills, and Emily reached for the stack, sorting through it as Matthew plowed through the rest of the box.

"Good grief," Emily said, holding up an electric bill dated May 17, 1975. "I'd say Miss Rosabel gave new meaning to the term *pack rat*. What's left in the box?"

"Looks like books and ledgers of some sort."

"Well, this stuff is just a bunch of junk," Emily said, disappointed.

"Not necessarily." Matthew had been riffling through the stack of papers on the table in silence for a moment, but now he withdrew a newspaper clipping and held it out to Emily. "Take a look at this."

Emily scanned the clipping. It was all about Jenny Wilcox's murder and how the police had questioned Miss Rosabel, Nella and Tony Vincent, all three of whom had seen the victim and the suspect, Wade Drury, the night of the murder.

Matthew handed Emily another clipping about the murder, and then another. She began to make a stack. Most of the clippings she'd already seen on her trip to the library, but the last clipping Matthew handed her wasn't about the murder at all.

It was about a family who had lived on the outskirts of Paradise and who had left town abruptly after the man was accused of stealing from his employer, Huntington Industries. The bank had had to foreclose on the property, and Huntington had generously agreed to pay off the mortgage and settle the back taxes.

The article was dated fifteen years ago, and Miss Rosabel, or someone, had scribbled in the margin one word: *Avengers.*

Emily looked up. ''Are you thinking what I'm thinking?''

Matthew nodded. ''What was it Miss Rosabel told us? Young boys beaten up? Property vandalized? One poor family run out of town?''

Emily frowned. ''Do you think she was talking about this family?''

''It's a definite possibility.''

''Why do you think Miss Rosabel kept all this stuff?''

Matthew shrugged. ''It appears she had a lingering interest in the murder. And in the Avengers. Possibly she was trying to find a connection between the two.''

''And the reason she left all this to me?''

Matthew picked up an envelope, glanced at the front of it, then tossed it back on the stack. ''Maybe she thought you could find what she couldn't.''

''She always did have more faith in me than most people in this town,'' Emily said, with a pang of sadness. She stared gloomily at the untidy pile of papers on her table. ''It'll take forever and a day to sort through all this stuff.''

''Well, maybe not quite that long.''

Emily heard the smile in Matthew's voice, and when she looked up, her heart tumbled inside her. She knew there could be nothing between them. She'd told herself that a hundred times, and Matthew had made it perfectly clear.

But…he could be so devastating when he wanted to be. Emily hadn't yet found a way to protect herself from his charm.

Take deep breaths, she told herself. *And pretend he's someone else. Someone like Trey Huntington. That should take the edge off.*

But it didn't work. Couldn't work. Because there was no way Emily could ever pretend that Matthew Steele was anyone other than himself.

With gritty determination, she got out her list of suspects and went over the details they'd jotted down before. At the bottom of the list, she wrote AVENGERS all in caps, then drew a big question mark beside the word.

Emily stared down at the question mark. "If the Avengers did have something to do with Jenny's death, what could their motive have been? She was a substitute schoolteacher who wasn't even going to be in town that long. Why would a vigilante group want to kill her?"

"Maybe she stumbled onto something."

Emily looked up. "Like what?"

"Like their identities. Or some of their dirty little deeds."

Emily let out a long breath, ruffling her bangs. "We've gone from a crime of passion to something completely different here. This is hardly a simple homicide, is it?"

"Murder is rarely simple," Matthew said. "Let's just do a little supposing." He sat back and steepled his fingers beneath his chin. "Let's suppose for a minute that the Avengers, whoever they were, *didn't* have anything to do with Jenny's death. Miss Rosabel said everyone in town believed Wade Drury was guilty. What if the Avengers believed that, too, and decided to take the law into their own hands, just like they'd done many times before? What if they killed Wade Drury, all in the name of truth, justice and the American way?"

Emily grew pensive. "Then we'd be looking for more than one killer. We'd have to solve two murders instead of one.'' She looked up and caught Matthew's intense gaze on her. ''What's wrong?''

He seemed at a loss for a moment. Then he said, ''The way you accepted my theory so readily. There would have been those in this town who would have been outraged by my suggestion.''

''I'm not like most people in this town.''

''So I've noticed.'' And without so much as a warning, he leaned across the table, took her face in his hands and kissed her tenderly on the lips.

Emily, dazed and more than a little confused, said breathlessly, ''What was that for?''

''For not being like most people in this town.'' His hands still cupping her face, he leaned down and kissed her again, harder, more urgently, this time. His tongue slipped between her lips, and Emily began to tremble. She raised a tentative hand to his arm, felt the flex and bunch of powerful muscles beneath his flannel shirt, and she thought, *Oh, Lord, I'm a goner.*

And then she didn't think at all, because the kiss deepened, intensified, and everything in Emily's head flew out the window.

Matthew groaned—it was a low, intimate sound of need—as he pulled Emily into his arms. He squeezed his eyes tightly shut as the tension inside him heightened. God, how he wanted her, he thought. She was so soft. So incredibly feminine.

And she could be his. He knew that. Sensed it in the way she sighed against his mouth, in the way her body strained against his. He could go on kissing her until this heat, this fierce, melting hunger, made them both desperately ready.

Without breaking the kiss, Matthew traced his hand up the front of her blouse, unfastened the top two buttons and slipped his hand inside. He found her breast, stroked, and her body instantly responded. She moaned into his mouth, and Matthew thought that nothing had ever excited him as much.

She was incredible, so sexy and sweet. It was all Matthew could do not to sweep her up into his arms and carry her off to the bedroom, strip off their clothes and make savage love to her all night long.

But Emily deserved more than that. She deserved more than a dishonest, dangerous man who could give her nothing more than a night or two of ecstasy.

Oh, but what ecstasy it would be, he thought, shuddering with regret as he moved his hands upward to wind through her hair. He lifted his lips from hers to skim kisses along the smooth, delectable line of her jaw.

Emily pulled back, thoroughly shaken. She gazed at him in rapture. "Matthew," she whispered, lifting her hand to touch his. "What was that for?"

"That one…" he said, in a deep, husky drawl that thrilled her all the way to her toes. "That one, my sweet Emily, was just for me."

"Oh," she said, and after that singularly expressive comment could think of nothing else to say.

"*There* you are!" said a voice from the kitchen doorway. "I've been looking *all over* for you!"

Like guilty conspirators, Matthew and Emily jumped apart as Mrs. DeVere sailed into the kitchen. In her purple chenille bathrobe and green hair curlers, she reminded Emily of some weird eggplant experiment gone awry. Emily had to control an almost hysterical urge to laugh. Or cry.

As unobtrusively as she could, Emily reached up to fasten her blouse. If Mrs. DeVere noticed, she gave no indication. She planted herself beside the table and stared down at Emily, seemingly oblivious of the mess on the table and the telltale blush on Emily's cheeks.

Emily said weakly, "My goodness, you're up late."

"My dear, I never doze more than two or three hours a night. The spirits are most active while the rest of us sleep, and so I've made it a point to adapt my schedule to theirs. But that's not why I've been looking for you," she said. "I've had the most wonderful idea, and I'm sure you will concur. We simply *must* hold a séance, here in this very house, to try and summon that poor murdered girl's lost spirit."

"A séance?" Emily repeated. "I don't know—"

"We simply must. There is no question about it."

"Well…" Emily glanced at Matthew, expecting to find him amused and perhaps a little annoyed at the interruption, but what she saw on his face made her catch her breath. It was as if, in the space of seconds, he had donned a mask—a cold, hard, fearsome-looking mask.

He pushed back his chair and stood.

"Matthew?"

"I'll say good-night," he said. "It appears you two ladies have something to discuss."

"But—" He had already disappeared through the swinging door of the kitchen before Emily could voice her protest.

She shrugged and smiled lamely at Mrs. DeVere, but Emily couldn't help feeling that something precious had just been lost to her. Something precious and wonderful and all too elusive.

MATTHEW OPENED the throttle on his motorcycle, letting the wind tear through his hair and sting his face into numbness. He only wished the rest of him was numb, but the adrenaline pumping through him brought his every nerve ending vitally alive.

Emily had done that to him.

With just one kiss, she'd made him realize how vulnerable he was. How weak he was. How very much he wanted her.

It was dangerous to want a woman that badly.

Matthew opened the throttle wider, sending the bike plunging through the darkness. He wanted the speed and the noise and the danger to drive the images of Emily Townsend from his mind, but her scent was all over him. The subtle fragrance seemed to embody her sweetness, her sexy innocence, reminding him all too vividly of what he might have been doing with her at this very instant if he hadn't stopped them.

What a mess, he thought grimly, barely slowing for a curve. The tires screamed in protest as Matthew leaned into the turn. Wind roared past his ears.

When he first came to Paradise and sought out Emily Townsend and her inn, he'd been perfectly willing to use her. Gaining her trust had been part of the plan. He'd had no idea he'd end up desiring more than just a room. More than just her help.

Everything had changed. Their relationship had been elevated to a new level. Deeper emotions were coming into play, and Matthew hated to think how hurt Emily would be when she learned the truth about him. There was still so much she didn't know.

But it couldn't be allowed to matter, Matthew resolved. He couldn't let anything get in his way. He'd come to Paradise for justice. For revenge. Emily was a means to that end.

Nothing more.

He didn't know how long he'd been on the road when

he discovered he had been driving steadily eastward. The foothills of the Ozarks were giving way to flat, monotonous bottomland. Soon he would be crossing the Memphis-Arkansas bridge.

There was someone he had to see in the city.

Someone from his past.

Someone who would remind him why he couldn't get involved with Emily Townsend.

Chapter Nine

"Is Earl Grey okay?"

"Perfect," Emily said, accepting the cup of tea Nella handed her. The library had just opened the following morning, and they were sitting in Nella's office. Emily gazed around curiously, noting how neat and orderly everything seemed. Just like Nella herself.

Nella took a seat behind her desk and smiled. "I'm so glad you came back. I did so enjoy our talk."

"I did, too. I don't know why I haven't made it a point to become acquainted with you sooner." Emily sipped her tea, then set the cup aside. She looked at Nella, taking in the trim gray wool skirt and sweater, the dainty pearl earrings—the librarian's only adornment—and wondered how to tell Nella about her aunt.

Finally Emily took a deep breath and said, "Have you been in contact with your Aunt Rosabel's nursing home lately?"

Nella's blue eyes clouded. A look of distress passed across her delicate features. She tucked a nonexistent strand of hair behind one ear. "No, I'm sorry to say I haven't. Aunt Rosabel and I had a...well, a disagreement...a few years ago. It was a silly thing, really, but it just seemed to escalate, and before I knew it, we were completely…estranged. You don't know how badly I've felt about the situation all these years, Emily, but I simply have not known how to fix it.'' She paused for a moment, then said, ''That must seem strange to you. I know how close you are to your brother.''

If you only knew, Emily thought. She understood exactly how fragile familial relationships could be. The animosity between her and Stuart had grown all out of proportion over the years, but neither of them seemed willing to meet the other halfway.

She said sympathetically, ''It doesn't seem strange at all. I know how easy it is to drift apart from someone you care about. But I'm afraid it doesn't make what I have to tell you any easier.'' She hesitated for a moment, then said in a rush, ''Nella, someone from Shady Oaks called me last evening. Your aunt Rosabel died the night before last.''

Nella stared at her in shock. ''Died? Aunt Rosabel's dead?''

Emily nodded. ''They think it was a heart attack. I'm sorry I couldn't tell you sooner. I tried to reach you last night, right after I found out, but you were out.''

''I had a meeting,'' Nella murmured. Her cup clattered against her saucer as she set her tea down. The liquid sloshed over the rim, onto her hand, but she seemed not to notice. ''I…don't understand. Why did the nursing home call you?''

''Evidently I was the last one who had been in to see Miss Rosabel. And…well, they didn't seem to have your name and number.''

Nella put trembling fingers to her lips, seemingly trying to quell her emotions. After a moment, she said, ''Did…Aunt Rosabel say anything about me when you last saw her? Did she mention me at all?''

Nella was obviously stricken with guilt and needed something, *anything,* for reassurance that her aunt had forgiven her. Emily's heart went out to her. She said softly, "Miss Rosabel mentioned you once or twice. I…never got the impression she harbored any ill feelings toward you."

Relief flooded Nella's eyes. "I suppose…there are arrangements to be made. And I'll need to pick up her personal belongings from the nursing home."

"Actually," Emily said, "that was another thing I wanted to tell you. Miss Rosabel left a box for me. I picked it up last night, after I got the news. It's just a bunch of old letters and newspaper clippings, some books, that sort of thing, but if you'd like to come by and look through the stuff yourself, you're welcome to."

Nella was gazing at her in surprise. "I didn't know you and my aunt were that close."

"We weren't. But, as I said, I'd been to see her recently, and I think she thought there might be some things among those letters and clippings that might help me with the investigation."

"Did you find anything?"

"Not really. There were some newspaper clippings about Jenny's murder, about you and Miss Rosabel being questioned by the police." Emily took a sip of her tea, then said tentatively, "This is probably not the right time to ask you, and if you don't want to answer, just say so. But you know how involved I am in the investigation of the murder and all, and I've been wondering something— just how well did you know Wade Drury?"

Nella picked up her teacup, but didn't drink. Her hand trembled slightly. "We were friends," she said.

"You weren't…in love with him?"

Nella's eyes, behind her glasses, rounded in shock. "In

love with him? Wherever did you get that idea? I hardly knew him, and what I did know—'' She broke off, shuddering delicately.

Emily said quickly, ''I'm sorry. I don't mean to pry, but your aunt said something that lead me to believe you might have…had feelings for Wade.''

''I had feelings, but not the kind you mean,'' Nella said. ''Wade Drury frightened me. I never said anything to Aunt Rosabel, because she was so obviously taken with him, but there was a darkness inside that man. He had secrets—'' Again she stopped short, her gaze meeting Emily's meaningfully. ''He had secrets, and a man with secrets can be a dangerous thing, Emily.''

A chill raced up Emily's spine. Just what was Nella trying to tell her? Was she talking about Wade Drury or Matthew Steele? Was she referring to her own past experiences or warning Emily?

Uncomfortable with her thoughts, Emily stood. ''Well, thanks for the tea. I have to be going. If there's anything I can do…''

Nella waved aside her offer. ''Thank you, but you've done enough already. Your kindness to my aunt in her last days…well, that means everything to me.'' She walked Emily to the door, then said, ''There is just one more thing.''

Emily turned expectantly. ''Name it.''

''You mentioned something about some books. My aunt had a family Bible in her possession. It was mine, actually, left to me by my mother. It was the only thing I had of hers, and somehow, when Aunt Rosabel and I…went our separate ways, the Bible got misplaced. If you run across it—''

''Say no more,'' Emily said. ''It's yours.''

Gratitude filled Nella's eyes. She clutched Emily's

hand. "Thank you, Emily. You've been such a good friend. I don't know how I can ever repay you."

"DO YOU KNOW what this has cost me?" Stuart threw the latest edition of the *Herald* across his desk. Emily winced. She'd already seen the headline: Innkeeper brings in psychic to help solve murder. Mike Durbin had really outdone himself this time, though how he'd found out about Grace DeVere, Emily had no idea.

Mike was no longer asking for Emily's help with his articles. He now seemed to have his own agenda. Emily shuddered to think what that agenda entailed. Or what Mike might be willing to do to achieve it.

Jumping up, Stuart began to pace his office. "Do you have any idea the damage you've done?"

Emily brushed her fingers through her short hair as she watched her brother's distraught movements. "You're making too much of this, Stuart. No one takes this kind of thing seriously."

"A *psychic,* for God's sake. What are you going to do, set up a fortune-telling booth at your grand opening?" His voice was heavy with sarcasm as he spun around to face her. "Just what the hell were you thinking, Emily?"

"I didn't invite her here," Emily said, annoyed with herself for sounding so defensive. "She just showed up. And I didn't tell Mike Durbin about her, either. I don't know how he got the information." It made her a little uneasy to think of Mike—as unscrupulous as she knew he could be—skulking about the inn without her knowledge.

"That man is a menace," Stuart muttered. "Someone ought to put a stop to this kind of garbage."

"Look," Emily said, trying to soothe him, "I'm as upset by this as you are. I'm hardly presented in a favorable light in that article. I sound like some kind of New Age nut, which is not at all the type of publicity I'd originally envisioned for the Other Side of Paradise Inn. But there is such a thing as freedom of the press, Stuart, like it or not. There's nothing you can do to stop Mike Durbin, so I don't see the point in getting yourself so worked up by all this.''

''Don't you?'' Stuart glared at her. ''Well, I don't see the point of your running around town with that stranger, making a spectacle of yourself on the back of his motorcycle.''

Emily just shook her head. ''Why do I even bother?''

''Because you know your brother is right,'' said a voice from Stuart's doorway. Emily froze at those smooth, liquid tones. The skin at the back of her neck crawled. ''And I'd like to know, too—just what *are* you doing with that stranger, Emily?''

There was a nasty insinuation in Trey Huntington's voice that Emily didn't like. He walked across the room to her, then bent and brushed his cool lips against her cheek.

It was all Emily could do not to jerk away from him. Sensing her distress, he laughed—it was a low, ugly sound—and straightened. ''Is our girl here giving you a hard time again, Stu?''

Stuart looked uncomfortable with the exchange that had just taken place. He glanced from Emily to Trey, and for a moment, it seemed to Emily that he was about to spring to her defense. Then he muttered, ''Some things never change,'' as he sat down in his chair. Trey rested one hip on the corner of Stuart's desk, folding his arms, and they both stared at Emily.

''I should have smelled an ambush when you called me down here,'' she said. ''What's this all about, Stuart?''

"Your brother and I feel you've gotten way out of line with this murder thing, Emily. All the area papers, not to mention the local radio ·stations, are in a feeding frenzy, and there are bound to be repercussions, come election day. For everyone's sake, we want you to back off."

In spite of Trey's easy tone, Emily knew the statement wasn't a request, but a command. She lifted her chin. "I have no intention of backing off. Matthew and I—"

"Matthew?" Trey's elegant brows rose, and he managed to imply a slyness with that one word that irritated Emily no end.

She snapped, "*Matthew* and I have come up with some very promising leads. I expect we're very close to solving this whole thing."

Stuart yanked at his tie. "Why do you insist on wasting your time with this nonsense? Everyone knows Wade Drury killed Jenny."

"Maybe because that's what everyone was led to believe." Emily paused for a moment, then said, "I understand you both got to know Jenny pretty well."

Stuart gaped at her. "Who told you that?"

"Miss Rosabel, who, by the way, died night before last. I thought you might like to know."

"I'm sorry to hear it," Stuart murmured, but Trey said nothing at all. After all the years she'd known him, his coldness still astounded Emily.

"Miss Rosabel told me that you two used to come by the inn to see Jenny until Tony Vincent laid his claim on her. Then you backed off."

Trey said in a bored tone, "Jenny Wilcox was a schoolteacher. What possible interest could either of us have had in her?"

Emily didn't want to point out that she'd been a college dropout when Trey asked her to marry him. Instead, she said, "From what I understand, she was a strikingly beautiful woman who could have had her choice of suitors. Did either of you ever ask her out?"

Stuart looked decidedly uncomfortable. He said irritably, "Where's this all leading, Emily?"

"I just want to make sure I understand the situation back then correctly."

"There was no situation," Trey said calmly. "Obviously, someone's been telling tales out of school."

"Okay," Emily said. "So neither of you had a thing for Jenny Wilcox. Let me ask you this. Have either of you ever heard of a group who called themselves the Avengers?"

The Mont Blanc pen Stuart had been holding fell to the floor and landed silently on the plush carpet. He bent to retrieve it as Trey said, "'The Avengers'? I believe that was an old TV show, wasn't it, Emily? I forget who the stars were."

Emily shook her head, not fooled by his innocent tone. "They were a group of modern-day vigilantes who operated right here in Paradise fifteen years ago. They vandalized property, beat people up, and word has it they even ran one poor family out of town."

"And just whose word would that be, Emily?"

"I happened across an old newspaper article about the family in a box of papers and letters Miss Rosabel left to me. You must have known them, Trey. The man worked for Huntington Industries, and H.I. acquired his property by paying off the mortgage and settling his back taxes after he left town. As I recall, Huntington expanded its facilities about fifteen years ago. That property, located out on the highway and all, must have come in real handy." Emily was taking a stab in the dark, but from the silence that followed she knew she'd hit a nerve.

"I think you and I need to have a little talk, Emily." Though his tone remained even, Trey's words were frost-coated and his eyes were like glaciers. All at once, Emily wondered whether she might have gone a little too far. No one knew better than she how dangerous Trey could be when pushed.

She stood. "I'd love to chat with you, Trey, but I have to be going." To Stuart, she said, "I trust you won't call me down here again concerning this matter. This has been a real waste of my time."

"I'll walk you out," Trey said.

"No need—"

"Oh, but there is." His hand was on her elbow, and though Emily made a point of moving away from him, he remained steadfastly by her side as they left the building and walked across the parking lot.

"Thanks for seeing me to my car," Emily said, her tone brimming with sarcasm. "You've always been such a gentleman."

Trey laughed. "You're not still holding that little incident in our past against me, are you, Emily?"

"Little incident?" Emily stared at him in open disgust. "You hit me, Trey. You hurt me. I thought you were going to kill me, you were so angry. I told you then I would never forgive you, and I meant it. You stay away from me, or I might just have Mike Durbin write up a little exposé on you. And he'd do it, too. Mike's very ambitious. He's one of the few people in this town who isn't afraid of you."

"The more fool he," Trey said, smiling slightly.

"What do you think the people in Paradise, not to mention Stuart's supporters, would think if they knew about that 'little incident' in your past?"

"Why, Emily." Trey's hand slid up her arm. "That almost sounds like a threat."

"That's because it is one," she said. "Take your hands off me, and don't you ever touch me again."

Trey's smile broadened into a malicious grin as his grip tightened on her arms. He held her still as his head moved toward her, and for a terrible moment, Emily thought he was going to try to kiss her. Everything inside her rebelled.

"She said take your hands off her."

At the sound of Matthew's voice, Trey froze. For one split second, he stared down at Emily, as if defying her to make a move. Then, slowly, deliberately, still holding her, he turned to face Matthew.

MATTHEW TRIED to control the murderous rage descending over him. He wanted to smash in Huntington's face for touching Emily. The strength of his emotion astounded him.

Trey said slowly, "I don't think you realize what you've just done. No one, I mean *no one,* in this town talks to me that way."

"I know exactly what I've done," Matthew assured him, trying to control the violent impulses surging through him. "I'll give you two seconds to get your hands off her. One."

"Your boyfriend's got a lot to learn about how things operate around here, Emily."

"That's two," Matthew said, slowly walking toward Trey. Matthew thought that it would give him the utmost pleasure to connect one of his fists with Huntington's nose. He almost hoped Trey wouldn't back down.

But that was asking too much. Trey let his hands drop from Emily's arms as he stared at Matthew with undisguised hatred. "You just made the biggest mistake of your life."

"I doubt that very seriously," Matthew said. "Now why don't you get the hell out of here, before I do something you might regret?"

"This isn't over, Emily," Trey said over his shoulder as he stalked toward his car. "Not by a long shot."

Matthew turned to Emily. "What did he mean by that?" he demanded. "He acts as if he has some kind of claim on you."

Emily laughed nervously. "I assure you, he doesn't," she said, but Matthew thought there was the slightest hint of fear in her eyes as she watched Huntington's Mercedes tear out of the parking lot.

What the hell kind of past did the two of them have? Matthew wondered, surprised by the fierce possessiveness he felt toward Emily. The urge to protect her had never been stronger.

Even though the afternoon was warm, he saw her shiver. Before he could stop himself, he reached up and tucked a strand of her dark, silky hair behind her ear. His voice softened. "Hey, you okay?"

She smiled. "I'm fine. Thanks for coming to my rescue, Matthew. I don't believe anyone's ever done that for me before."

The look in her soft brown eyes as she gazed up at him took Matthew's breath away. He'd never felt more heroic. Or more humble.

He said gruffly, "You need to be more careful about the company you keep."

"I didn't know Trey would be here," she said. "I came to see Stuart." She waved a hand toward the office building behind them.

Matthew couldn't keep his eyes off her, and he was

having a hard time keeping his hands away. She looked so vulnerable today. So sweet and inviting.

She was dressed in one of the flowing print dresses she seemed to favor. This one buttoned all the way up the front, but several of the buttons at the bottom had been left undone, giving Matthew tantalizing glimpses of her slender legs every time a breeze caught the hem. The denim jacket she wore for warmth did little to hide the tiny indentation of her waist, the soft swell of her breasts.

Desire tightened inside Matthew. At that moment, he thought her the most beautiful woman he'd ever seen. No one else even came close.

Not even Jenny.

HE WAS STARING AT HER so strangely, Emily thought, as if she were a delectable morsel and he a starving man. The image made her blush. She put a nervous hand to her throat. "So what are you doing here, Matthew?"

He shrugged, and the intensity in his eyes began to fade. "Looking for you. I just came from the coroner's office. The cause of Miss Rosabel's death is being listed officially as a heart attack. The funeral's tomorrow."

"Did you tell him our suspicions?"

"Her. The coroner was a her," Matthew said. "There wasn't any evidence of foul play, and at Miss Rosabel's age, no reason to order an autopsy."

"So we may never know for sure what happened to her."

"I guess not."

Emily leaned back against her car, pulling her denim jacket around her as a brisk breeze blew through the trees. She saw Matthew's gaze drop to her legs, and she shivered. "I can't help feeling responsible," she said.

"There was nothing you could have done for her."

"I know. But if I hadn't gone to see her, if I'd never asked her all those questions, then no one would have had any reason for wanting her dead." Emily bit her lip, feeling tears sting behind her eyes. The day had been emotionally trying, to say the least. The conversation with Nella, the fight with Stuart, the scene with Trey and then Matthew's unexpected rescue—all were conspiring against Emily's composure. She wiped the corner of her eye as unobtrusively as she could.

"For all we know, she did die of a heart attack," Matthew said softly. "Just like the coroner said. You can't start second-guessing yourself, Emily. Believe me, that road leads nowhere fast."

The bitterness in his voice drew her gaze, and as Emily stared up him, she somehow knew that he was thinking about the woman he'd told her about. The woman who'd died because of him.

Matthew's eyes were bleak as he gazed at the distant mountains, and Emily wondered whether she would ever find out what had really happened to that woman. And whether she would ever get to know the real Matthew Steele.

And as she studied his stark profile, searching for answers, something Nella told her earlier came back to her.

A man with secrets can be a dangerous thing, Emily.

THAT NIGHT, Emily was again startled awake by the sound of shattering glass, this time followed by a small explosion. Her first thought as she jumped up in bed was *Oh, no, not again.* Fearing the worst, she hurried down the hallway.

Just as she entered the living area, the smoke alarms began to blare. Across the room, a small blaze ignited a rug on the floor, and as Emily watched, the fire spread rapidly, racing along the floor to snare the lace curtains hanging at the broken window.

Heart pounding, Emily grabbed the nearest fire extinguisher and screamed at Mrs. DeVere, who was now standing petrified at the top of the stairs, "Get out! Hurry!"

Emily's command seemed to spur the older woman to action. She hurried down the stairs, her purple robe billowing out behind her. "I'll call 911."

"We don't have 911. Just get yourself out."

"Aren't you coming—?"

"Just go!"

For what seemed like minutes, but must have been only a second or two, Emily struggled with the release on the fire extinguisher. She cursed, pleaded, sobbed—and then, suddenly, the extinguisher was ripped from her hands. Matthew shouted, "Get the hell out of here!"

"Let me help you—"

"Go, Emily!" he commanded, just as she had with Mrs. DeVere.

Knowing that they were wasting precious seconds arguing, Emily turned and ran. There was another extinguisher in the kitchen. She got it and ran back, and together she and Matthew doused the flames.

Everything was over in less than five minutes, but the adrenaline rush was still incredible. When they knew the blaze was out completely, Matthew took her arm and led her outside. The crisp night air felt wonderful on her face, and she breathed deeply, trying to calm her racing pulse. Then she collapsed to the ground, ignoring the cold.

Matthew was wearing his leather jacket, as if he'd just come in, and he took it off and wrapped it around Emily's shoulders. She shivered, not from the cold, but from the warmth that clung to the jacket. She could almost pretend it was Matthew himself holding her.

"Are you okay?"

"You seem to be asking me that a lot," she said, her smile weak. She pushed back her hair from her face. "I'm fine, but I can't even bear to go back inside and survey the damage."

"What happened?" Matthew asked. "I was driving up when I saw the blaze."

Emily shivered, huddling inside her cotton nightgown. Her feet were bare, and she knew her hair was a total mess. But right now, all she could think was how very glad she was that Matthew had come back when he did. She didn't even stop to question where he had been at this late hour. "I'd already gone to bed," she explained, "when I heard the window break. And then some kind of explosion. I came out and found the fire, and..." She trailed off, her teeth chattering, more from shock than cold.

"I'm going back in to check around," Matthew said. "You stay out here."

"But, Matthew—"

"You have a guest to attend to," he reminded her, nodding toward Mrs. DeVere, who stood wringing her hands in the middle of the street.

Matthew was right. Emily had some reassuring to do. This was her job, and she rose, literally and figuratively, to the occasion. By the time she reached Mrs. DeVere, Matthew had already disappeared inside the inn. Emily laid a hand on Mrs. DeVere's arm. "I'm so sorry this happened," she said. "Are you all right?"

Mrs. DeVere had been looking at the house, but now she turned toward Emily, her eyes bright with excitement.

"This is thrilling," she said. "Absolutely thrilling. Wait until I tell the others."

It wasn't quite the response Emily had been expecting. She said hesitantly, "If you would like me to find you another place to stay for the night, I'll certainly understand."

"Another place to stay?" Mrs. DeVere looked aghast. "Surely you realize this is the first contact we've made. I wouldn't dream of leaving now."

"But you don't think a…a spirit caused the fire. Mrs. DeVere—"

"My dear." Mrs. DeVere placed a calming hand on Emily's arm. "A spirit can manifest its displeasure in many ways—cracked mirrors, shattered glass, even spontaneous combustion. You have a very angry ghost living in your house. The séance is more important than ever. We must proceed at once with our plans."

Emily started to protest, but just then Matthew came out on the porch and motioned them inside. Emily wanted to cry when she saw the damage wrought by the fire.

Having been given the all clear by Matthew, Mrs. DeVere went straight up to her room, but Emily couldn't move. She stood staring at the ruined rug and curtains, and all she could think about was her dwindling bank account.

The grand opening was less than a week away. She had dozens of people coming for the open house. How in the world would she ever get this mess cleaned up in time? The thought of having to cancel the open house and the other plans she'd made was more than Emily could bear.

"I'll drag the rug and curtains outside," Matthew said, still poking through the rubble. "That'll help with the smell."

"Can you tell what happened?"

Matthew glanced up. "Do you know what a Molotov cocktail is?"

"No, but I think I could use one right now," Emily said dryly.

"You just had one," he informed her. "A Molotov cocktail is a sort of homemade hand grenade."

Emily stared at him for a moment. "You mean like in the movies, where they put gasoline in a bottle and stuff a rag in the top for a fuse? *That's* what happened here?" At this point, Emily didn't think she could take another shock.

Matthew kicked aside a shard of glass with his toe. "Either we just got another warning, or someone wants to run you out of business," he said, his tone forbidding.

"But who?" Emily asked desperately. "Who would do something like this?"

"That's what we have to find out. When I pulled up, I thought I saw someone skulking about in Cora Mae's yard."

"Could you tell who it was?" The thought crossed Emily's mind that it might have been Mike Durbin. The reporter seemed to have an uncanny ability to be at the right place at the right time.

But, of course, if you created your own story, it would be easy to be on the scene, Emily thought with a shiver.

Matthew shook his head. "I don't know who it was. I didn't get a good look, because I wanted to get inside and make sure you were all right."

He gazed about the room, seemingly unaware of what he'd just said. Or of the impact his simple statement had on Emily. Her heart thumped against her chest. He'd wanted to make sure she was all right. Emily tried not to read too much into it, but it was hard not to, especially when she wanted to so badly.

"If it *was* Cora Mae out there, then I think she has some explaining to do," Matthew was saying.

"You don't think she's responsible for this, do you? I mean, I know she has it in for me and all, but this—" Emily gazed at the damage in despair. "Someone really sick has to be behind this."

"I'm not accusing Cora Mae," Matthew said. "Though after having met her the other day, there's very little I'd put past her. But if she was the one in her yard tonight, she might have seen something, and I'd like to know why she doesn't appear to be coming forward on her own."

"Why don't we just go over and ask her?" Emily said impatiently. "Right now. Tonight."

"Because it's after midnight," Matthew pointed out. "And if it wasn't Cora Mae I saw, then she's probably fast asleep by now. We'll talk to her tomorrow. Meanwhile, we'd better make a call to the sheriff."

"For all the good that will do," Emily muttered. She sighed. "Okay. We'll go talk to Cora Mae first thing in the morning."

Matthew was kneeling again, examining something on the floor. "The afternoon would be better," he said, without looking up. "I think we should go to Miss Rosabel's funeral in the morning, and then after that, there's someplace I have to go. I probably won't make it back before four."

"Four! But I don't want to wait that long. I thought we were partners, Matthew," Emily blurted out, then blushed fiercely when she heard the way she sounded—like a nagging wife who didn't trust her husband.

Matthew stood up. His eyes softened. "We are partners, Emily. This has nothing to do with the investigation. Or you."

"Okay," she said, but it wasn't okay. Not even when

he walked over and put his arm around her, drawing her close. Not even when he gazed down at her tenderly and murmured, "You've had a hard day, Emily. Why don't you go back to bed?"

It wasn't okay, because all Emily could think about, wonder about, was this mysterious business of his. If it didn't have anything to do with her or the investigation, what did it have to do with? Another woman? Was that where Matthew went when he disappeared from the inn?

Well, what did you think? Emily asked herself furiously as she strode down the hallway to her room. *That he was a monk?*

Matthew Steele was an attractive, sexy man, and there were bound to be women in his life. Lots of women. It was stupid to feel jealous. Stupid and childish and Emily had no right. No right whatsoever. What was wrong with her anyway? She was acting as if...as if...oh, Lord.

She was acting as if she were in love with the man.

Chapter Ten

She couldn't be in love with him, Emily decided as she and Matthew drove into Batesville the next day and located the funeral home where the memorial service for Miss Rosabel would be held.

She couldn't be in love with him because she hardly knew him. It was a ridiculous notion.

She couldn't be in love with him because if she were, she wouldn't be able to sit here beside him so coolly and calmly and rationalize her feelings for him. Not Emily. She knew herself too well. If she were in love with him, she would probably be doing something stupid, like begging him to elope with her.

No, she wasn't in love with him, Emily thought as she studied Matthew's silent profile. He was dressed in a dark double-breasted suit, white cotton shirt and a dignified striped tie. She almost hadn't recognized him when he'd come down the stairs earlier, and then she'd tried to tell herself it was impossible that he looked even more handsome in a suit. She'd decided the first moment she laid eyes on him that he was at least a ten in his leather jacket and jeans. How could he look any better?

Matthew pulled her VW into the parking lot, killed the engine, and turned to her. His light gray eyes swept her with a smoldering look of approval. She was wearing a short black dress, complete with black stockings and black pumps. Emily had never thought black was her color, but Matthew's eyes told her otherwise.

She saw his gaze linger on her legs, and her heart thudded against her chest. Her mouth went dry and her stomach fluttered with awareness.

So much for cool and calm.

"Ready to go in?" he asked, lifting his gaze to meet hers. There was something warm and dark in his eyes. Something that looked like desire.

Emily tried to remind herself they were here for a funeral. She should conduct herself accordingly. But her hands were trembling as she fumbled with the door handle.

Matthew reached across her and opened the door. His arm skimmed her breast, and something like an electrical shock passed through Emily. She longed to have him touch her again, ached for more than a brief, accidental contact.

She wanted him to pull her into his arms and kiss her as he'd kissed her that night in the kitchen, when her whole being had been turned inside out. She wanted him to touch her all over, make her burn with desire for him. She wanted—

"Emily? You okay?"

His words broke into her fantasy, shattering the titillating images her mind had conjured up. Her face flamed with color as she glanced at him.

"I'm fine," she said curtly, slipping from the car. But the moment he took her arm to usher her into the building, the images began to build again. His very nearness became an exquisite torment.

The funeral, however, brought her crashing back to

earth, and made Emily realize, as funerals usually did, how fleeting life can be. Even though Miss Rosabel had lived a long and seemingly content life, Emily couldn't help wondering if the old woman had been ready to die. If her time had really come, or if someone had cruelly snuffed out what remaining months or years she might have had.

The only people Emily recognized at the somber gathering—other than Matthew—were Thelma Dickerson from the nursing home and Nella.

Nella, also dressed in black, sat in the front row with her head bowed, obviously overcome by grief. She looked up when Matthew and Emily walked in, nodded, then dropped her gaze back to her lap. Emily couldn't help wondering what Nella must be feeling, considering her estrangement from her aunt. The guilt must be unbearable, and it made Emily think about her own situation with Stuart. Would she one day be filled with bitter regrets?

After the short ceremony, she and Matthew walked out into the brilliant fall sunshine. He tugged at his tie, loosening the knot and unbuttoning the top button of his shirt.

"I wanted to talk to Nella," Emily said, gazing around. "But I don't see her anywhere."

"She made a beeline out of the chapel as soon as the service was over," Matthew said. "I wonder what her hurry was."

"I think she was just overcome with grief," Emily said. "And guilt. I told you about her relationship with Miss Rosabel."

Matthew nodded. "Well," he said. "I don't suppose we accomplished much today other than paying our last respects."

"I'm glad we came, though," Emily said. "It's always better to say goodbye."

There was a haunted look in Matthew's gray eyes that tore at Emily's heart. She wondered what he was thinking. Wondered if there had been someone in his life he hadn't been able to say goodbye to.

Because I killed her.

The memory of his tormented words was like cold water to Emily's senses, reminding her once again how very little she knew about the man who stood beside her.

He turned to her, his gaze sweeping over her again, making her shiver. "I have to go now," he said. "I'll drop you back at the inn and get my bike."

"Fine."

"I'll try to be back before four. But if I'm not, I want you to wait for me."

"Why? Cora Mae's an old woman, Matthew. Surely you can't think she'd do me any harm. All I want to do is ask her a few questions."

"Just promise me you won't do anything impulsive, Emily. Promise you'll wait for me. We'll go see her together."

Emily bristled at his imperious tone. If he really cared, he'd go with her right now, she thought. Or at the very least, he'd tell her where—or who—he was hurrying off to.

She lifted her chin, annoyed with herself for her feelings of possessiveness. Feelings she had no right to be feeling. "I promise I won't do anything impulsive," she said.

BUT PATIENCE HAD never been one of Emily's virtues, and as the hour hand on her mantel clock crept past three and edged toward four, she became more and more edgy. Where in the world was Matthew? Did he think she had nothing better to do than sit around and wait for him?

Which was exactly what she had been doing ever since they'd returned from the funeral and Matthew had hopped on his bike and driven off. Emily's imagination had gone wild, conjuring up all sorts of possibilities. He was with a woman. A beautiful, thin, irresistible woman. Emily just knew it.

And as the day wore on, she became even more certain. If Matthew hadn't been going to see a woman, then why was he keeping his whereabouts a secret?

Her visit to the sheriff's office right after Matthew left had been just as frustrating. She'd gone to report the fire last night, but Sheriff Willis had been his usual helpful self, inviting Emily to file a report which she was sure he would toss in the trash as soon as she left his office. She hadn't even bothered, remembering Miss Rosabel's assertion that the sheriff had been in "up to his eyebrows" with the Avengers.

When the clock chimed four, Emily decided she'd waited long enough. She was not going to wait one minute longer for Matthew. Why should she? She was a grown woman, perfectly capable of asking Cora Mae Hicks a few questions. What harm could there be in that?

Emily left the inn and marched across the street to knock on Cora Mae's door, which stood ajar and swung inward when Emily gave it a little push. She stuck her head inside and called, "Cora Mae? You here?"

No response, but somewhere in the house Emily heard a television. She stepped across the threshold. It wasn't like she was trespassing in a private home or anything, she reasoned. Cora Mae ran a business, same as Emily did. She never locked the front door of the Other Side of Paradise Inn. There'd never been a reason to. Until now.

"Cora Mae?"

Emily gazed around, her curiosity getting the better of

her. The house was larger than hers and surprisingly charming. The perpetual air of gloom the house wore outside had been subdued within by the clever use of rugs and throw pillows, baskets of chrysanthemums and beautiful hand-painted pottery.

Cora Mae certainly had the touch, Emily noted in surprise, taking in the smallest detail with an innkeeper's critical eye. No wonder the This Side of Paradise Inn had been the premier bed-and-breakfast in town for over twenty-five years.

But as Emily walked slowly through the house, she began to get a funny feeling that something was wrong. In the offseason, Cora Mae was completely alone in her big old house. And she was getting on in years. What if something had happened to her, a heart attack or a stroke or something?

As she went out into the kitchen, Emily's fears seemed justified when she saw that a plate of food and a glass of milk, still cold, sat waiting on the dinette and the cellar door was standing open. She called down into the darkness, but there was still no answer. Everything was ominously silent.

By now, Emily was almost sure something bad had happened. Cora Mae might have fallen down the cellar stairs and been badly injured. She might be lying down there now, bleeding and unconscious. As Emily considered her options, she decided the best thing to do was go down and investigate the situation herself.

Finding a string pull, Emily turned on the light, then made her way down the steps. The bare bulb dimly illuminated the cellar, and there was just one small window that let in only a glimmer of faded sunlight. One wall contained shelves of tools and equipment, but the rest of the space was crowded with shelves of canned fruits and vegetables, household solvents and gardening chemicals—some of which had been stored in jars and cans with handwritten labels.

A fire marshal would have a field day in here, Emily thought, gazing at the assortment of flammable products. If Cora Mae had wanted to make a homemade hand grenade herself, she certainly had the ingredients readily available.

The stairs creaked behind her, and Emily whirled toward the sound just as the light in the basement went out, plunging her into darkness.

''Cora Mae?''

No answer.

Footsteps sounded on the stairs.

Fear froze Emily's blood. ''Who's there?'' she called out.

Emily backed away, searching for a place to hide. She stumbled over something lying on the floor—a shovel, she thought—and before she could regain her balance, a figure flew down the steps and shoved her backward. The momentum knocked Emily off her feet, and she fell with a bang against a shelf of cleaning solvents. Glass shattered against the concrete floor. Then footsteps clattered back up the stairs, and the door at the top slammed shut.

Instantly, a noxious odor permeated the air, tearing Emily's eyes. She had no idea what kind of chemicals Cora Mae had kept stored in the containers, but Emily suspected they could be dangerous. Maybe even deadly.

Coughing and trying to quiet her racing heart, she pulled the ruffle at the neck of her cotton dress up over her mouth and nose and, using the window to guide her, made her way back up the stairs. The door at the top was locked from the outside. Panic exploded inside her as she rattled the knob and banged her fist against the door.

"Cora Mae! Open the door! It's me, Emily!"

There was no answer, and the fumes inside the tightly closed cellar were growing thicker, stronger, deadlier. Emily struggled for breath. She stumbled back down the stairs, looking about frantically for another way out.

"Help!" she tried to scream up at the window, but it only came out as a hoarse croak. "Someone help me!"

Still coughing and gagging, Emily began to push with all her might on one of the shelves. Fruit jars crashed to the floor, but she paid them no mind. Finally, she managed to get the shelf positioned under the window. Forcing herself to remain calm, she located the shovel on the floor and hurried back to the window.

By that time, less than a minute or two had passed, but it felt like hours. Emily's head was spinning even more crazily, and for a moment she doubted her ability to haul the shovel up onto the shelf. Trying to will away the dizziness, she managed to climb the shelf and bang the blade against the window. The glass shattered, and a rush of cold air poured in.

With a cry of triumph, Emily threw down the shovel. Gulping the sweet, clean air, unmindful of the cuts and scraps she received on her hands, she pulled herself up and shimmied through the small opening to collapse on the ground.

Blue sky and sunshine had never looked so good. Emily took one long look, one deep breath, and then everything around her faded to black.

ALMOST BY INSTINCT Matthew found Emily, lying unconscious near the broken basement window. The print dress she wore was splotched with blood from the cuts on her hands, and her face looked deathly pale. Matthew knelt and felt for her pulse, then listened to her heart, prepared to give CPR if necessary. But she was breathing. Thank God, he hadn't found her too late.

He remembered what Emily had said the night before, during the fire, about the town not having 911 emergency service. He had no idea whether there was even a doctor in this godforsaken place.

Not knowing what else to do, Matthew picked Emily up—she was so light!—and strode around Cora Mae's house, across the street and up the steps to the Other Side of Paradise Inn.

Mrs. DeVere was sitting in the garden alcove, all alone, when Matthew burst through the front door carrying Emily. The psychic jumped up and hurried across the room toward him, the lavender caftan she wore billowing around her legs like a parachute.

"What happened?" she asked.

"I don't know," Matthew told her. "She's unconscious. We need to get a doctor over here right away."

"I'll go next door," Mrs. DeVere said, heading for the front door. "They'll know how to get hold of the town doctor."

Matthew laid Emily on the sofa and covered her with the crocheted afghan draped across the back. Then he elevated her legs and monitored her breathing and pulse, treating her for possible shock. The cuts on her hand were minor, the least of his worries right now.

Where the hell was the doctor?

This was all Matthew's fault. He shouldn't have been late. He should have known it was just like Emily to throw caution to the winds and go without him. Her impulsiveness was one of the things he found so endearing about her. But there were other things, so many things he couldn't have begun to count them.

He gazed down at her, and a wave of tenderness

washed over him. Gently, he smoothed away the dark hair from her forehead, then ran his finger along the contour of her jawline. He hadn't expected to ever feel this way again. He wasn't sure he'd ever felt precisely this way. Emily was like no woman he'd ever known before. She was so sweet and warm and trusting…

And he'd let her down. The last time he'd failed some-one the result had been tragic. He couldn't let that happen again. Not with Emily. Because if anything happened to her, Matthew knew he would never be able to live with himself.

EMILY SIGHED IMPATIENTLY as Dr. Sheldon took his time listening to her heart. Finally he removed the stethoscope from his ears and made his pronouncement. "She'll be fine. All her vital signs are stable. In a day or two, she'll be good as new."

Stuart had come in shortly after the doctor arrived, and now he and Matthew stood at opposite ends of the couch, gazing down at Emily worriedly.

Matthew said, "Are you sure she shouldn't go to the hospital?"

"Nothing more we could do for her there," Dr. Shel-don assured him. "Just make sure she gets plenty of rest."

"She'll come and stay with Caroline and me," Stuart said. "We'll keep a close eye on her."

"That might not be a bad idea," the doctor agreed.

Emily hated the way they were all talking about her as if she weren't even there. She'd been unconsciousness for only a minute or two, but they were all acting as if she had been at death's door.

She pushed the afghan away and sat up on the couch. "I have no intention of going home with you, Stuart," she said. Then, turning to Matthew, she went on, "Or of going to the hospital with you. There's nothing wrong with me. I'm perfectly fine.''

''You're not fine,'' Matthew said. ''When I think what might have happened—''

''Don't.'' Emily reached for his hand. His fingers closed around hers, warmly, protectively, making Emily's heart race. ''This wasn't your fault,'' she said. ''I don't want you blaming yourself.''

''I'm finding it hard not to,'' he said, his eyes dark and fathomless, regarding her with an intensity that stole Emily's breath away. She couldn't stop looking at him.

Was this what being at death's door did to one's senses? Emily thought in wonder. If so, perhaps the risk had been worthwhile.

Stuart, who was standing at the end of the couch, frowned, his gaze going from Emily to Matthew and then back again, clearly not liking what he was seeing. Or hearing. His voice sounded strained when he said, ''How do you really feel, Emily?''

''My head hurts,'' she admitted, finally able to tear her gaze away from Matthew's.

''I'll give you something for that,'' Dr. Sheldon said. He placed a small vial of capsules on the coffee table. ''Just follow the directions. You'll feel better in a few hours.''

He got up, packed his bag and started for the door. Stuart said, almost reluctantly, ''I'll see you out.''

When they'd disappeared out the front door, Emily turned back to Matthew. ''I didn't want to say anything in front of them, or in front of Mrs. DeVere before the doctor got here, but I think it was Cora Mae who pushed me into that shelf and locked me in her basement. She knew those chemicals were there. Who else could it have been?''

"That's what I've been wondering," Matthew said, his expression grave.

"That old woman tried to fumigate me, Matthew. She's got enough chemicals and cleaning solvents in her basement to blow up half of Paradise. You should see what all she's got down there." Their eyes met again, and she knew Matthew was thinking, just as she was, about the Molotov cocktail someone had thrown through her window last evening.

But neither of them said anything, because just then Stuart came back into the room. "What the hell's been going on around here?" he demanded, loosening his tie. "I dropped by here to invite you to dinner tonight, and I find the place looking like a war zone and you out cold on the couch." His gaze shot to Matthew. "Would one of you mind filling me in on a few details?"

"Someone threw a Molotov cocktail through Emily's window last night," Matthew said bluntly. "They deliberately set the place on fire."

"*What?*" Stuart's voice sounded shocked. Frightened. "Is that true, Emily?"

"Of course it's true. You can see for yourself." She motioned wearily toward the broken window and the remains of the fire. The acrid smell of smoke still clung to the air, in spite of Emily's best efforts. "And then today, when I went over to ask Cora Mae if she might have seen anything last night, someone locked me in her basement after pushing me into a shelf of chemicals. The fumes could have killed me."

All the color drained from Stuart's face. He said hoarsely, "My God, Emily. I had no idea things had gone this far."

Emily folded her arms and glared at him. "Now do you believe me, Stuart? Now do you believe that something sinister is going on in this town? Someone is going to extreme measures to try to get me to drop my investigation into Jenny Wilcox's murder, which only proves that Matthew and I are on the right track. We're close to solving the murder.''

Stuart looked downright sick. He dropped down in a chair and said weakly, ''Emily, you've got to stop this nonsense. You could have been seriously hurt—''

''I could have been *killed,* Stuart, which is exactly my point. If someone didn't have something to hide, then he—or she—wouldn't care how much I investigated the murder. Don't you see?'' she asked, her tone growing a little desperate. ''There's something wrong in this town, Stuart. Very, very wrong. I always thought it was just me, but now I know why I never fit in here. I can't hide things. I can't keep all those dirty little secrets like everyone else does. Who were the Avengers, and why will no one in town talk about them, still, to this day? It's almost as if everyone's trying to protect them,'' she finished in disgust.

''If the townspeople still try to protect the Avengers,'' Stuart said, ''maybe it's because the Avengers tried to protect this town.''

Matthew said, ''So you admit to knowing about a group of vigilantes operating in Paradise who called themselves the Avengers.''

Stuart, ever the lawyer, responded, ''I admit to nothing.''

''But you just said—'' Emily began.

Stuart exploded. ''Drop it, Emily! For God's sake, what are you trying to do to me? To this town? Do you hate us all that much?''

Emily gaped at her brother in shock. ''This has nothing to do with my feelings for you or for Paradise.''

"Of course it does! That's why you bought this house in the first place. So you could flaunt it before the whole town. Rub our noses in a past we'd all like to forget. Well, you've made your point, Emily. We know you don't give a damn what the rest of us think. Now it's time to forget all this nonsense about the murder, before you do something we'll all live to regret." Without another word, he got up and stomped out of the room.

Emily didn't quite know what to say. Or to think. Why was Stuart acting so defensive? She'd never seen her brother so agitated. What in the world was going on in this town? And exactly where did Stuart fit into the picture?

Emily glanced up, only to catch Matthew staring down at her. There was a look in his eyes, a strange little glimmer of something that almost seemed like pity.

MATTHEW STAYED WITH EMILY until Caroline Townsend, who had no doubt been sent by Stuart to try to talk some sense into Emily, arrived, and then Matthew excused himself from the two women and went outside.

He didn't tell Emily where he was going, but he wanted to have a look around Cora Mae's basement before the sheriff got there. Avoiding Cora Mae's front door, Matthew went around back to the basement window and let himself in.

The fresh air from the broken window had diluted the fumes by this time, but the harsh smell still lingered. Using his flashlight to guide him, Matthew located the containers of chemicals Emily had told him about.

The glass jars had been smashed against the concrete, but the cans were still intact. Matthew sifted through the debris, reading the handwritten labels. Toluol, zylene, methylene chloride. What in the world was Cora Mae doing with such strong chemicals? They were hardly typical household products, and any one of them could prove deadly in the wrong hands.

Matthew reached for another container, then froze. The door opened at the top of the stairs. The light came on. Silently he doused his flashlight and turned from the shelves, slipping into the shadows near the stairwell as he listened to the telltale creak of the wood as someone slowly descended the steps.

When the footfalls stilled at the bottom, Matthew stepped out of his hiding place to confront the intruder. Almost too late he saw the gleam of a knife blade arc through the air toward him.

Chapter Eleven

Matthew reacted instinctively. He grabbed her arm and wrenched the knife away. Cora Mae howled in pain.

"You broke my wrist!" she screamed, holding her arm as she backed away from him.

"It's not broken," Matthew said, putting the butcher knife on one of the top shelves. Cora Mae would have to stand on something to retrieve it, but Matthew didn't care. He felt safer with the blade out of the woman's reach. "You've got a little explaining to do, Cora Mae. You tried to kill Emily earlier, and now me. You want to tell me what's going on, or shall we wait for the sheriff?"

Cora Mae glowered right back at him. "I don't feel like talking to nobody. I just got back from the post office, and I saw you climbing through my window, busting into my house. I was trying to protect myself. I didn't try to kill nobody."

"Then why did you lock Emily in your basement earlier?" He pointed toward the broken jars and metal cans on the floor. "She could have died down here. In case you didn't know it—but I'm guessing you do—those fumes could have been lethal."

Cora Mae's chin shot up. "I don't know what you're talking about. Are you telling me Emily Townsend was over here, prowling around in my basement? Is she the one who made this mess?'' Cora Mae's eyes narrowed as she glared at Matthew. ''What are you two trying to pull here?''

''Nice try,'' Matthew said. ''But attempted murder is a very serious crime, Cora Mae.''

''Now see here—''

''*You* see here. I might be willing to buy your story that you thought I was an intruder, and I might be able to persuade Emily to forget what happened earlier…in exchange for a little information.''

Cora Mae wasn't persuaded. Her black eyes gleamed like marbles in the murky light. ''I got no information,'' she said. ''And I got nothing to hide. You and Emily Townsend trespassed on my property. I could have you both arrested if I wanted to.'' She folded her arms over her shriveled bosom and stared at Matthew in triumph. ''Go ahead and call the sheriff.''

Matthew had to hand it to her. She was a tough old bird, and he knew when he'd been outmaneuvered.

Sensing her advantage, Cora Mae shook a bony finger at him. ''If you ask me, the two of you are just begging for trouble, snooping around people's private property, asking a bunch of questions that are none of your concern. You best be careful. You could end up like those other two.''

''What other two?''

''Jenny Wilcox, and that Drury fellow. They asked a bunch of questions, too, and look what happened to them.''

''Jenny was murdered,'' Matthew said. ''But no one knows what happened to Wade. Are you implying that he was murdered, too?''

Cora Mae pressed her thin lips together. She looked as

if she'd said a good deal more than she meant to. "I've said all I'm going to say. Now you git!"

"Now, are you sure you'll be all right?" Caroline asked sweetly as she shot Matthew a cool, appraising glance. She picked up her sweater and purse and made ready to leave.

Emily reclined against the headboard of her bed. She'd changed from the blood-streaked dress to a pair of jeans and a T-shirt emblazoned with the slogan Another Day in Paradise, but Caroline had still insisted that she rest in bed. Emily found it easier not to argue. She waved an impatient hand at her sister-in-law. "I'm fine, Caroline. All this clucking about is making me nervous. Go on home to the kids."

Again Caroline threw Matthew, who was standing in the doorway of Emily's bedroom, a less-than-friendly glance. "Well, all right, if you insist. I do have to make some treats for Charles's preschool class tomorrow."

"Go on, then," Emily said tiredly, relief washing over her as she watched Caroline disappear through the doorway. Matthew stepped aside to let Caroline pass, then folded his arms and leaned against the frame.

He smiled at Emily.

Emily smiled at him.

"Hey," she said. "Where'd you disappear to?"

"I went over to check out Cora Mae's basement," he said. "I wanted to get there before the sheriff did. The old bat actually tried to attack me with a butcher knife."

Emily stared at him in horror. "Matthew! Are you okay?"

"I'm fine, but you're lucky you got out of there alive."

Emily's hand went to her heart. "I can't believe this is

happening,'' she said. "Do you think Cora Mae was be-hind it?''

Matthew shook his ahead. "Not really. I know all the signs point to her, but unless we have more than one cul-prit operating here, I don't see her being able to rig up that boulder to roll down the cliff toward us, no matter how feisty she still is.''

"Then someone else must have followed me over there,'' Emily said. "Someone was watching me.'' A chill crept down her spine at the thought that someone had deliberately stalked her with the intent to kill.

Matthew straightened and walked into the room. He sat down on the edge of Emily's bed and took one of her hands in his. "I'm really sorry I wasn't there, Emily. I feel responsible for this.''

Emily squeezed his hand. "Remember what you told me yesterday? Second-guessing yourself gets you no-where fast. You're not responsible for me, Matthew. I'm a grown woman.''

He smiled, his eyes flickering over her in a way that made her heart leap. "Believe me, I'm aware of that. But we are partners, and partners should be able to count on one another. From now on, I think we should stick to-gether. No more going off on our own.''

"That's fine by me,'' Emily said, but she couldn't help wondering whether what he said meant he intended to curtail his own disappearing acts from now on. She gazed up at him, then glanced quickly away, afraid her heart might be in her eyes.

She took a deep breath and said, "Even if Cora Mae wasn't the one who locked me in the basement, she still tried to stab you. That's pretty serious business, Mat-thew.''

"She claims she thought I was an intruder, that she was only protecting herself."

"Do you believe her?"

Matthew shrugged. "I don't know. But she thinks fast on her feet, I'll give her that."

Emily sat up in bed suddenly. "Do you remember the warning Miss Rosabel gave me about Cora Mae? She said she wouldn't have been surprised to learn that Cora Mae was the one who killed Jenny, just to drive Miss Rosabel out of business."

"Right," Matthew agreed. "I've seen Cora Mae's bitterness, and that almost obsessive competitiveness of hers, firsthand. Just because I think it highly unlikely she's behind everything that's happened, doesn't mean I'm ready to discount her altogether."

Emily sank back against the pillows. "It's really scary, you know? To think that someone in this town—maybe someone I've known all my life—is capable of murder. In a way, I can almost understand why the townspeople were so willing to believe Wade Drury was guilty. It's easier to accept that kind of darkness in a perfect stranger than it is in one of your neighbors." She paused for a moment, her mood pensive. "Matthew, do you suppose there's a chance that we're simply on a wild-goose chase with this investigation? What if Wade really did kill Jenny?"

"He didn't."

The adamant denial in his voice made Emily glance up. A shiver ran down her spine, raising goose bumps along her arms. "How do you know? How can you be so sure?"

He remained silent for a moment, just sat there staring at her. Then, finally, he said, "Because Jenny was Wade's wife. He was crazy about her."

It was Emily's turn to stare at him. "His *wife?*"

Matthew got up and paced to the window. He stood gazing out with a brooding frown as Emily watched him from her bed, stunned. "Wade and Jenny were *married?* How do you know this?"

Matthew said nothing for a moment. Then, slowly, as if feeling his way along, he began to talk. "Wade Drury was my brother, Emily. When he disappeared, I was sixteen years old. I vowed I would someday come here and find out what really happened to him and to Jenny."

Emily could hardly believe what she was hearing. "That's why everyone acted so strangely when they first saw you. Miss Rosabel and Nella and the others. They saw Wade when they looked at you."

Matthew nodded. "I deliberately fed the illusion by coming here on a motorcycle, just like the one Wade rode, and wearing clothes similar to the way I remember he used to dress. I wanted to shake people up. I wanted to look them in the eye and see what they saw when they thought they were looking at Wade."

"Is your real name Drury?"

"No. My real name is Steele. Drury was my mother's maiden name. Wade used it a lot when he was working undercover."

The word sent a shiver up Emily's spine. "Undercover?"

Matthew turned to face her. His eyes looked grim, and the expression on his face told Emily that in a lot of ways, the fifteen-year-old tragedy was still fresh to him. "Jenny and Wade were both FBI agents."

"FBI agents?" Emily knew she sounded like a parrot, but she couldn't help it. Everything Matthew was telling her was such a shock. She drew a long breath and released it. "I can't believe any of this. FBI agents in Paradise? What were they here for?"

"Jenny's assignment was to infiltrate the Avengers. According to eyewitness accounts, some of the members of the group were heavily arming themselves with military-type weaponry, and the FBI is always concerned about any secret organization that appears to be stockpiling weapons, because of the threat it might pose to national security. There were several similar operations all over the country back then, and Jenny's assignment was coordinated with the others, so that none of the target groups would become prematurely suspicious."

"This is crazy," Emily said. "Like something you see on TV. It's not the sort of thing you associate with your own hometown."

The silence that fell between them was disturbed only by a car passing on the street. It was still daylight outside, but just barely. The fading light slanted through the window, casting deep shadows on Matthew's face where he stood staring out. It was hard to tell what he was thinking. What he might be feeling.

After a few seconds, Emily said, "You said coming to Paradise was Jenny's assignment. Why did Wade come down here?"

Matthew threw her a quick glance and shifted, so that he could lean his shoulder against the window frame. "He was worried about her. He'd had a similar assignment some months before, and he knew how dangerous it could be. Jenny was down here on her own, working without backup. That was the way it had to be. Alone, she had a much better chance of infiltrating the group. She was young, beautiful, and seemingly unattached. As far as the FBI knew, the Avengers were all men. I'm sure you can see the reasoning behind sending Jenny," he said dryly.

She could also see why Jenny's husband would have been worried.

"Wade disregarded direct orders from his superior and followed Jenny down here on his own. By the time he hooked up with her, Tony Vincent was already sniffing around and sensed something was going on between Wade and Jenny. Vincent became insanely jealous, and he and Wade eventually came to blows." Matthew's eyes were on the falling twilight outside the window.

Emily was mesmerized. "Keep going," she said. "Tell me everything." The story itself was fascinating, but now that the initial shock was over, she also had an idea that she might gain some valuable insight into the man who was telling the tale. Perhaps more than she bargained for, she thought with a shiver, gazing at his dark countenance. But that was a chance she had to take.

"There's not a lot more to tell," Matthew said. "After Jenny's body was discovered, Wade called home, almost beside himself with grief. He said he'd written down everything and was sending us a letter, detailing all the events that had occurred since he and Jenny arrived in Paradise. If anything happened to him, we were to take that letter to his section chief at the Bureau. He also told Mom that he wasn't going to leave Paradise until he found out who killed Jenny." He paused. "We never heard from him again."

Matthew's story was so compelling, the images he evoked so vivid, that Wade Drury and Jenny Wilcox were almost living, breathing entities in the room with them. The sensation was so powerful that Emily found herself glancing around, and she wondered if Matthew felt it, too. Wondered if he was remembering, as she was, that Wade and Jenny had last seen each other alive in this very house.

Emily got up from the bed and walked across the room to stand behind Matthew. She put out a tentative hand to touch his arm, needing to connect with him. He didn't turn to look at her, but his hand closed over hers.

"I'm sorry," she said gently. "It must have been awful for you."

"My mother was devastated," he said simply. "I guess we both were, but kids are resilient. I got over it, but I don't think she ever did."

"A mother never gets over the death of a child," Emily said, thinking of the children she'd once planned to have, and feeling the loss.

"I suppose not," Matthew said. "My father died when I was nine, and my mother and I had both looked to Wade as the man of the house. He was always there for us. And Jenny…Jenny was an angel. We all adored her. Her death was such a waste." There was no grief in his voice, no sense of tragedy, but in some strange way, that almost made it seem worse. The casual way he retold the story made Emily wonder how many times he'd gone over it in his head. How many times he'd thought about it over the years.

After a moment, she said, "What happened to the letter?"

"When my mother and I took it to the FBI and tried to convince them to conduct an investigation into Jenny's murder and Wade's disappearance, we were informed that Wade had acted in an improper and dangerous manner. His reckless and irresponsible disobedience of a direct order had resulted in the death of an agent. As far as the Bureau was concerned, Wade Drury was considered a fugitive."

"You've got to be kidding!" Emily cried, outraged. "But they had his letter!"

"Which they kept. We never saw it again, but my mother had had the foresight to make a copy. We had that, and the first time I ever saw her crying over that letter was when I vowed to come here someday and find out what really happened. For her.''

Emily's heart went out to him, and to the woman—to the mother—whom she'd never even met. ''How could they do that?'' she asked helplessly. ''How could the FBI just sweep it under the rug like that?''

''They were afraid a full-scale investigation into Jenny's murder would have threatened not only the operation in Paradise, but all the other ones around the country, as well. They had to keep it a secret in order to protect the lives of the agents who'd infiltrated the other groups.''

Darkness had gathered outside, and the first star twinkled out. The distant shimmer of light seemed like an omen, but whether it was good or bad, Emily couldn't have said.

She looked up at Matthew. ''And so, after all these years, you've come here—for what?'' she asked him softly. ''Revenge?''

He shrugged. ''Maybe, in a way. My mother died two years ago, never knowing what happened to her oldest son. Wade's disappearance and Jenny's death had a profound effect on both of us. I guess I just decided it was time for the truth to come out.''

''But why *now?*'' Emily couldn't help asking. ''Why fifteen years later?''

A brief smile touched his lips. He lifted his hand and stroked her cheek in a butterfly caress that seemed infinitely tender. ''That, my sweet Emily, is the sixty-four-thousand-dollar question, isn't it?''

A QUESTION he wasn't sure he was prepared to answer. The gentle warmth and compassion in Emily's eyes drew Matthew like a magnet, but he knew he had to be careful.

There was still so much he hadn't told her, couldn't tell her, and the last thing he wanted was to play fast and loose with her feelings.

With a measure of regret, he let his hand fall away from her.

"I could use some air," he said. "Why don't we take a walk in the garden?"

He saw the flicker of confusion in her eyes, but she shrugged. "Okay. Sure."

Emily grabbed her denim jacket from the closet and slipped on her shoes, and then they went down the hallway and out into the garden, through the French doors in the living area. Darkness had fallen, but just over the mountains the sky still glowed with red and gold streaks of fire, remnants of what had probably been a spectacular sunset. A current of air drifted through the trees, carrying the nostalgic scent of autumn and the darker, deeper hint of winter.

Together they sat down on a wrought iron bench, and Emily seemed content to sit in the deepening twilight and watch the stars twinkle out one by one. After a while she said, "I love this time of year here. The fall was what I missed most when I left Paradise. I don't believe there's anywhere in the world that smells quite like the Ozarks in autumn."

"Why did you leave?" Matthew asked, partly because he wanted to delay the rest of his story, but mostly because, suddenly, he wanted to know everything there was to know about Emily Townsend.

She shrugged her thin shoulders, her eyes fixed on the moon just rising over a mountaintop. "I was young, and like a lot of teenagers, I couldn't wait to get out of my hometown, see the world. The summer I turned nineteen, I was very unhappy. I'd dropped out of college, couldn't find a job, and there were a lot of…other pressures on me. When Eugene—my ex-husband—came through here, I guess I saw him as my way out.''

''Was it love at first sight?'' Funny how disturbing that notion was, Matthew thought.

But Emily was shaking her head. ''Hardly. Lust at first sight, maybe.'' She laughed in self-derision. ''And that didn't last long, believe me, but by the time I'd gotten over it, it was too late. We were married. It didn't take either one of us long to realize we had absolutely nothing in common, except… I guess we were both running away from our families. Eugene's father had kicked him out of the house a few months before, and Stuart…Stuart wanted me to marry Trey Huntington. In fact, both he and Trey were…adamant about it.''

She was still staring at the moon, never glancing his way, but Matthew thought that she had grown quite tense. It seemed he wasn't the only one with secrets. Emily wasn't telling him everything, either.

''What happened?''

She gave him an ironic smile. ''In a nutshell? I turned Trey down, and let's just say he wasn't happy about it. Trey doesn't like rejection, and rather than have to face him—and Stuart—I left town with Eugene. I stayed away for seven years, and then—I don't know—I guess, like you, I thought it was time for the truth to come out.''

''The truth?''

She hesitated only fractionally. ''The truth about myself. I'd made a mistake. My marriage was a failure, and it was time to come home and take my medicine.''

''Lots of people make mistakes, Emily,'' Matthew said. ''Lots of people get divorced. You shouldn't be punished for it.''

She laughed. It was a brittle little sound that had nothing to do with mirth. "Eugene was hardly my first mistake. I seem to have a talent for making the wrong choices." She turned to him in the moonlight, saying softly, "I just hope I'm not about to make another."

And what was he supposed to say to that? Matthew asked himself miserably. Was he supposed to rush to reassure her?

He couldn't do that. There was no way he could promise Emily she wouldn't be hurt by him, because when this mess was over, when all was said and done, she would probably look back on her time with him and wonder if it wasn't perhaps the biggest mistake of her life.

He felt her eyes on him in the darkness. "Matthew? May I ask you something?"

"What?"

"Did your decision to come here now have anything to do with the woman who died?"

"In a roundabout way." He turned his head and stared at her. "There's still a lot you don't know about me, Emily."

"I haven't exactly shared all my deep, dark secrets with you, either. Maybe some things are best left unsaid. You don't have to tell me anything you don't want to."

And that simple statement suddenly made Matthew want to tell her everything. Reveal every last one of his secrets. His suspicions. Everything he had to hide. But subterfuge had been too deeply ingrained in him for far too long. There was only so much he was prepared to disclose.

He drew a deep breath and then expelled it. "When I told you that solving mysteries is a hobby of mine…that wasn't exactly the truth. I'm a federal marshal, Emily."

Even though he wasn't looking at her, he could sense her startled reaction. Still, she said nothing.

He ran his hand through his hair, wondering how to proceed. "I guess law enforcement runs in our family. For years, I was drawn to that type of life, probably because of Wade. I got caught up in the excitement and challenge of my own career, and over the years, my memories of Wade and Jenny faded. I hardly ever thought about them.

"Then, a few months ago, I was assigned to guard a federal witness, a woman who had agreed to testify against her husband about his involvement in organized crime. We had Christine—that was her name—and her five-year-old daughter, Rachel, sequestered in a safe house, just outside of Memphis. There was a leak somewhere. The husband found out where we were keeping her, and he had his thugs attack the house. Christine was killed instantly, and Rachel—'' He broke off, closing his eyes briefly as he relived the horror of that night. The blood. The screams. The terrible guilt.

Matthew rubbed his hands over his eyes, trying to banish the images, but they were indelibly marked on his memory.

He felt Emily's hand on his arm, and her voice, gentle and soothing, said, "You don't have to go on if you don't want to."

He shook his head. "No, it's okay. Rachel was hit twice, once in the shoulder and once in the lower back. She's undergone three surgeries in the past several months, and for a while the doctors weren't sure she would ever walk again."

"And now?"

"She's been undergoing intensive physical therapy, and she was making remarkable progress until just a few weeks ago. She had a setback—more mental than physical, her doctors said. For some reason, though God knows why, she seems to be comforted by my presence, and so I've been trying to go see her as often as I can.''

"So that's where you go," Emily murmured, almost to herself. Then, "None of this is your fault, Matthew. Surely you know that."

"It *was* my fault," he said harshly. "Christine and I—" He stared at the ground. This was the part that was hardest to admit. Especially to Emily. He glanced up at her. "We never stepped over the line. I want you to know that. Nothing ever really happened between us, but it…could have. A life-and-death situation is always emotionally charged, and when you're sequestered with someone night and day…" He trailed off and sighed. "Anyway, when I came to in the hospital, I had a lot of time to think, and I couldn't help wondering if my attraction to Christine had somehow made me let my guard down. If it had made me careless. It was my duty to protect her and Rachel, and I let them both down. I failed them."

Emily's first instinct was to rush to reassure him again, but something he'd said made her ask instead, "What did you mean, when you came to in the hospital? You were injured, too?"

He nodded, his expression grim. "I was a lot luckier than Christine or Rachel. I was out of the hospital in a few weeks, but I couldn't go back to my job. I didn't trust myself anymore, and so I took a leave of absence, bummed around the country for a while. Then, a week or so ago, I saw Mike Durbin's article in the paper. I don't know why, maybe because of everything I'd just been through, but it seemed the right time to come here. To resolve the past, once and for all. Does that make any sense?"

Emily sighed. "It makes perfect sense to me. You have

to lay the old ghosts to rest before you can deal with the new ones. I think that's why I came back here, too.''

Their gazes met in the darkness, and it came to Emily that she had never felt so connected to anyone in her life. Never had anyone shared with her something that was so personal, so profound. She was deeply moved. ''Thank you for telling me,'' she said softly. ''It means a lot to me.''

''There's no need to thank me. I wanted you to know.'' Matthew's hand closed over hers on the bench, and though Emily couldn't see his face clearly, she knew that his eyes, on her, were intense, darkly seductive.

She caught her breath as he said her name, very softly, in the darkness. His voice was like a caress, like a whisper of air against her neck, and a thrill of excitement shot up her spine.

''Matthew, I—''

Emily hadn't a clue as to what she was about to say, but it didn't matter, because the words were no sooner out of her mouth than Matthew gave a little tug on her hand and suddenly, somehow, she was in his arms.

His touch was electric. Emily's breath rushed out of her as her every nerve ending sprang alive, waiting for his kiss. But for a moment, for an eternity, all he did was stare deeply into her eyes, searching her face in the darkness. Emily didn't know what answers he hoped to find, didn't take time to consider what might happen if he found them. She slid her hand around the back of his neck and pulled him toward her, until his lips were only a breath away from hers.

''Emily.''

''Don't say it,'' she whispered. ''Don't say it can't happen.''

She saw him smile in the moonlight. "I was going to say I think it's time to go in now."

THEY TOOK THEIR TIME undressing. The slanting moonlight in Emily's bedroom cast interesting patterns of light and dark on Matthew's face as he gazed down at her, watching her every movement with a passion that captured her breath. They weren't even touching each other, and yet the buildup was incredible, the tension deliciously prolonged.

Emily shivered as she shed the last of her clothing, and then, drawing a long breath, she stepped into Matthew's arms. He held her for a long time, skimming his hands along her back, whispering his lips through her hair, letting their bodies become accustomed to each other before he kissed her. And when he did kiss her, it was a long, slow, deliberately unhurried exploration that made Emily's heart pound frantically inside her. He buried his hands in her hair, holding her face still as his lips worked their sinful magic.

"Are you sure this is what you want?" he murmured, raining kisses along her jawline and down her neck until Emily could hardly think at all.

She pressed herself against him, wanting more of him. Needing all of him. "Yes," she whispered, letting her head fall wantonly back so that the column of her neck was completely exposed to his kisses. "I've never been so sure of anything."

"Thank God," Matthew muttered, just before his mouth claimed hers again in a kiss that dissolved any lingering hesitation.

Emily gave herself completely to the sensation. Thrill after thrill raced through her as Matthew picked her up, wrapped her legs around him and carried her to the bed.

EMILY AWAKENED. She couldn't seem to move, and for a moment, panic swamped her. Then she realized the weight holding her down was Matthew's arm. Her back was to him, and he was holding her close, as if he would never let her go.

Emily snuggled closer, and his arm tightened around her.

"This is nice," she murmured.

His breath was hot against her cheek as he bent to skim the shell of her ear with his tongue. "I've been lying here dying for you to wake up," he said in a low, intimate tone.

Emily laughed. The low, throaty, sexy sound of it surprised her. "Why didn't you wake me up?"

"I thought you might need your rest," Matthew said, his hand applying the lightest, most exquisite pressure to her breast. Emily shuddered in delight, and Matthew drew her closer, letting her feel the evidence of his urgency.

A thrill of desire shot through Emily. She turned in his arms so that she could gaze into his eyes. "Matthew," she said, "rest is the last thing I want right now."

MATTHEW AWAKENED, startled to find Emily staring down at him. He was lying on his back, and she was propped on her elbow, tracing lazy patterns on his bare chest with her finger. She smiled when she saw that he was awake.

"I've been lying here," she said, "dying for you to wake up."

Her hand skimmed lower, disappearing beneath the sheet, and Matthew's body instantly responded. Emily's brown eyes deepened knowingly.

"Why didn't you wake me up?" he asked hoarsely as her hand continued to explore.

"I thought you might want to sleep."

Matthew kicked off the sheet and lifted her on top of him, letting their bodies become reacquainted all over again.

"Emily," he said, his breath coming out in a gasp as she began to move against him, "sleep is the last thing I want right now."

Chapter Twelve

"What does one do at a séance?" Emily asked as she lit candles and placed them strategically around the parlor.

"There are no hard-and-fast rules," Mrs. DeVere said as she made her final preparations for the evening. She glanced up at Emily, her eyes dark and mysterious in the candlelight. "I'm so glad you agreed to hold the séance this evening. I feel sure we'll make contact. I can already feel the vibrations."

Emily could feel the vibrations, too, but she didn't think hers had anything to do with spirits. She was still basking in the afterglow of her and Matthew's lovemaking the night before. Every time she thought about it, shivers of delight raced all through her.

"I'm sure tonight will be an evening to remember," she said, pretending more interest than she actually felt.

Nella Talbot was the first guest to arrive. Dressed in a subdued navy wool dress, with her blond hair pulled back into a bun, the librarian looked quietly pretty, as always. But her deep blue eyes, behind her wire-rimmed glasses, appeared anxious.

"My," she said, glancing around, "it's dark in here."

"All for effect, I assure you," Emily said. "Come on into the parlor. It's a little bit lighter in there."

"I didn't quite know... Am I dressed okay?" Nella stammered shyly.

"Lord only knows," Emily said, glancing down at her own broomstick skirt, long black sweater and lace up boots. She hadn't exactly known how to dress for the spirit world, either. "You look great," she assured Nella. "Let me introduce you to Mrs. DeVere, our guide to the netherworld this evening."

"I brought you this." Nella held out a loaf of home-made pumpkin bread.

"Why, Nella, you didn't have to do that." Emily was touched by Nella's thoughtfulness. She started to take the bread, but just then the doorbell rang.

"Shall I put it in the kitchen for you?" Nella asked.

"Can you find your way in the candlelight? Be careful," Emily called as Nella turned away.

Mike Durbin was at the door, and he, too, was bearing gifts. "I don't know if a bottle of wine is appropriate for a séance or not," he said. "But I brought red."

No one, including the hostess, seemed quite sure of the proper etiquette for a séance. Emily took the wine from Mike as he strolled into the parlor. She'd had grave reservations about inviting him tonight, but at the last minute she'd decided she could keep a closer eye on him this way. Maybe she could steer the article he was certain to write about the night's events in a more flattering direction.

By the time Emily returned to the candlelit parlor with a tray of wineglasses and Mike's wine, Stuart and Caroline had arrived. She'd been hesitant about inviting them, also, but Mrs. DeVere had insisted they needed at least five people, besides herself, and Emily hadn't known who else to coerce into coming.

Actually, she was a little surprised that Stuart and Caroline had agreed. She suspected curiosity had gotten the better of them. It wasn't every day a séance was held in Paradise.

Stuart, looking even more sober than usual, and extremely put out, said, "For God's sake, can't we have some lights on in here?"

"That would spoil the ambience," Emily assured him, offering both him and Caroline a glass of wine.

"Got anything stronger?" he muttered, yanking at his tie.

"I'm sorry, I don't."

"I'd rather just have tea," Caroline said, gazing around the room in obvious disapproval. She seemed at a loss for anything else to say.

Emily said, "I'll go make you some. Be right back."

"No, don't bother," Stuart said. "I'll go."

"I've got candles lit in the kitchen," Emily informed him. "Please don't turn on the lights. Mrs. DeVere said—"

He cut Emily off with a look, muttering a word under his breath that Emily was sure he rarely used in front of his wife. And, indeed, Caroline did look quite shocked. Her eyes rounded, and her mouth thinned in distress.

She turned on Emily. "What is *he* doing here?"

Emily glanced over her shoulder, almost expecting— and hoping—to see Matthew, but it was Mike Durbin who had garnered Caroline's attention. Across the room, he raised his wineglass in a salute.

Caroline said scathingly, "Do you know what that man is trying to do to Stuart? He's trying to ruin him, that's what. I can't believe you'd have him in your home."

"He's just a reporter," Emily said, trying to curb her exasperation. "You and Stuart are making too much of Mike's influence on the voters."

"That's easy enough for you to say," Caroline replied primly. "You've never cared one whit what anyone thinks about you. Who else in Paradise would hold a séance in her own home?"

"Would you rather I have it in yours?" Emily couldn't resist asking. "Excuse me," she said. "I need to talk to Mrs. DeVere for a moment."

Emily headed across the room, away from Caroline. As far away from Caroline as she could get. Mike Durbin drifted up to her.

"Interesting little gathering, Emily. So that's your psychic." He stood with one hand in his pocket, the other hand nursing his wineglass, as he gazed across the room at Mrs. DeVere, who looked quite regal in a flowing purple caftan and turban. Mike turned backed to Emily. "A little on the flamboyant side, wouldn't you say?"

"She's very charming," Emily said curtly. Then, after a moment's hesitation, she added, "How are you going to handle this story in the paper tomorrow?"

"What makes you think this little event is worthy of an article?" There was a smirk of amusement in Mike's eyes, probably because he already had the story written, Emily decided.

"I hope you'll at least keep an open mind."

"I always keep an open mind," Mike assured her. "And I fully expect this to be a night of surprises. We might even learn who the real killer is this evening." He tipped his glass to his lips and drained the contents.

Emily scowled. "You don't really believe Mrs. DeVere can tell us that, do you?"

"We don't need a psychic to tell us anything," Mike said. He crooked a finger and chucked her under the chin. "I'm one hell of an investigative reporter, Emily. Pretty soon, the whole damn state is going to remember just how good I am.''

"What do you mean?'' A strange feeling of foreboding crept over Emily. Mike was up to something, and she was fairly certain she wouldn't like whatever it was.

He hesitated for a moment, drawing out the anticipation. Then he grinned. "I know who the killer is.''

"What?'' She stared at him, in shock, not knowing whether to believe him or not. "Who is it? How do you know? What are you—?''

Mike's grin disappeared as he put up a hand to calm her storm of questions, casting an uneasy gaze around to see who might have overheard them. "Not so loud,'' he warned. Then, lowering his own voice mysteriously, he said, "You'll find out everything, all in good time. Why do you think I agreed to come to this sideshow tonight? I fully expect to have all my facts corroborated before the evening is over. Tomorrow, I'll be able to write my own ticket to any newspaper in the state. Hell, the country.''

"Who's going to corroborate your story?''

"A good reporter always protects his sources, Emily.''

"Are you telling me that you're meeting your…source here at the séance?''

"According to the note I received today.''

"What note?''

Mike patted his jacket pocket. "As I told you earlier, I have a feeling tonight will be full of surprises. Let's just wait and see what happens.''

"But—''

He held up his empty wineglass. "I need a refill before the fun starts.''

Emily stared after Mike as he drifted out of the room, wondering how much of what he'd told her was the truth and how much was just empty boasting. He seemed to have an ego that rivaled his ambition.

But had someone really sent him a note about the murder? Did someone here tonight really know who the killer was?

Emily started to follow Mike out, to ask him point-blank just how much he knew about Jenny Wilcox's murder, but another man had come into the room, and Emily frowned in displeasure.

Trey Huntington was the last person she'd expected to see here. Since the confrontation with Matthew in the parking lot outside Stuart's office, Trey had kept a surprisingly low profile. But Emily wasn't fooled. She knew he hadn't forgotten or forgiven. He was simply biding his time.

The thought filled Emily with unease as she watched him stroll across the room to join Caroline. He bent and kissed her cheek, and in the candlelight Caroline's eyes glowed with pleasure.

They chatted for several minutes, until Stuart came back in. He handed Caroline her tea, then promptly turned his back on her as he and Trey became embroiled in a heated discussion. Some political intrigue, no doubt, Emily thought acerbically.

She walked up behind them. "What are you doing here, Trey? You weren't invited," she told him rudely.

Stuart said, "Emily," in a warning tone, but she ignored him.

Trey turned and stared down at Emily. He wore a charcoal double-breasted suit, a white shirt and a silver-and-red silk tie. His appearance, as always, was polished perfection, and his smile was carefully calculated to charm. Emily despised the sight of him. "I was sure my invitation had gotten lost in the mail,'' he said. ''And I certainly didn't want to disappoint you.''

''Always considerate,'' Emily said dryly.

Stuart said, with obvious irritation, ''I invited him, Emily. I didn't think you'd mind. He and I have business to discuss later, and I thought it would be convenient to meet here. Is there a problem?'' His tone implied that, if there was a problem, it was Emily's.

For two cents, I'd tell them all to get lost. But she had no desire to create a scene in front of Mike Durbin—and have it all end up in the paper tomorrow—so she gritted her teeth and shrugged. ''I guess you can stay.''

''How can I turn down such a gracious invitation?'' Trey said, his eyes mocking her. Before Emily could move away, his hand reached out and snared her arm. His fingers tightened, but to anyone looking on, the two of them would appear to be immersed in an intimate little chat. Trey knew all about appearances.

He bent low and whispered in her ear, ''Where's your boyfriend? He hasn't walked out on you, has he? First your husband, and now your new boyfriend. What is it about you, Emily?''

She wanted to slap him so badly her palm itched, but she deliberately turned away, and Trey was forced to release her. She couldn't wait to get away from him.

As Emily walked away, she saw Nella wandering around the room alone. She seemed nervous, anxious, running her fingertips over a table surface here, the back of a chair there. Emily wondered whether Nella's inexperience with social gatherings was what made her so uneasy, or whether it was returning to this house. Being here was bound to stir up memories.

Emily stepped up beside her. ''So what do you think of the place?''

Nella turned and stared blankly at Emily for a moment, then seemed to catch herself. "I'd almost forgotten what a wonderful old house this is. You've done a beautiful job, Emily. It looks so romantic by candlelight. I just wish—" She cast her eyes downward. "I wish Aunt Rosabel could have seen it one last time before she died."

"I'm sorry I didn't get a chance to talk to you at her funeral," Emily said. "But the service was lovely."

"Thank you. It still seems hard to believe she's gone." Nella paused for a moment, as if gathering her courage to broach an unpleasant subject. Then she said hesitantly, "Did you ever have a chance to look for the Bible I mentioned? I don't mean to pester you about it, but it does mean a lot to me."

"I'm sorry, Nella, I haven't looked through all the books yet. It may still be in the box. I'll give you a call if I run across it."

Nella looked relieved. "Thank you, I do appreciate it." She smiled and drifted away again.

By nine o'clock, Emily had to conclude that Matthew was a no-show.

She tried to curb her disappointment as she doused all the candles in the parlor except the one Mrs. DeVere placed in the center of a drop-leaf table.

Earlier, Emily had pulled the drapes at all the windows, also per Mrs. DeVere's instructions, and now, with the lights out and only one candle, the room—so charming in sunlight—took on a forbidding air.

The purple candle dancing in its holder in the center of the table sent long shadows creeping up the walls. A thin, pungent trail of smoke curled upward from the brass incense burner Mrs. DeVere had also placed on the table, along with a notebook, a silver pen and a crystal hand mirror.

"Shall we begin?" Mrs. DeVere said. "Please sit any-where you feel comfortable." She sat down at the table, and the flickering candlelight made her face look ghostly pale, even a little demonic.

Mike Durbin came up beside Emily and hummed the "Twilight Zone" theme beneath his breath.

"May we please have silence?" Mrs. DeVere com-manded. Her expression was stern as she glared at Mike and Emily. Emily felt as if she'd just been caught passing a note in class. A flush crept up her cheeks, but Mike just chuckled. Emily cringed to think what she would find in the paper tomorrow about this entire proceeding.

But if Mike was right and the identity of the killer was revealed tonight, the séance would surely not be a priority item in his article.

There was a bit of shuffling about as everyone found seats. Caroline and Stuart sat on the couch, Nella pulled out the piano bench, Mike Durbin took the wing chair Mrs. DeVere had vacated and Trey stood at the fireplace, his arm draped over the mantel as he viewed the whole gathering with an air of amused disdain. Mrs. DeVere motioned Emily to sit at the table with her.

Satisfied that she had everyone situated and their un-divided attention, Mrs. DeVere said, "I would like for each of you to close your eyes and concentrate on clearing your mind of any negative thoughts. If you need help, try thinking about a person or an event or a specific time in your life that brought you great happiness. Open your mind to the positive energy that abounds all around us."

Emily, feeling a little foolish but nonetheless game, closed her eyes and thought of Matthew, and how happy she'd been last night, when he told her about Jenny and Wade, and later about his own tragic experience. She'd been happy because she knew his openness meant that he trusted her. He'd wanted her to know everything about him before they grew any closer. Before they made love.

Emily felt a warm little glow just thinking about later that night, after their talk had concluded. Matthew had been an incredible lover, both generous and demanding, tender and possessive. He'd been everything she'd ever dreamed a lover should be, and afterward, when he held her in his arms while she drifted into sleep, Emily had thought drowsily that at last, at long last, she knew what real love was all about.

She wished he was here right now. She wished—

Somewhere deep in the house, a floorboard creaked. Emily's eyes flew open. The stealthy sound would have gone unnoticed at any other time, but now, in the silent darkness, it seemed ominous.

The candle in the center of the table danced wildly, as if caught in a draft. Emily started to get up to go investigate, but Mrs. DeVere, her eyes still closed, whispered sternly, "Do not let your concentration be broken. No matter what."

Emily wilted in her chair. She gazed around the room. Mike Durbin's face was cast in shadows, his expression unreadable. Nella's eyes were tightly shut, but whether in concentration or in fear, Emily didn't know.

Surprisingly, both Stuart and Caroline had closed their eyes, as well, but Trey's eyes were wide-open. The candlelight reflected in those dark depths seemed sinister. He held Emily's gaze for a long moment, then turned his head toward the door, as if he, too, had heard the noise.

As if he'd somehow been expecting it.

Emily felt the draft on her face now. A door had definitely been opened somewhere in the house. Her first thought, that Matthew had come back, was followed by a little niggling suspicion that perhaps Mrs. DeVere was setting them up.

Then, suddenly, the psychic stiffened, her head rolled back, and she moaned. The low, plaintive sound sent a chill racing down Emily's back.

Mrs. DeVere said nothing, but for several seconds the moaning continued until Mike Durbin whispered loudly, "I can't tell whether the old broad's in agony or ecstasy."

Emily opened her mouth to scold him for his irreverence, but then, all of a sudden, the candle on the table went out. With the lights extinguished and the drapes drawn at the window, the room lay in pitch blackness.

Someone—it sounded like Caroline—screamed. Stuart said, "What the hell?" and Emily jumped up as Mrs. DeVere commanded, in a booming voice, "Don't break the concentration!"

"I think we should turn on the lights," Emily said. "I don't like this. Someone's in the house."

There was a flurry of activity around the room as everyone stood or shifted in their seats. Someone coughed. It was strange to hear every nuance of sound but not be able to see anything.

Then Caroline screamed again. It was a hair-raising sound that brought gooseflesh to Emily's neck. "What's wrong?" she called out in alarm.

"Someone touched me," Caroline said. "Brushed right by me. Stuart? Stuart, where are you?"

Stuart said, "I'm over here." His voice sounded muffled, strained. He didn't say anything else.

Emily didn't like any of this. "I'm going to turn on the lights." She didn't care what Mrs. DeVere had to say about it. She turned to ask Mike Durbin to open the drapes.

"Mike?"

When he didn't answer, Emily felt a ripple of panic inside her. She turned and felt her way in the darkness until she reached the wall switch. She flipped it, but nothing happened. She flipped it several more times.

"The lights are out," she said, trying to control a deepening sense of danger.

Mrs. DeVere said in the darkness, "She's here. That's her sign. Please. Don't anyone move."

"I'm going to check the breaker," Emily said, ignoring the psychic's plea. Enough was enough. Emily was no longer amused. In fact, she was becoming increasingly alarmed. Except for Mrs. DeVere, everyone else had grown strangely silent. "Don't worry," she told them. "I'll have the lights on in a minute."

Some of the candles in other parts of the house had gone out, as well. As Emily passed through the living area, there was a noise on the stairs that set her heart to pounding. She told herself it was just the house settling, showing its age.

But the hair at the back of her neck prickled as she felt her way through the dining room and kitchen and out the back door, to the screened porch where the breaker box was located. After several minutes of fumbling about in the dark, Emily discovered that the main switch had been thrown.

She was gone no more than seven or eight minutes, but it seemed longer by the time she returned to the parlor. Everyone was still sitting in the dark. No one had thought to flip the switch.

Emily turned on the light as she came back into the room, and she couldn't help noticing the different reactions. Nella blinked her eyes several times, Caroline gave a little squeal, Stuart cursed under his breath, and Trey—

still standing at the fireplace—smoothed back his immaculately styled hair, then straightened his tie.

Only Mrs. DeVere seemed unfazed by the sudden harsh glare of light. She sat behind the table staring straight ahead, as if still deeply ensconced in her trance.

Emily walked over to the table. "Mrs. DeVere, are you all right?"

Emily's voice seemed to bring the psychic around. She raised her eyes and stared at Emily. "You shouldn't have turned on the lights," she said accusingly. "Now we'll never know what Jenny had to tell us." -

Suddenly weary of the whole thing, Emily said, "I'm sorry. I guess I panicked. I thought I heard someone moving about in the house."

"It was probably just Matthew," Mrs. DeVere said. "I don't know why the dear boy didn't come down and join us."

"Perhaps he was afraid," Trey said dryly. "You are a psychic of formidable talent, I understand. Maybe he didn't want you exposing his secrets."

Emily said coolly, "I don't think Matthew has anything to hide. He simply isn't here."

"Don't be naive, Emily." Trey smiled. "We all have something to hide."

Emily started to retort, but then decided against it. Trey had no way of knowing that Matthew had confided in her, and Emily hugged her knowledge to herself. She and Matthew had shared something so wonderful, so special, so profound, that a man like Trey Huntington—with all his secrets and lies—could never possibly understand it.

Stuart rose from the couch. "This is all just a bunch of nonsense, if you ask me. I don't know how I let you talk me into this, Emily." He turned to his wife. "Get your coat, Caroline."

"I left it upstairs," she murmured, then quickly left the room.

Across the parlor, Nella rose reluctantly from the piano bench. "Perhaps I should be going, too."

"You don't have to," Emily said. "Stay and have a cup of tea." With both Nella and Mrs. DeVere present, Emily was certain Trey would leave.

And, sure enough, he undraped himself gracefully from the mantel, remarking slyly, "I must say, it was a thoroughly Emily Townsend evening. I wouldn't have missed it for the world."

Emily just shrugged, refusing to rise to his bait. "I can't imagine what you all did for entertainment before I moved back here."

Trey grinned. "Oh, it was deadly boring, I assure you."

Behind her, Stuart grumbled, "What the hell is keeping Caroline?"

Glad of an excuse to leave, Emily said, "I'll go see about her." She started out of the room, but a piercing scream, echoing eerily through the house, stopped her in her tracks. Her heart started to pound with fright. "Caroline," she said.

"My God!" Stuart exclaimed.

"What the hell—?" Trey muttered as he brushed past Emily and started up the stairs. Stuart was right behind him, followed on his heels by Emily and then Nella and Mrs. DeVere, bringing up the rear.

Caroline was standing in the hallway, her hand clapped to her mouth as if to stifle another scream. The door to Matthew's room was open, and her eyes were fixed on something inside. The moment Stuart reached her side, she began sobbing and turned her face into his shoulder. Stuart's arms came around her, holding her gently and more protectively than Emily had ever seen him. But he, too, was staring at something inside Matthew's room. Staring in horror.

Emily hurried past them, then stopped dead. A scream rose in her throat, and like Caroline's, Emily's hand flew to her mouth, as if she could physically hold back the sound.

Trey stood just inside the room, but beyond him, Mike Durbin lay sprawled on the floor, his clothes covered in blood, his eyes open and staring. And kneeling over the body, his hands bloody and his expression grim, was Matthew Steele.

Chapter Thirteen

A dark cloud hung over Paradise. A cloud that could not be so easily dispelled this time. Two murders, fifteen years apart but undeniably linked, had been committed, and both remained unsolved. Paradise's image would never be the same.

But, as if to show they had nothing to hide, the whole town turned out for Mike Durbin's funeral. Emily stood beside Matthew at the graveside service and thought about everything that had happened in the three days following Mike's murder.

Her life had turned into a nightmare. She'd been staying with Stuart and Caroline, because not only was the Other Side of Paradise Inn a crime scene, it had also been besieged by the media and by the gruesomely curious.

It was hard to believe now that Emily had ever wanted to tap into that morbid curiosity for the sake of publicity, but she also knew that her perspective on the fifteen-year-old murder of a stranger had been far different from her feelings about the slaying three days ago of someone she knew. Mike Durbin had certainly had his faults, but he hadn't deserved to be stabbed to death with a butcher knife from Emily's kitchen. No one did.

It was the knife that had seemed to interest Sheriff Willis the most that night, when he finally arrived on the scene. "Do you have any idea how long that knife has been missing from the kitchen?" he'd ask Emily. "Could someone have taken it before tonight?"

"It's possible," Emily had to admit. "I didn't use that particular knife very often."

"So in other words, anyone who had access to your kitchen could have come in and taken it—say a week ago—and you might not have missed it. Someone—let's just say for the sake of argument—who was staying at your inn."

Emily knew what Willis was driving at. Someone like Matthew Steele. He had found the body. There had been blood on his hands, and just as his brother had been fifteen years ago, Matthew was a stranger in Paradise. No one knew anything about him. Who better to point the finger at than him?

As she thought about the night of Mike's murder, Emily's gaze traveled over the people standing around Mike's grave, studying this one, lingering on that one, and she couldn't help but wonder if she was staring into the face of a murderer.

Everyone who had been at the séance was present today except Mrs. DeVere, who had packed her bags that night and left the inn, muttering something about negative vibrations as she beat her hasty retreat.

And so the Other Side of Paradise Inn was completely deserted. No one was allowed inside the inn until the sheriff had finished his investigation. Matthew had moved temporarily into a motel on the outskirts of town, and Emily had hardly seen him at all in the past three days. She'd missed him terribly.

After the service, Matthew took Emily's arm and

steered her toward her car, trying to avoid the crush of reporters, but Sheriff Willis waylaid them.

"I need a word with you, son." He put his hand on Matthew's shoulder.

"I've been in twice to talk to you in the last three days," Matthew said, and Emily shuddered, remembering how Willis had taken Matthew into custody the night of the murder. She'd been frantic, not knowing what to do to help him, but Matthew had been released a few hours later.

"There's nothing more I can tell you," Matthew said now.

"Why don't you let me be the judge of that?" Willis's hand rested heavily on Matthew's shoulder, as if he were afraid Matthew might try to make a run for it. "I got a real interesting fax this morning from the state capital. I think you might like to take a look at it. In fact, I think I'm going to have to insist."

"All right," Matthew said, with an edge of exasperation. "Give me a minute, will you?"

"A minute's about all I got, boy. Make it snappy."

Matthew took Emily's arm and guided her away from Willis. Emily stared up at him, her eyes full of concern. "What's going on? Why does he want to talk to you again?"

Matthew shrugged. "He said something about a fax from Little Rock. I'll go along with him and see what he's found out."

Emily bit her lip. "Matthew, I think it's time we called in a lawyer. Maybe I should talk to Stuart about it."

"Don't worry about me," Matthew assured her. "I'm not about to be railroaded into anything."

"Yes, but Wade probably thought that, too, and look what happened to him."

"Wade misjudged what and who he was up against in this town. I won't make that same mistake."

"Matthew—" Emily broke off, unable to voice her fears. The thought of something happening to Matthew, of her never seeing him again, was almost unbearable.

As if sensing her deep emotion, Matthew gazed down at her tenderly. He took her hand and lifted it to his lips, skimming her fingers with a kiss so soft, so gentle, Emily's eyes teared.

"Nothing's going to happen to me," he said. "I've got too much to live for. Now."

Emily's breath caught in her throat. What was he saying? Was he talking about…her? Emily hardly dared believe it. Hardly dared hope that he could feel for her what she felt for him.

"I'll be back as soon as I can." He bent and brushed his lips against hers.

Such a light kiss, Emily thought, to cause such explosions of excitement inside her.

As Matthew walked away, Stuart and Caroline came up to Emily in the parking lot.

"I'm glad you're here, Stuart," she said. "I need your advice."

Stuart looked stunned. "Do you feel okay?"

Emily barely registered his sarcasm. "I really do need to talk to you."

Stuart shrugged and turned to Caroline, handing her the keys to his BMW. "Why don't you go ahead and start the car? I'll be right there."

Caroline tossed Emily a curious look, but took the keys and did as she was told. Stuart turned back to Emily. "I expect this has something to do with Steele and Willis leaving together?"

Emily nodded. "This is the third time Willis has had

him come in for questioning. How long does Matthew have to put up with this harassment?''

"It's not harassment," Stuart told her. "Matthew Steele is a suspect in a murder investigation." When Emily started to protest, he held up his hand. "We all are. Everyone who was present that night. But Steele even more so, because he was found with the body."

"His fingerprints weren't on the knife," Emily pointed out.

"No one's were. The knife had been wiped clean."

"But that doesn't prove anything. Matthew didn't kill Mike. In fact, he tried to revive him."

"So he says. But for all we know, he could have gotten that blood on his hands when he stabbed Durbin."

Emily stared at Stuart for a moment. "Matthew's not a killer, Stuart."

"How do you know that? How much do you really know about this guy?"

"I know I trust him." She lifted her chin, gazing at her brother in defiance.

"And love him?"

"Maybe.... Yes.... I don't know!" Emily finished in a burst of frustration. The days since the murder had been agony without him. "I think I do."

"For God's sake, Emily." Stuart ran a hand through his thinning hair as he released a long, weary breath. "This is just like your Eugene Sprague debacle all over again. You didn't know anything about that guy, either, and look what happened."

"Matthew isn't anything like Eugene," Emily said defensively. "If you knew him at all, you'd realize that. And besides, I'm not nineteen anymore. I've learned a few things along the way. I learned them the hard way," she finished, with a touch of uncharacteristic bitterness.

"I know." Stuart's smile was sad. "I could see it in your eyes, when you first came back to town. It hurt me to see what that man had done to you, Emily."

His words surprised her. They were so unusually perceptive, so tender, for Stuart. Emily's eyes smarted with sudden tears, and for the first time in years, she wanted her brother to take her in his arms and hold her, as he'd done years ago, when he told her their parents were dead.

But open displays of affection were as out of character for Stuart as spontaneous bursts of devotion were perfectly natural for Emily. And besides, there'd been too many years of estrangement. One hug wouldn't fix everything that had gone wrong between them.

But, for the first time in a long time, Emily felt a glimmer of hope that someday, just maybe, she and her brother could be close again.

Stuart cleared his throat awkwardly, as if the moment had affected him, too. "I'll talk to Willis, see if I can get him to back off a little. I can't make you any promises, though."

Emily felt a rush of gratitude. She reached out and touched her brother's sleeve. "Thank you, Stuart. I just don't want Matthew to be railroaded like his...like Wade Drury was."

"I'll see what I can do," Stuart said. He hesitated, as if there were something else he wanted to say. Then, with a shrug, he turned and strode across the parking area to join Caroline in the car, calling over his shoulder, "I'll see you back at the house."

By the time Emily had climbed inside her own car, most everyone else had already left the cemetery. Though it was only about four o'clock, the overcast day made it seem much later. Emily turned on her lights as she pulled out on the highway and headed back toward town.

Fog, rolling down from the mountains, curled like smoke in the beams from her headlights. The heater in the Volkswagen was still on the blink, so the defroster didn't work. Emily leaned forward and wiped her hand across the windshield, trying to improve her visibility. It didn't help much, and neither did the wipers.

The car picked up speed going downhill, and Emily applied light pressure to the brakes, to slow in time for the turn she knew was coming up. The car didn't respond.

Emily pressed the brakes harder. The Volkswagen continued to gain speed.

In a full blown panic now, Emily pumped the brakes furiously, but to no avail. To her right was the limestone face of the cliff. To her left, the steep drop-off. She was approaching a hairpin turn, and she knew she couldn't make the curve at this rate of speed.

Trying to calm herself, Emily gripped the steering wheel. Maybe if she could somehow bounce the right front fender off the cliff, just graze it, the car would slow enough for her to make the turn.

Emily eased the wheel to the right, a little more, until she heard the scrape of metal against rock. The jolt snapped her head back, then forward, but for a moment Emily thought her plan had worked. The car slowed.

But as the tires once again connected with the wet pavement, they went into a spin. The steering wheel whirled in her hands. Emily valiantly fought for control, but the car skidded sideways on the slick road, spun completely around, and then took a nosedive off the embankment.

For what seemed like an eternity, the car plunged down the hillside at a dizzying speed, bouncing over rocks and tree stumps, careening wildly first one way, then the other.

A tree loomed before her, and Emily screamed, throwing her arm up to protect her face as the Volkswagen slammed into the trunk. She heard the awful sound of crunching metal and shattering glass, and then, as the car's engine sputtered out, all was silent.

The impact had knocked the breath out of Emily, and for a moment she couldn't move. All she could do was sit there and wonder how badly she was hurt. Strangely, she didn't feel much pain. Gingerly she moved her arms and legs. She felt a few twinges here and there, but nothing major. No broken bones, she was fairly certain.

It came to her suddenly that she needed to get out of the car. She'd seen enough action movies to know that crashed cars sometimes exploded. The door was stuck, but, using her shoulder, she finally managed to free it and tumble out onto the slippery hillside.

The fog was even thicker down here. Emily could barely see the road above. Slipping and sliding, sometimes having to use tree roots for leverage, she managed to climb up the embankment to stand on the side of the road. She swiped her hair back with a muddy hand. Surely someone would be coming by in a moment. At the very least, the men who'd stayed behind to cover the grave would be along shortly.

Sure enough, Emily had been on the side of the road no more than three or four minutes before she heard the sound of an engine. From the position of the headlights as the vehicle came around the curve, Emily thought it must be a truck. She stationed herself on the side of the road and began to wave and shout frantically, fearing that she might not be seen in the fog. But as the truck lumbered around the curve, she heard the driver downshift and apply pressure to the brakes.

The vehicle was a tow truck with heavily tinted windows. Emily couldn't see anyone inside, and for a long moment, the driver remained obscured.

A shiver skittered down Emily's back as the window rolled down slowly and a familiar voice said, "Have a little accident?"

Emily's heart pounded in terror as she gazed at Tony Vincent, but she tried to hide her fear. Tried not to think about how very vulnerable she was at the moment.

"What happened?" he asked.

"The brakes went out on my car. I—I lost control," she stammered. "It went over the embankment." She pointed downhill, shivering.

"Wow," Tony said as he got out of his truck. He peered down the embankment, where Emily's car was barely visible in the fog. "You could have been seriously hurt." He turned to her, and though Emily couldn't see his expression clearly in the misty twilight, she could hear the frustration in his voice. "How many lives have you got, anyway?"

Her fear gave way to panic. Emily began to back away from him. "Wh-what do you mean?"

Tony took a step toward her. "I mean, anyone else would have been dead right now. But not you. You're like a cat."

"You did that to my car," she said hoarsely. "Why?"

"Because you ask too many questions. You just have to keep prying into affairs that are none of your concern, don't you? I guess there's only one way to shut you up for good."

Emily whirled and tried to make a run for it, but Tony, in spite of what his drinking had done to his body, was still quick and strong, still very much an athlete. He caught her easily, pinning her hands behind her back as he jerked her toward his truck.

Emily struggled, tried to break free, but his hands on her wrists were like vises. He dragged her toward the truck, and Emily held back, making it as difficult as possible for him.

Releasing her with one hand, he opened the truck door, and as he did so, Emily turned and kicked him as hard as she could. She'd been aiming for his groin, but the slippery pavement gave her very little purchase. She connected with his knee instead, but Tony howled in pain, screaming over and over, "My knee! My knee, you bitch!" And Emily suddenly remembered that the injury that finally ended Tony's football career had been a shattered kneecap. Purely by accident, she'd found his Achilles' heel.

He fell to the ground, clutching his knee, and Emily didn't waste time. She jumped over him and headed down the highway, hoping the mist would swallow her up before Tony was able to pull himself together.

But she'd gone only a few yards when she heard him running behind her. If he caught her this time, Emily knew he wouldn't let down his guard. She'd wouldn't stand a chance. She had to get away from him now.

Heart hammering in her chest, she abandoned the road for the embankment, slip-sliding her way downhill, using the fog for cover. She heard Tony up on the highway, cursing her, but she knew he wouldn't be fooled for long.

A tree root snagged her foot, and Emily pitched forward. She lay frozen on the ground, catching her breath as she listened for any sound of pursuit. All was silent for a moment, but then she heard it—the telltale snap of a twig as Tony made his way down the embankment toward her.

Even with a bum knee, he would catch her. Emily looked around desperately, searching the murky hillside for a place to hide. A dead tree, split by lightning, lay a few feet away, and she scrambled toward it, drawing herself up into the small cave created by the cleaved trunk. She lay there shivering, watching the mist swirl around her.

Tony ran past her, breathing heavily. The flight down the embankment had taken its toll on him. He was limping badly, and Emily thought desperately that if she could make it back up to the highway, she could drive away in his truck. Out here, she didn't stand much of a chance against him. Even with darkness coming fast and the fog like a heavy blanket around her, the embankment offered very little cover. He would find her, and soon.

Slipping from her hiding place, Emily began the long climb uphill. Earlier, after the accident, it had been difficult enough, but now she was terrified and exhausted, and the misty darkness tangled around her like a web. The highway was in sight now, and there, rising out of the fog, stood Tony's truck. Freedom. Emily tried not to gasp for breath as she pulled every ounce of her energy and courage together. She could make it. Only a few more feet. Another few seconds—

And then a hand grabbed her foot, and Emily lurched forward. Clawing at the ground, she screamed as Tony pulled her toward him.

Emily fought him like a wildcat. He tried to pin her to the ground, but she lashed out with her arms and legs, making it as difficult as she could for him to get a hold on her. Finally, he grabbed her wrists and straddled her. Beneath his weight, Emily was helpless.

"Bitch," he muttered, staring down at her in the darkness. "No one would ever have known if you hadn't started asking all those questions. I won't go to prison," he said through gritted teeth. "My old man died in the joint. I'm not following in his footsteps."

He dragged Emily to her feet, pulling her arms painfully behind her back. He pushed her forward, up the embankment, toward the highway. Emily stumbled once, and he jerked her upright. White-hot pain shot up her arms.

He was going to kill her. Emily knew that. But as she frantically cast her eyes about for a means of escape, a sound came to her. A low thrum that steadily grew louder. A motorcycle. A motorcycle in Paradise.

Matthew!

Tony heard it, too. He pulled her to a stop, cursing under his breath as he listened to the sound, which was growing stronger by the second. It was right above them, and for a moment, Emily was afraid Matthew would ride by them. But as he reached Tony's truck, the Harley came to an abrupt halt and the motor was killed. In the screaming silence, Emily heard the sound of her heart beating wildly in her ears.

Tony yanked her behind a stand of cedar trees, whispering against her ear, "Don't make a sound, bitch." And then she felt the cool metal edge of a knife thrust against her throat.

Emily dared not even swallow. She could feel the blade biting into her skin, and knew that Tony would have no compunctions about using it. He was a desperate man. A killer.

"Emily?" It was Matthew's voice, calling to her from the highway. Emily wanted to sob out his name. He was so close! So close, and yet she could do nothing to bring him to her.

Emily heard him scramble down the embankment toward her car, heard the sound of the door being wrenched open and then slammed shut again. For a moment, for an eternity, everything was silent. The knife bit into her neck, warning her. Emily closed her eyes tightly, willing Matthew toward her. But she could hear him moving back up the hillside, toward the truck.

''Damn,'' Tony muttered. He hesitated, as if trying to decide the best course of action. ''We're going down,'' he said, jerking his head toward the valley. ''Don't try anything stupid.''

Emily nodded as they began their awkward sliding shuffle downhill. Tony, still limping badly, lowered the knife from her throat to her side, making the trek a little easier for both of them. They'd gone perhaps a hundred yards or so when Emily slipped on the wet ground. As she fell, her weight put added pressure on Tony's already weakened knee as he grabbed for her, and they both lost their balance.

Tony hit the ground with a thud, and his grip on Emily loosened. She scrambled away from him, screaming Matthew's name as she got to her feet.

''Emily!'' His answering call was so close, Emily wondered how she had not heard his pursuit. Tony got to his feet, head lowered, shoulders forward, ready to charge. The knife glistened in his hand as he eyed Emily for a long moment, ready to spring.

Matthew came out of the mist behind her. She saw Tony's head lift, and his body went still. Emily thought she heard him mutter, ''Drury,'' in a voice edged with fear and anger and maybe just a hint of wonder.

For the longest moment, no one moved a muscle. Emily strained to see Matthew's face in the darkness, but his expression was veiled by the mist. He might have been nothing more than a ghost.

The illusion must have held for Tony, too, for he said thickly, ''Why did you come back? Why couldn't you let her rest in peace?''

Matthew said calmly, "You killed her, didn't you, Tony?"

"Why did you have to come back?" Tony's voice was a hoarse plea that sent a shiver scurrying down Emily's back. It was eerie, those disembodied voices, those dark silhouettes facing off in the misty night.

Then, like a flash of lightning, Tony lunged forward. He tried to grab Emily, but she stepped backward, stumbling over a boulder.

Matthew came at him like a freight train. The collision knocked the knife from Tony's hand, and the momentum carried them both several feet away before they crashed to the ground, rolling over and over in their deadly embrace.

A cold feeling went through Emily as she heard fists connect with flesh, grunts of pain, the sharp intake of someone's breath—her own, perhaps.

And then Tony screamed in pain, and Emily thought Matthew had probably found the injured knee. She staggered forward, trying to see what was happening, to see whether she could somehow help Matthew, but as she drew near the two men, she saw that the fight was all but over. One of them lay doubled up on the ground, clutching his knee to his chest, while the other, gun gleaming dully in his hand, stood over him.

Emily gave a little gasping sob as she ran forward.

Matthew said, "Are you all right?"

But all she could muster was a weak little nod that she wasn't even sure he could discern in the darkness.

Tony was still alive, but all the fight had drained out of him. He lay on the wet ground, groaning in agony. Both men were breathing heavily. Matthew's arm came around Emily and he drew her close as they stared down at Tony.

"What do we do now?" she finally managed to ask.

"Now we let Tony tell us everything we want to know. Right, Tony?"

The beaten man glared up at him.

"You might as well come clean," Matthew said conversationally. "They'll let you take the rap for everything. First murder, and now attempted murder. You're in big trouble, Tony, but if you cooperate, I might be willing to help you."

"How can you help me?" Tony said sullenly. He sat up on the wet ground, still grasping his knee.

With his left hand, Matthew dug in his back pocket for his wallet. He brought it out, flipped it open and handed it to Tony. "I'm a federal marshal."

Emily saw Tony's shock. He brought the wallet close to his face, squinting. "I can't see anything."

"You'll have to trust me, then," Matthew said. "I can do you a lot of hurt or a lot of good. It's your call."

"If you're a federal marshal," Tony said suspiciously, "what the hell are you doing in Paradise?"

Matthew flipped his wallet closed, then stuffed it back in his pocket. His arm came back around Emily, and she shivered. "I think the answer to that question is obvious. I came here to solve a fifteen-year-old murder. Jenny Wilcox was an FBI agent."

"You're lying," Tony said desperately. "She was a schoolteacher. I knew her. I knew her better than anyone."

Matthew shook his head. "She came here to infiltrate a group of vigilantes calling themselves the Avengers. I see that name means something to you," he said when Tony visibly reacted. "I thought it might. I imagine Jenny did, too. That's why she struck up a…friendship with you."

"She was in love with me."

Matthew just shook his head. "She used you, Tony, because that was her job. She was in love with her husband."

"Husband?" The word was almost a whisper.

"Wade Drury."

Tony tried to get up, but Matthew took a warning step toward him, motioning with the gun. "No, I think I like you there just fine."

Tony slumped back to the ground. "I need a drink, man."

"Not yet," Matthew said, in a tone that was oddly soothing. "Just a few more questions, and then we'll get you that drink." Matthew began to move around a bit, as if he were a lawyer questioning a witness on the stand. The effect was at once lulling and intimidating. Emily had to admire his technique. "You knew about Wade and Jenny, didn't you, Tony?"

"No! I thought she was in love with me. I thought she wanted me—"

Again Matthew shook his head. "You never thought that. You wanted it to be true, but you never really believed it, did you? Is that why you killed her?" Though the bluntness of the question shocked Emily, she had to marvel at the calmness in Matthew's voice. Nothing in his tone gave away what he had to be feeling.

Tony's voice trembled. "I loved her! She was the only woman I ever loved! There's been no one else since her. I dream about her every night. Every time I close my eyes, I see all that blood on my hands—" He stopped suddenly, as if realizing what he'd just said. Then he drew a shaky breath. "I didn't mean to do it," he whispered in despair. "You gotta believe me. I was drunk. I didn't know what I was doing—"

"Who were the other members of the Avengers?"

Tony balked on that question. Emily could sense his hesitation, his almost palpable fear. She peered through the darkness, trying to read his expression.

He said, "I can't tell you that. We were sworn to secrecy."

"By whom?"

Again he faltered.

"They can't help you now, Tony. I'm probably the only one who can help you."

Tony stared up at Matthew. "You know who they were, man. Everyone knows."

"Was Sheriff Willis involved?"

"Yes."

"Trey Huntington?"

Emily caught her breath. Trey, an Avenger? But why should that notion shock her? It made so much sense. He'd always thought he owned Paradise. Using violence to coerce the townspeople into doing what he wanted them to, accepting what he wanted them to accept—

Somewhere deep inside her, Emily realized she had always suspected the truth.

"Was Trey Huntington involved?" Matthew asked again.

"Yeah. He was involved," Tony said at last. "The whole thing was his idea."

"Did he know you killed Jenny?"

"He knew. He agreed to help me, because we were brothers, Avengers. We always had to stick together, that's what Trey said. He said he would take care of everything, and he did. He gave me an alibi for that night, and then he came up with the idea of framing Wade Drury for Jenny's murder."

"What happened to Wade?" No one but Emily would have noticed the catch in Matthew's voice.

Tony said, "I don't know what happened to him, and that's the God's truth. They went out to find him the night after the murder. Someone told them he'd been seen down by the river and—"

"Wait a minute," Matthew said, interrupting him. "You said they. Are you talking about Huntington and Willis?"

"Yeah. And Stuart Townsend."

The name was like a physical blow to Emily. She felt Matthew's body tense. His arm tightened around her.

"You're lying," she said, glaring down at Tony. "Stuart would never have condoned a group like the Avengers. He abhors violence, and to even suggest he might have had something to do with Wade's disappearance is utterly ridiculous." She turned to face Matthew in the darkness. "How can we believe anything he's said now? He's obviously lying to cover his own tracks."

"Emily." That was all Matthew said, just her name, but there was something in his voice that reminded her of the day she'd been locked in Cora Mae's basement, and afterward, when Stuart had left so abruptly. Matthew had been looking at her with pity in his eyes then, and she heard that same sentiment in his voice now.

Emily spun back around to face Tony. "You're lying about Stuart!" she cried. "Tell him. Tell him the truth. Stuart wasn't involved. He couldn't have been...."

She saw Tony shrug in the darkness. "He was one of us. I don't know what he and Trey and Willis did to Drury that night. We never talked about it again."

Emily put both hands to her mouth. She couldn't believe it, couldn't accept what the man was saying. He was a murderer, after all. He'd just owned up to killing Jenny Wilcox. How could they believe anything he said?

And why was Matthew still listening to him? Acting as if what Tony said had credence?

Matthew said quietly, "You tried to kill us, too, didn't you, Tony? That night out on the highway. You loosened that boulder. Was it your idea, or Huntington's?"

"He said we had to find a way to stop you two. You were asking too many questions. If the truth came out, we'd all be ruined."

"So you followed us out of town, rigged the boulder somehow, then waited for us to come back."

Tony's voice took on a whining note. "We just wanted to scare you. Then."

"Then?"

"Trey got the idea that if we ran Emily out of business, she'd give up the investigation. Forget all about the murder. And if she didn't have her business, no means of support…" He trailed off on a shrug.

Matthew swore. "If she had no way to support herself, then she would be forced to turn to Trey, is that it?"

"He didn't like anyone rejecting him," Tony explained. "He said Emily…needed to be taught a lesson."

"So you threw the rock through her door and the Molotov cocktail through her window. Then you locked her in Cora Mae's basement. Only you went a little too far that time, didn't you? Emily almost died. And then there was Mike Durbin. What happened, Tony? Did he find you out?"

Tony said incredulously, "I didn't kill Durbin, and I didn't lock Emily in any basement. I don't even know what you're talking about."

"Don't stall on me now, Tony. We've come too far," Matthew warned.

"I'm telling you the truth!" Tony all but shouted. "I've admitted what I've done, but I won't take the rap for something I didn't do."

"Why is it I find myself not believing you?"

"It's the truth! I swear to God!"

There was a tremor in Emily's voice when she spoke. "You said Trey wanted to frighten me out of business so I'd drop the investigation. Did…did Stuart know about that, too?"

Tony didn't say anything, but his silence said it all. Emily covered her face with her hands. She felt like weeping. She'd never felt so betrayed.

"Emily, I'm sorry," Matthew said softly.

She raised her head and stared at him, suddenly realizing why he had looked at her with pity that day at the inn, why his voice now held so much remorse. "You knew, didn't you?"

Matthew let out a breath. "I suspected."

"Why didn't you tell me?"

He made a helpless gesture with the hand that held the gun. "I couldn't. I had no proof, just a gut feeling."

"And how long had you had this gut feeling?" *Don't ask the question unless you want to know the answer,* Emily thought fatalistically, but it was too late. Matthew was already gazing at her with a mixture of pity, regret, and guilt. *Guilt.*

"You knew all along, didn't you?" Emily whispered. "Even before you came here?"

Matthew nodded. "I'd done a lot of research. I had my suspicions."

"And that's why you came to me. You thought…what? That I would somehow lead you to Stuart? Inadvertently give you the proof you needed? Is that why you—?" She stopped herself before saying more in front of Tony Vincent than she would ever be able to forget. She had to somehow save whatever shreds of pride might still be intact.

She turned away from him. "What happens now?"

"I think it's time to call the state police," Matthew said, his voice heavy with regret.

AFTER Matthew had filled in the two state troopers who responded to his call and Tony Vincent had been carted away, Matthew took Emily down the mountain, back to Stuart's house.

"What a mess this has all turned out to be," he said as they stood on the front porch. "There'll be a dozen state troopers in Paradise within the hour. All hell is going to break loose."

"What will happen to them?" Emily asked, hugging herself against the chill in her heart.

"Willis will be formally relieved of his duties, pending a hearing, and both Huntington and...your brother will eventually have to face charges of conspiracy, obstruction of justice, perhaps even murder. The list is pretty long. I'm sorry, Emily."

"Why? You got what you came for, didn't you?"

He drew his hand through his hair, gazing down at her in the dim light from the street lamp. "I never wanted you to get hurt."

"How could I not be hurt?" Emily asked in anguish. With her fingertips, she wiped away a tear spilling down her cheek. "You used me to get to my brother. You were willing to do whatever it took to find out the truth, and that included sleeping with me. Didn't it? *Didn't it?*" she almost screamed.

"It wasn't that way—"

"Then why didn't you tell me the truth before we made

love? You told me so many things that night, Matthew. You shared so much of yourself with me. I thought it was because you trusted me. I thought you…cared about me. I thought we had something special, but I was wrong, wasn't I? It was all just a part of your plan for revenge.''

''Emily, no…'' He reached for her, but she backed away from him, not daring to let him touch her. If he touched her, she knew, her resolve would melt, and where would she be then?

''What we have is special,'' Matthew said softly. ''It means everything to me. For the first time in a very long time, I feel as if I can go on again. Like my life has purpose. Don't diminish what we have, what we've shared. Please.''

Emily closed her eyes, steeling herself against the traitorous emotions raging through her. Even now, she still wanted him. What kind of fool was she?

Matthew said, ''I'm moving back into the inn tonight. Willis has given his okay. If you need me, call me there. I'll come right over.''

Emily opened her eyes and stared up at him. ''Don't hold your breath,'' she said coldly. ''I'm going in to see Stuart now. Don't try to stop me.''

''I NEED to talk to Stuart alone, Caroline.''

Caroline started to protest. Then, glancing again at Emily's ravaged face, she shrugged. ''He's in the study.'' She turned on her heel and disappeared back into the kitchen.

Emily walked down the hall to Stuart's office and knocked on the door. Without waiting for an answer, she opened the door and stepped into the darkly paneled room.

Stuart, leafing through a folder, looked up in surprise. Then, seeing her face, her muddy clothes, he set the folder aside. ''What's wrong? Has something else happened?''

"Like what, Stuart?"

"I don't know. Another accident?"

"What makes you think there'd be another accident?" Emily couldn't believe how cool she sounded, when her insides felt as if they were coming apart. When her heart had just been smashed into a million tiny pieces and then stomped on.

Stuart came around the desk and faced her. "Emily, what's this all about? What happened to you?"

"What happened to Wade Drury?" she blurted out.

A dozen emotions flashed through Stuart's eyes before he turned away from her. "How should I know?"

"Because you and Trey and Sheriff Willis went to see him down by the river the night he disappeared. What happened, Stuart? Did you find him? Did you kill him?" The calmness in Emily's voice fled. She sounded almost hysterical, even to her own ears.

Stuart looked at her in shock. "What the hell are you talking about? Are you crazy?"

"No, I'm not crazy," Emily said, striving for a measure of control before she picked up something, anything, and hurled it across the room. "I'm shocked. I'm disillusioned. I'm more hurt than you could ever possibly know. But I'm not crazy, Stuart."

"You're not making any sense. Let me have Caroline make you a cup of tea. Something to calm your nerves. Let's sit down and talk about what's gotten you so upset."

"I don't want to sit down." Emily began to pace, glaring at him through tearstained eyes. "But I'll tell you why I'm so upset. Matthew and I have just had a conversation with Tony Vincent. He tried to kill me tonight. I'm hoping, I'm *praying,* you didn't know anything about it, Stuart."

Stuart looked speechless. Sick and speechless. "Emily, my God, it can't be true."

"It's true. And tonight wasn't the first time he tried to do me in. He says you and Trey knew all about the other times. How could you, Stuart? I'm your sister, for God's sake." Her voice broke, and Emily put her hand to her mouth, trying to quash the emotions rushing through her. She wanted to slap Stuart. She wanted him to put his arms around her and deny everything. She wanted this night never to have happened.

"Tony told us everything," she said, her voice quavering with suppressed emotion. "The state police have arrested him, and I imagine they'll be here soon to talk to you."

Stuart let out a long breath as he sat down behind his desk. He looked like a man who had just had the wind knocked from his sails. "I never dreamed it would go this far. We just wanted to scare some sense into you. Make you stop asking so many questions."

"How could you?" Emily whispered again. "You knew how much the inn meant to me. You knew how much I wanted to succeed. *Needed* to succeed. How could you try to drive me out of business like that?"

"I thought it was for the best," he said desperately. "I was thinking about your future. Trey said—"

"Trey said! Trey said! Do you know why I left town seven years ago?" She flung the question at him. "Because Trey hit me when I told him I wouldn't marry him. I thought he was going to kill me. I had to get away from Paradise because I was terrified of the man you wanted me to marry."

Stuart's face was completely white now, his pallor intensifying the raw emotion in his eyes. "You never said anything. Why didn't you come to me?"

"Because I was afraid to," Emily told him. "I was afraid you wouldn't do anything about it. It was Trey Huntington, after all."

Stuart's eyes closed in agony. He put a trembling hand to his temple. "My God, Emily. I didn't know. I swear to you—" He took a deep breath and looked up at her. "I'm truly sorry. For everything."

"Tell that to Jenny Wilcox's family," she said coldly. "And Wade Drury's."

"I didn't have anything to do with their deaths. You have to believe that."

"*Their* deaths? Then Wade *is* dead?"

Stuart nodded miserably, his gaze distant. For a long moment, he didn't say anything, and then he began to talk, quickly, as if the contents of his conscience had been under pressure for too long, and once the stopper was released, it all came out in a rush. "Tony killed Jenny, or at least that's what Trey told me. He said we had to help Tony, because if we didn't, we could be in for a lot of scrutiny. The identities of the Avengers could be uncovered, and then we'd all be in a lot of trouble. Our careers would be ruined. I was just out of law school, Emily. I had to think of my future."

"How did you get talked into joining a group like that in the first place?" Then she said in derision, "Trey, of course."

"It started when we were all in college," Stuart said. "It seemed harmless enough at first, a sort of fraternity pledge. We patrolled the campus, made students feel safe. We did some good."

"Go on."

"Then, when we graduated, we all moved back here— Trey and I right away, and then Tony a couple of years later. Trey came to us one day with the idea of resurrecting the Avengers. I didn't want to at first, but he, well, he convinced me it would be for the best. Later, I found out that what he really wanted was a piece of land out on the highway for Huntington Industries' expansion. The Avengers was a cover to get that property.''

Emily narrowed her eyes. ''The property belonged to the family that was driven out of town by the Avengers because the man was accused of stealing. That was all just a ruse?''

Stuart nodded. ''When I found out, I felt terrible about it, but by then, there wasn't anything I could do. Trey had too much on me. And it just kept getting worse. Pretty soon, there wasn't a way out.''

Emily could hardly believe her ears. ''You mean Trey Huntington has been blackmailing you all these years? That's the control he's had over you? Why in the world did you ever want me to marry a man like that, Stuart?''

''I'm finding that a little hard to understand myself right now.'' He looked at her beseechingly, found no sympathy, then sighed. ''I know how all this must sound to you.''

''Do you? I don't think so.'' Emily could hardly stand to look at him, but she wouldn't let herself turn away. She wanted him to have to face her, to look her in the eye and admit what he'd done. All of it. ''I don't think you have any idea how I feel right now. All these years you've sat in judgment of me, Stuart. You've made me feel worthless, like a failure, when all along you were doing Trey Huntington's dirty work—not the least of which was shielding a murderer.''

Stuart winced, as if he had never quite let himself think of his actions in those terms.

Emily was relentless. ''What happened when you went to see Wade Drury that night?''

Stuart rubbed his temples. ''Trey had gotten a call from

someone, I don't know who—I don't think he knew—that said we could find Drury hiding out down by the river. I think Trey had some vague notion of coercing Drury into leaving town, but when we got there, when we found him, he was dead. He'd been stabbed in the back. I swear, Emily, we had nothing to do with Drury's death."

In spite of herself, Emily found herself thinking of Matthew and how this news would affect him. He'd always known, of course, that the chances of Wade being alive after all these years were very slim, but to know for sure, to hear how his brother had died, was bound to have a profound effect on him.

And to think that her brother—*her brother*—had known all along.

"What did you do?" she asked in a wooden voice.

"We buried him," Stuart said. "Trey said it was meant to be. Everyone would think Drury skipped town because he was guilty, and Tony would…go free."

"And you never wondered who murdered Wade?"

"We assumed it was Tony."

Emily scrubbed back her hair. "My God, you're an officer of the court, Stuart. How could you justify that?"

"As I said, I didn't have much of a choice by then. I was in too deep. We all had to help each other and keep our mouths shut."

Emily closed her eyes briefly. "How do you sleep at night? How have you lived with yourself all these years?"

Stuart looked unutterably weary, and ten years older than when Emily had first stepped through his door. "I haven't had a good night's sleep in years," he said. "Believe it or not, I feel almost relieved that the truth has finally come out."

Chapter Fourteen

Emily walked the few short blocks from Stuart's house to the inn, wishing she felt relief. She didn't. The truth had at last come out, and the mystery of Jenny Wilcox's death and Wade Drury's disappearance had been solved, but all Emily felt was betrayed, first by Matthew and now by Stuart. She wondered if her life would ever be normal again, if she would ever be able to trust anyone.

As hard as it would be to face Matthew again, she knew she had to see him, to tell him what she'd learned about Wade. He had a right to know the truth about his brother. Emily just wished she didn't have to tell him about her own brother's involvement.

But then, Matthew already knew about Stuart. Or at least he suspected. That was why he'd gotten close to her. That was why he'd led her to believe he cared about her. So that he could find out more about Stuart.

Impatiently Emily wiped at the dampness on her face. She wasn't sure whether it was mist or tears. She felt too numb to cry. Too dazed to do anything more than go home, crawl into bed and pull the covers up over her head.

The yellow crime-scene tape had been removed from her door when Emily arrived, and the lights were on in the inn. Matthew must already be there, she decided as she bent to pick up a package that had been left by her front door. Then she let herself in and sighed deeply as she gazed around the room that had once given her so much pride. How everything had changed in just the space of a few short hours.

Emily glanced down at the package. It didn't have a return address, and she couldn't imagine what was inside. She didn't remember ordering anything.

Normally she loved surprises, but today she'd had just a few too many. She carried the package with her to her bedroom, avoiding looking at the stairs and the door beyond the landing as she made her way down the hall.

First she'd change out of her damp clothes, and then she'd go find Matthew. As much as she wanted to postpone their meeting, she knew she couldn't. Better to just get it over with now.

Changing into jeans and a sweatshirt and pulling on warm white socks, Emily once again picked up the package. Maybe just a peek wouldn't hurt before she talked to Matthew.

Ripping open the brown paper, Emily stared at the Bible she'd revealed, recognizing instantly that it must be the one Nella had asked her about. Emily flipped the paper over and noted that the postmark was from several days ago, before Miss Rosabel died. Had she mailed Emily the Bible from the nursing home? Or had someone else mailed it for her?

Well, Emily thought, this was just another detail she'd have to take care of. She'd call Nella first thing in the morning. Tonight, however, she didn't feel like talking to anyone. Her pride had taken too much of a beating.

As Emily leafed through the old Bible, a newspaper clipping fell out and drifted to the floor. She stooped to pick it up, then scanned the headline and first few lines of the article. The clipping was about a science teacher in a small Louisiana town who had been embroiled in some scandal with a student, and had subsequently been found stabbed to death. His wife was the chief suspect.

There wasn't a date on the paper. Emily had no idea how old the article was or why Miss Rosabel had felt it significant enough to keep in the Bible, but something about the article touched a memory inside Emily. There was something she should remember. Something Miss Rosabel had told her.

Emily struggled to grasp the elusive memory, but she couldn't quite put her finger on it. Couldn't quite remember what it was she should remember—

And then, without warning, the lights in the inn went out. Emily stood in complete darkness, the newspaper article about a murder clutched in her hand.

MATTHEW BRUSHED past a surprised Caroline, not waiting for her to invite him inside. "Is Emily here? I have to talk to her."

"Just who do you think you are, bursting in here like this?" Caroline demanded.

A weary voice from the hallway said, "It's okay, Caroline. Let him in."

"He's already in," she grumbled as she made a sweeping gesture with her hand, motioning Matthew toward the hallway. "I'd like for someone to please tell me what on earth is going on around here."

Matthew strode down the hallway to the open doorway. Stuart had already gone back inside his office, and Matthew followed him in, closing the door behind them.

"Where is she?"

Stuart didn't try to pretend ignorance. "She's gone.

Left about fifteen minutes ago. I was hoping she was with you.''

Matthew raised his brows at that, but let the comment pass. ''What happened?''

''We had a…fight of sorts,'' Stuart said. ''She stormed out of here. I wanted to go find her myself, but I've… Well, Caroline and I have to talk.''

''Do you have any idea where she was going when she left here?''

Stuart shook his head, his expression uneasy. ''I thought she might have gone back to the inn, but I've been calling ever since she left. There's no answer. I think you'd better get over there, Steele. She shouldn't be alone right now.''

Matthew knew he was the last person Emily wanted to see, but he didn't mention that fact to Stuart. He said instead, ''The state police have Tony Vincent in custody. He's admitted everything.''

Stuart nodded. ''Emily told me. But I still don't think she should be alone. Especially not now.'' There was an odd note of urgency in Stuart's voice. For the first time, Matthew felt a small prickle of panic inside him.

''What aren't you saying?'' he demanded.

Stuart closed his eyes briefly. ''Trey,'' he said simply. ''When he finds out—''

Matthew didn't wait for the rest. He spun on his heel and strode out of the room.

''Matthew? Is that you?'' Emily stood at the bottom of the darkened stairway and gazed upward, to the landing. She'd heard a noise a few minutes earlier and, locating a candle and matches, she'd made her way out of her bedroom, first to the breaker box on the back porch and now to the stairway.

The noise had sounded as if it came from upstairs. She wondered whether Matthew might be looking for a candle, too.

''Matthew, are you all right? I've tried the breaker, but that didn't work. I guess a transformer blew or something. I'll call the power company.'' But when Emily picked up the phone, the line was dead. The fear that she had been keeping at bay since the lights went out a few minutes ago mushroomed inside her.

Her gaze lifted again to the stairway, and this time she gasped. In the flickering light of her candle, she could see someone standing on the landing, staring down at her. Dressed all in black, with a black ski mask pulled over the face, the figure looked like a demon, some dark specter spawned by the night.

The figure didn't say a word, just stood there looking down at her. Slowly, painfully, Emily's heart began to pound inside her chest. She was paralyzed by fear, rooted to the spot for what seemed like an eternity, but when the figure started down the stairs toward her, Emily sprang into action. She whirled and rushed for the door.

Footsteps clamored down the stairway behind her as Emily ran through the living area into the foyer. The door wouldn't open, and she realized someone had locked it. Her shaking fingers closed on the bolt, but before she could release it, something hit her. Hit her hard, on the back of the head.

Pain knifed through her, and as Emily lifted her hand to her head, her fingers found something warm and sticky. And then the darkness around her deepened as her knees buckled and she slipped to the floor.

EMILY HAD no way of knowing how long she'd been out, but when she came to, she found herself in bed, in a candlelit room that looked vaguely familiar. She tried to sit up, but the room spun out of control. Collapsing back against the pillow, she moaned and closed her eyes. When she opened them again, she tried to concentrate on a small area of the room at a time.

The lace curtains at the window directly in front of her. The patchwork quilt on the bed. The pine armoire to her left.

Then Emily knew. She was in Matthew's room. Jenny Wilcox's room. The murder room.

And as her eyes became even more accustomed to the dim candle glow, she saw something else. The figure was standing in a corner, watching her through the eerie slits in the ski mask.

Seeing that Emily was awake, the figure glided across the floor toward her. Something flashed in one of the gloved hands. Something bright and metal and…sharp. Deadly-looking. A knife. A long-bladed butcher knife.

Slowly, ever so carefully, the other gloved hand came up and tugged off the ski mask. The woolen fabric slipped over the head and a tumble of blond hair spilled out.

"Nella!" Emily gasped.

"I found the Bible," she said. "And the clipping. You had it all along, didn't you? You knew about me."

Emily shook her head in desperation. "No! I received the Bible in the mail today. The clipping fell out, but I didn't know what it meant. I didn't know it was you…." She trailed off, remembering suddenly what she had been trying to recall earlier. Miss Rosabel's words came rushing back to her.

She'd had…infatuations before, you see, one rather serious. That's why her father had sent her to me that year. She'd fallen madly in love with one of her teachers, and there was some trouble, because the man was married.

*There was a lot of talk, and, well, we decided—my brother
and I—that it would be best for everyone if Nella came
to stay with me until all the fuss blew over.*

"He didn't love me, so I killed him," Nella said, so
calmly her words were even more chilling. "I had to,
don't you see? It was all meant to be. I had to get rid of
him so I'd be sent here and meet Wade. He was the one.
The real one. The others…" She shook her head. "I knew
it the moment I first laid eyes on Wade, but *she* tried to
come between us. *She* tried to take him away from me."

"Who?" Emily's mind was working frantically. She
had to get out of here, but her head was still pounding,
and every time she moved a wave of dizziness swept over
her.

And Nella had a knife. In her weakened state, Emily
would never be able to overpower her. The best she could
do was to keep Nella talking until…until… Oh, God. Until what?

Matthew, Emily silently cried. *Where are you? I need
you!*

Nella was staring down at her strangely. *"Who?"* she
repeated incredulously. "Why, Jenny, of course. She pre-
tended to be my friend, but she wasn't. She just wanted
to get me out of the way so she could have Wade all to
herself."

"So you killed her," Emily whispered in horror.

"I had to."

"And Tony Vincent? How did you manage to convince
him he'd killed Jenny?" *Think!* Emily commanded herself
desperately. How was she going to get herself out of this
mess?

Nella smiled a little half smile that made Emily's blood
run cold. "I don't mind telling you. That's why I waited
for you to wake up. So I could explain it all to you, and

then you'd understand why you have to die. I owe you that much, since we're friends.'' Nella's eyes glowed with madness in the candlelight, and Emily gasped. Any hope of talking rationally to the woman evaporated, and fear exploded inside Emily again.

''Tony was in a drunken stupor that night,'' Nella went on conversationally, staring down at Emily. ''It was easy to plant Jenny's blood all over him, put the knife in his hand and, when he awakened, tell him that I'd seen him leaving Jenny's room. He couldn't remember anything, and his temper had gotten the better of him before. He believed everything I told him.''

''You had it all planned out, didn't you? Every last detail.'' Emily forced a note of admiration into her tone. ''And Wade? What happened to him?''

Nella's blue eyes grew dreamy in the candlelight. ''We were free to be together. I'd removed every last obstacle. Everyone thought he'd killed Jenny, but I told him I'd help clear his name. That could have brought us even closer, if he had just told me he loved me. But he wouldn't. Even after everything I'd done for him, for *us,* he wouldn't say it.'' There was a note of wonder in her voice, as if, after all these years, she still couldn't quite believe it.

Emily took a deep breath, mustering her courage. She eased herself up against the pillows. ''So you lured him to the river that night and waited for him. You were the one who stabbed him in the back.''

Nella shrugged. ''He wasn't expecting anything like that from me. I took him by surprise. That's always the key, you know. Surprise. I surprised you tonight, didn't I?'' She seemed like a child eager for approval. Her vivid blue eyes gleamed in the candlelight.

Emily nodded, swallowing past the knot in her throat.

Slowly, inch by inch, she drew up her knees. "Yes," she murmured. "You really surprised me. So you just left Wade's body there for the Avengers to find. You were the one who called Trey about Wade, weren't you?"

"Everyone suspected Trey Huntington was behind the Avengers, but no one would ever come right out and say so. I decided to find out for sure. I called him, then waited for him to find Wade's body. Trey and the sheriff…and your brother." Again her eyes shimmered with satisfaction as she waited for Emily's reaction. When the desired result wasn't forthcoming, Nella frowned in displeasure. "You knew!"

"I'm still surprised," Emily said quickly, tensing her muscles. "Especially at how you managed to pull everything off. You killed Wade and Jenny, and no one ever suspected. You killed Mike Durbin, too, didn't you?"

"He'd dug up all that stuff about my past, before I came here. He even found out my father had committed me to a mental hospital for a while. My own father! Can you imagine that, Emily? Can you imagine what that betrayal did to me?"

Emily was imagining it, all right, and the visions were anything but reassuring.

"I knew Mike had gone to talk to Aunt Rosabel. She never trusted me, you know. Never really liked me. She was always watching me like a hawk. I knew she suspected something when I found that clipping in her Bible. But then she hid it, the old battle-ax, and I could never find it again."

Emily gazed at Nella in horror. "You didn't…kill Miss Rosabel?"

Nella smiled. "Didn't I?"

"But how?"

"It was easy," Nella said, with a complacent shrug that

sent a cold chill along Emily's spine. "She was old. She couldn't fight me. A pillow to her face, and it was all over. You can see why I had to get rid of her, can't you? She was talking to people, saying too much. I couldn't have that, could I?"

Fear rushed through Emily as she realized how truly demented Nella was. How cold-blooded. "You were the one who locked me in Cora Mae's basement, weren't you?"

"I heard you talking after the funeral," Nella admitted. "I knew you planned to go see Cora Mae, so I got her out of the house. Then all I had to do was wait for you. I knew the first time I saw the two of you together that I would have to get rid of you, so that he could see how much he loves me."

"Matthew?"

"Not Matthew. *Wade. Wade.* He's come back. He's come back to me. And now," she said, taking a menacing step toward the bed, "now you have to die."

As Nella lifted the knife, Emily grabbed the candle from the bedside table and threw it as hard as she could into Nella's face. It caught her by surprise more than anything else, but that was what Emily had been counting on.

Surprise was always the key.

MATTHEW PULLED to a stop in front of the inn and climbed off the Harley. He stood gazing at the darkened house for a moment, sensing that something was terribly wrong. He looked up at his bedroom, and a shadow passed in front of the window. Emily?

The shadow had been too tall for her. Someone was in the house with her. Someone who wanted her dead…

In less than half a dozen strides, Matthew was up the

walkway and on the front porch. He pushed on the door, but it was locked. Emily never locked her front door.

Matthew didn't take time to check the French doors or even for an open window. He picked up one of the wicker rockers and hurled it toward the stained-glass door Emily had just had reinstalled. The glass shattered into a million pieces.

Matthew reached inside, unlocked the door and pushed it open. He stepped inside the foyer, and drew his gun as he cautiously made his way through the darkened house.

AT THE SOUND of shattering glass, Emily jumped. She put a hand to her mouth to hold back a scream as she huddled in the linen closet at the end of the hallway, watching the flicker of candlelight through the louvered door. The light alternately grew brighter and dimmer as Nella methodically searched the hallway and the other bedrooms, slowly making her way down the corridor to where Emily hid in the dark.

The breaking glass meant that someone else was in the house now. Matthew? Did she dare call out to him? Did she dare not? Emily wondered frantically. She needed to warn him about Nella. Matthew had no idea who the real murderer was, or that somewhere in the darkened house she was stalking them both, with a knife she had used before.

But if Emily called out to Matthew, her hiding place would be given away. Nella was only a few feet away, and Emily was still weak from the blow to her head. She might not be able to get away this time.

Matthew, she silently screamed. *Be careful....*

SLOWLY, his every muscle tense and ready, Matthew climbed the stairs. The house was silent and dark. *And waiting,* he thought. Waiting for him. He had the eerie sensation that with every step he took, he was walking toward his destiny.

At the top of the stairs, he paused, getting his bearings, listening to the silence for a moment before making his way down the hallway. He wished he'd thought to bring along a flashlight, but it was too late to go back for one now. His every instinct was warning him that Emily was up here somewhere, and he had no intention of leaving without her.

The door to his bedroom was open, and he walked inside. Like the rest of the house, the room lay in darkness, and the mist outside partially obscured the moon. He could make out nothing more than hazy shadows. The hair on the back of his neck prickled, and as Matthew started to walk back toward the door, a shadow moved in the hallway.

"Matthew, watch out! She has a knife!"

"Emily!"

Something rushed out of the darkness toward him. Matthew barely had time to brace himself before that something crashed into him and knocked him to the floor. His gun went flying out of his hand, and he cursed.

He tried to spring up, ready himself for another onslaught, but the assailant, fast as lightning, was on him. Matthew had just a glimpse of her face in the darkness, just a hint of blond hair and demented eyes that caught him off guard.

"Nella?" he whispered, just before he felt the sharp sting of a blade as it ripped through his side.

Dazed, Matthew fell to the floor, his hand automatically going to the deep wound. Blood gushed through his fingers as he tried to roll away from Nella and the blood-stained knife she held in her hand. A wave of darkness swept over him, but he tried to fight it. He couldn't lose consciousness now. Emily still needed him. Emily…

Nella was standing over him. A drop of blood fell from the point of the knife and landed on Matthew's face. "Say it," she whispered. "Say you love me, Wade. That's all I want."

Matthew lunged upward and, with his last ounce of strength, grabbed Nella's arm. The knife went flying. It crashed to the wooden floor and skidded through the open French door, onto the balcony. Nella gasped and tore herself away from Matthew. She scrambled across the room, toward the knife, and picked it up, standing silhouetted in the open doorway.

The blackness was rushing up to meet him, but Matthew tried to fight it. He steadied himself as best he could for Nella's attack, but it never came. Another shadow flew past him. It was Nella who was caught off guard this time, and the momentum of the impact as the two bodies collided sent her flying through the French doors. She crashed into the balcony railing, and for no more than a second or two, she hovered against the splintered wood, the knife still grasped in her hand.

Then the wood gave way, and without a sound Nella fell backward into the darkness.

Chapter Fifteen

Emily knelt in the hospital chapel and closed her eyes. She wanted to pray, wanted to beg God to spare Matthew's life, but all she could think was that she'd made a mess of everything again, and this time the results had been tragic. Nella was dead, Mike Durbin was dead, Matthew was in surgery, fighting for his life, and Stuart's life was in ruins. If Emily had never come back to Paradise, none of these terrible things would have happened.

"Emily?"

At the sound of her brother's voice, Emily raised her tearstained face.

"I thought I might find you in here," he said. He knelt beside her. "How's Matthew?"

"He's still in surgery," Emily said numbly. "The doctors won't tell me anything."

Stuart patted her hand, as if at a loss to know what to do for her. "He's strong, and I've never met a man so determined. I'm sure he'll be all right."

"Well, I'm not," Emily said bitterly. "You were right about me, Stuart. I've always been a failure. I always screw things up, and now Matthew might die because of me."

Stuart looked at her in genuine astonishment. "If anyone's to blame, it's me. I'm the one who screwed up, bigtime. But you—'' He spread his hands. ''You saved a man's life, Emily. Nella killed Jenny and Wade all those years ago, and then she killed Mike Durbin when he dug up too much about her past in Louisiana. She even killed her own aunt. Do you think she would have hesitated to finish off Matthew? You're anything but a failure, in my book.''

''I…I can't believe I'm actually hearing you say that,'' Emily said, feeling a glimmer of hope ignite somewhere in the bottom of her heart.

''I'm finding it hard to believe a lot of things these days,'' Stuart said gravely. ''Mostly things about myself. I've been such a pompous bastard, Emily. Holding myself up as a role model to you, when all along—'' He broke off, glancing away. He shook his head. ''You always stood up for what you believed in, while I…I took the easy way out.''

''What's going to happen to you?'' Emily asked, feeling a genuine sorrow for her brother and for the fragile closeness between them that had come too late.

''I'm sure I'll face disbarment. Beyond that, I don't know. I haven't formally been charged with anything yet, but the investigation has just begun. Trey, of course, is denying everything, but I'm through lying for him.'' A ghost of a smile touched his lips. ''I think it's about time I become my own man, don't you?''

Emily touched his cheek with her hand. ''I think you already have,'' she whispered.

''MATTHEW?''

The voice, as soft as a butterfly's wing, fluttered through his mind, teasing him awake. Matthew struggled to rise from the darkness. Slowly, he opened his eyes.

"Matthew, it's me. Emily. Can you hear me?"

Emily? He had to be dreaming. Emily wanted nothing to do with him. He'd lied to her. Deceived her. She was the last person who would be sitting by his bedside.

But it was such a wonderful dream, having her so near, that he didn't want to wake up. He closed his eyes and let the darkness take him. When he woke up again—several hours later, he was told—Emily was gazing down at him.

"Are you real?" he whispered through dry lips.

Tears filled her eyes. "I used to wonder that same thing about you," she said. She wiped away a tear from her cheek with the back of her hand.

Matthew couldn't stop looking at her. Her warm brown eyes. Her sweet smile. Her funny little haircut. He adored everything about her.

"I didn't think you'd come," he said at last. "I didn't think you'd ever want to see me again."

She glanced away from his face, her gaze drifting downward, to where a thick white bandage wrapped around his middle. She bit her lip as her eyes met his again. "I made a deal with God," she said, her voice trembling.

Matthew wished he could take her in his arms, kiss away her fears, but all he could do was ask hopefully, "What did you bargain for?"

Emily stared at her hands. "That if he'd make you okay, if he'd let you live…I wouldn't let my pride stand in the way of telling you how I felt."

Matthew didn't think it would be possible for his heart to beat any harder. "How *do* you feel, Emily?"

Her eyes grew soft, misty. She put her fingertips to her lips, trying to quell their trembling. "I love you," she whispered. "I have from the first moment I met you. I came back to Paradise looking for something that was right here all along.'' She touched her heart with her hand. ''You helped me find what I was looking for, Matthew. Faith in myself.''

Matthew closed his eyes as a wave of joy swept over him. He didn't deserve this. He'd lied to her. Deceived her. Almost gotten her killed. He didn't deserve her love, but, dear God, he wanted it. Wanted it more than anything.

He took her hand and brought her fingers to his lips. ''I love you, too, Emily. More than I ever thought possible. I came to Paradise looking for something, too. I was looking for a reason to go on, trying to justify why I'd been allowed to live and Christine hadn't. And I found that reason. In you.''

''Oh, Matthew!'' Emily threw her arms around him and kissed him soundly on the lips. Ignoring the jagged edge of pain that shot through him as she pressed a little too hard against him, Matthew wrapped his arms around her and held her close, not wanting to let her go. Ever.

When Emily pulled away, he said, ''I had a dream earlier. I was dreaming about you and Rachel. We were all together, healthy and happy. It was so peaceful, I didn't want to wake up.''

Emily smiled down at him. ''Perhaps the dream was prophetic,'' she said. ''Rachel's doctor called earlier, to let you know how much better she is. Dr. Klein thought it might help your own recovery to know. He let me talk to Rachel. She's a remarkable little girl.''

''Yes, she is. She has a very special place in my life, Emily. I'd like for her to have a place in yours, as well.''

''You mean—''

''When I get out of here, I'd like to see about making

my dream come true. I'd like us all to be together. I know that's asking a lot. You've never even met her.''

"Oh, Matthew." Emily's beautiful eyes were liquid with emotion. "Do you know how long I've been praying for a family of my own? It's all I've ever wanted." Tears spilled over and ran down her cheeks. "Will you marry me, Matthew?"

He grinned, reaching up to run his fingers through her dark hair. "How like you to go about this unconventionally," he said. "But if you're willing to take a chance on a decrepit federal marshal with an uncertain future, then my answer is yes. I'll marry you, Emily Townsend. You just say when."

"When," she murmured, before she bent and kissed him again.

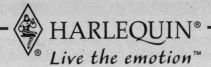

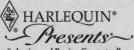

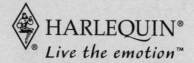

HARLEQUIN®
INTRIGUE®

BREATHTAKING ROMANTIC SUSPENSE

Shared dangers and passions lead to electrifying
romance and heart-stopping suspense!

Every month, you'll meet six new heroes
who are guaranteed to make your spine tingle
and your pulse pound. With them you'll enter
into the exciting world of Harlequin Intrigue—
where your life is on the line
and so is your heart!

THAT'S INTRIGUE—
ROMANTIC SUSPENSE
AT ITS BEST!

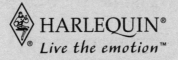

HARLEQUIN®
Live the emotion™

www.eHarlequin.com

INTDIR06

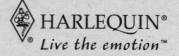

Harlequin® Historical
Historical Romantic Adventure!

Imagine a time of chivalrous knights and unconventional ladies, roguish rakes and impetuous heiresses, rugged cowboys and spirited frontierswomen— these rich and vivid tales will capture your imagination!

Harlequin Historical... they're too good to miss!

www.eHarlequin.com

HHDIR06

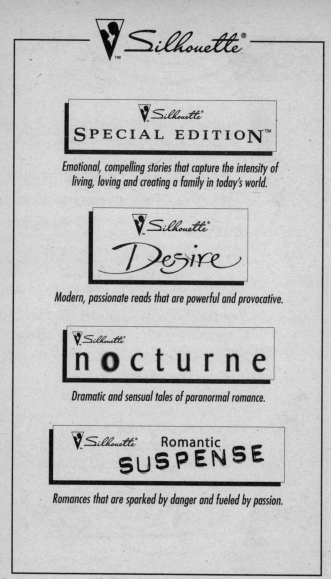

Silhouette®

SPECIAL EDITION™

Emotional, compelling stories that capture the intensity of living, loving and creating a family in today's world.

Silhouette® Desire

Modern, passionate reads that are powerful and provocative.

Silhouette® nocturne

Dramatic and sensual tales of paranormal romance.

Silhouette® Romantic SUSPENSE

Romances that are sparked by danger and fueled by passion.